THE CAMELO

ABOUT TOWN: Camelot, Virginia

Could the rumors be true?

Is Camelot's favorite son in a hot relationship… with his housekeeper's daughter? Reliable sources claim just that. Senator Gabriel Kendrick, some would say the future governor of Virginia, has been seen in the company of one Addie Lowe, the Kendrick estate groundskeeper and child of household staff. A photographer at *The Crier* caught them in an intimate pose on a garden path. Gabe has claimed the two are "just friends," but if a picture is worth a thousand words, the one above is screaming something more than friendship. Is the honorable senator involved in a clandestine affair? Or has he really fallen for the lovely Miss Lowe?

Dear Reader,

It's spring, love is in the air…and what better way to celebrate than by taking a break with Silhouette Special Edition? We begin the month with *Treasured*, the conclusion to Sherryl Woods's MILLION DOLLAR DESTINIES series. Though his two brothers have been successfully paired off, Ben Carlton is convinced he's "destined" to go it alone. But the brooding, talented young man is about to meet his match in a beautiful gallery owner—courtesy of fate…plus a little help from his matchmaking aunt.

And Pamela Toth concludes the MERLYN COUNTY MIDWIVES series with *In the Enemy's Arms,* in which a detective trying to get to the bottom of a hospital black-market drug investigation finds himself in close contact with his old high school flame, now a beautiful M.D.—she's his prime suspect! And exciting new author Lynda Sandoval (look for her Special Edition novel *One Perfect Man,* coming in June) makes her debut and wraps up the LOGAN'S LEGACY Special Edition prequels, all in one book—*And Then There Were Three.* Next, Christine Flynn begins her new miniseries, THE KENDRICKS OF CAMELOT, with *The Housekeeper's Daughter,* in which a son of Camelot—Virginia, that is—finds himself inexplicably drawn to the one woman he can never have. Marie Ferrarella moves her popular CAVANAUGH JUSTICE series into Special Edition with *The Strong Silent Type,* in which a female detective finds her handsome male partner somewhat less than chatty. But her determination to get him to talk quickly morphs into a determination to…get him. And in Ellen Tanner Marsh's *For His Son's Sake,* a single father trying to connect with the son whose existence he just recently discovered finds in the free-spirited Kenzie Daniels a woman they could *both* love.

So enjoy! And come back next month for six heartwarming books from Silhouette Special Edition.

Happy reading!

Gail Chasan
Senior Editor

Please address questions and book requests to:
Silhouette Reader Service
U.S.: 3010 Walden Ave., P.O. Box 1325, Buffalo, NY 14269
Canadian: P.O. Box 609, Fort Erie, Ont. L2A 5X3

The Housekeeper's Daughter

CHRISTINE FLYNN

Silhouette®

SPECIAL EDITION®

Published by Silhouette Books

America's Publisher of Contemporary Romance

For my walking buddy and dear friend, Wendy Graham.
Thanks for mile after mile of conversation, motivation
and for being the caring person you are.

 SILHOUETTE BOOKS

ISBN 0-373-24612-9

THE HOUSEKEEPER'S DAUGHTER

Copyright © 2004 by Christine Flynn

This edition published by arrangement with Harlequin Books S.A.

® and TM are trademarks of Harlequin Books S.A., used under license.
Trademarks indicated with ® are registered in the United States Patent
and Trademark Office, the Canadian Trade Marks Office and in other
countries.

Visit Silhouette Books at www.eHarlequin.com

Printed in U.S.A.

Books by Christine Flynn

CHRISTINE FLYNN

admits to being interested in just about everything, which is why she considers herself fortunate to have turned her interest in writing into a career. She feels that a writer gets to explore it all and, to her, exploring relationships—especially the intense, bittersweet or even lighthearted relationships between men and women—is fascinating.

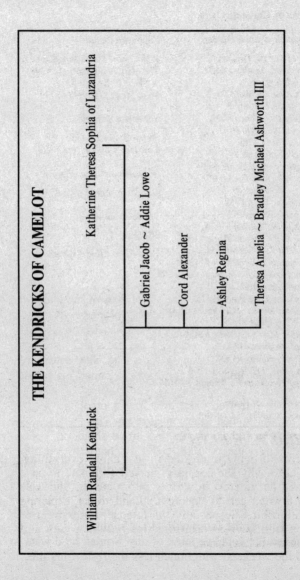

THE KENDRICKS OF CAMELOT

William Randall Kendrick

Katherine Theresa Sophia of Luzandria

Gabriel Jacob ~ Addie Lowe

Cord Alexander

Ashley Regina

Theresa Amelia ~ Bradley Michael Ashworth III

Chapter One

They said he needed a wife. A woman of breeding who wouldn't mind spending her evenings alone or entertaining on a moment's notice. A special woman who could withstand the scrutiny of his family, the press and his constituents. According to the polls, men who were settled projected a better image and more easily gained the public's trust.

A frown furrowed Gabe Kendrick's broad brow as he stood at the arched bedroom window, his hands in the pockets of his khaki slacks, his broad shoulders straight beneath his white polo shirt. As a senator in Virginia's General Assembly, he was well aware that political decisions could often be cold and calculated. But adding "find a wife" to his list of things to do hadn't been the advice he'd expected from his father and his uncle Charles when he'd arrived at the family estate last night.

Offhand, he couldn't think of any woman he'd want to spend the weekend with, much less the rest of his life.

The thought deepened the furrows. Last night's discussion had been a long-range planning session, one of those discussions that went beyond immediate needs to set smaller goals on the way to a larger one. He already had an excellent reputation. He had money. And heaven knew he had name recognition. From the moment his mother had relinquished her claim to the throne of the kingdom of Luzandria to marry his father thirty-five years ago, the Kendrick name had been a household word.

His father, now retired, had been a young senator himself at the time. Not much older than Gabe's own thirty-three years. His mother was one of the most photographed women in the world. He, his brother and both of their sisters had grown up on the covers of magazines. Press and paparazzi followed them nearly everywhere.

Name recognition, he definitely had.

All he needed was the perfect woman. He just had no intention of addressing the wife issue now. He had no time for a relationship. He would have even less after he announced his candidacy for governor. He barely had time for his own family as it was.

The thought had him glancing at his watch and wincing at the time. He was supposed to be joining them for breakfast at that very moment.

He loved his family. The good-natured competition between them energized him, and he hadn't seen certain aunts, uncles and cousins in months. He was even looking forward to a little rough and tumble with his young second cousins out on the manicured lawn. But, having arrived late last night from Richmond, then being up until two in the morning with his father and uncle, he wanted nothing more than a little peace before he joined the myriad relatives gathered below.

Always mindful of what others expected of him, he prepared to abandon the view of magnificent gardens beyond the leaded glass. Peace would have to wait.

Or so he was thinking when he caught sight of a small, slender figure moving from behind the gazebo. The family's young groundskeeper moved methodically as she tended the wide flower border, reaching to snag a weed, pinch a dead bloom.

He couldn't help the smile that erased his fatigue. His mother never had been able to get Addie Lowe into a uniform. With the exception of the stable master, every other member of the Kendrick estate's staff wore a uniform appropriate to his or her position. Bentley, the mechanic and chauffeur, wore tan in the summer and black in winter. The maids wore black dresses with white collars and aprons. The cook wore white. Gardeners wore tan jumpsuits.

Except for Addie.

The jumpsuits his mother preferred were apparently sized for men and didn't come small enough for her. As quiet and unassuming as the youngest staff member tended to be, she managed to blend in even in her usual chambray and denim. But Gabe thought it appropriate that she had escaped having to conform. He'd always thought her spirit too gentle to box in.

He hadn't even realized he'd been looking for her until he'd seen her.

He crossed the room, his footsteps soundless on the antique-gold rug and opened the door to the long, door-lined east wing. The other doors along the wide burgundy carpeted hallway were closed, hiding the unmade beds the maids would tackle now that everyone was up and moving.

The entire Kendrick clan had descended on the 125-acre estate in Camelot, Virginia, for the social event of the year. Gabe's youngest sister, Tess, was marrying Bradley Michael Ashworth III tomorrow on the north lawn. According to the schedule of events he'd found waiting for him on his pillow last night, rehearsal was at three o'clock this afternoon. The rehearsal dinner was at a restaurant in town at six-thirty that evening. Breakfast had started fifteen minutes ago.

The tantalizing aroma of coffee drew him down the steps of the double, carved and curving staircase that embraced the marble foyer. The scent mingled with the fragrance of an enormous bouquet on the round glass table centered in the echoing space before he pushed through a small door beneath the stairs. By using the butler's door, he could avoid the breakfast room.

Voices drifted toward him as he moved through the halls at the back of the house. The servants' areas were separate from the family's, but he was close to the breakfast room here. The clink of fine silver on china underscored animated conversation as he stepped into the brightly lit kitchen.

"Gabriel Kendrick."

His name held a blend of surprise and pleasure as the pleasantly plump Olivia Schilling turned from her sauce on the eight-burner stove. That stove was in the middle of the huge, white-tiled center island. Copper pots hung from the high ceiling above it. Fresh herbs lined the long, multipaned window over the triple stainless steel sink.

Grinning, he buzzed a kiss over her cheek. "How's my favorite chef?"

The Kendricks' cook of twenty-five years smelled of soap and vanilla, just as she always had. And, just as she always had, she replied, "She's just dandy," and smiled back.

Olivia's short, ruthlessly permed salt-and-pepper hair didn't budge as she turned back to her task. A white apron, pristine except for a streak of egg yolk, protected a starched white blouse and black skirt. Her white running shoes sported a defiant slash of neon green.

"We heard you might be late rising this morning," she informed him, referring to herself and the young maid backing through a swinging door with a silver tray of pastries. "I was just thinking I should set aside a tray for you. What do you need over there?"

"Not a thing," he replied, heading for the coffeemaker under a long line of white birch and glass cabinets. "I just want some coffee."

"Isn't there any in the other room?" she asked, glancing toward the still-swinging door. "Hold on and I'll have Marie refill the service."

"I haven't been in the other room. I'm avoiding it. Marie is new," he observed, as much to avoid making excuses for why he wasn't joining his family as to acknowledge new staff. "Is she permanent or just here for the weekend?"

"Permanent. She replaced Sheryl."

"Sheryl." He repeated her name flatly, trying to remember if he'd met her. "Didn't Mom just hire her?"

"Three months ago. I swear we've gone through one after another since Rita retired."

"So why did she quit?" Gabe asked, filling a thick ceramic mug his mom would never have allowed on any of her tables.

"She didn't. Mrs. Lowe fired her," she said, speaking of the head housekeeper. "She caught her snooping through a guest's handbag and let her go on the spot." Lifting her wooden spoon from the pot, she touched her finger to the thick sauce clinging to it. Frowning when she tasted it, she reached for a lemon. "She and your mom hired Marie a few weeks ago."

The door swung back open. "She's doing a fine job, too," Rose Lowe announced, her voice low. "I just hope she works out. With the social season beginning, there will be teas, dinners and parties, and it's so much easier to work with people familiar with the way we do things here.

"Hello, Gabe," she continued, offering him a polite smile on her way to the paper towels.

The head housekeeper wore the same style of black dress as the maid, only without the white collar and apron. In the thirty-some years Addie's mother had worked for the family, Gabe had rarely seen anything on her reed-thin body with much color to it. The past several years, she'd even worn black to the employees' Christmas party.

The overhead lights caught hints of platinum in her dark and tidy bun as she ripped off a dozen sheets of towling. He had known Mrs. Lowe most of his life, too. But the incredibly efficient, fifty-something matron maintained a formal reserve around family that Olivia often did not.

"Now that you're up," she continued, folding the sheets as she retraced her steps, "we can set out fresh eggs Benedict. Olivia, we need more sausages, too. Young Trevor reached across the sideboard and knocked the pitcher of orange juice into the chafing dish. Miss Amber added milk."

Trevor was his cousin Nathan's youngest son. If he remembered correctly, Trevor had just started school. Amber was younger and belonged to his cousin Sydney.

He had a few other young second cousins in there, too. No doubt the twenty-some adults gathered around the table were reminding them all of their manners right about now.

"Don't set out anything on my account." Pulling his mug from beneath the tap on the industrial-size coffeepot, he headed past the pine table where house staff shared their meals. With the touch of chaos going on in the other room, no one would even miss him. "I'm just passing through."

Olivia visibly stifled the urge to tell him he needed to eat. Mrs. Lowe said nothing. Her mouth just pinched the way it inevitably did when he spoke. He had no idea why that was. But, more often than not, she tended to regard him with that faint but distinct disapproval.

Too accustomed to the look to think anything in particular of it now, he excused himself with a nod. "Ladies," he said, and headed for the back door.

"If you run into Addie out there," he heard Olivia call, "ask her about her news."

"What kind of news?"

"Let her tell you."

"He doesn't need to take Addie from her work," he heard Mrs. Lowe insist.

"She can work while they talk."

"She doesn't need the distraction."

"Oh, lighten up, Rose," Olivia insisted right back. "It'll take all of a minute."

"Will do," he called back, intending to talk to Addie, anyway, and let the door bump to a close on their debate.

Taking a sip of Olivia's wonderfully strong coffee, he stepped into the late-September sunshine. The spicy scent of petunias drifted on the warming morning air. Huge pots of the thick white blooms lined the sprawling verandah with its wicker tables and lounging chairs. The lawn spread like a thick emerald carpet past the reflecting pond and formal gardens lush with color.

Addie would have been responsible for all of it, he thought, crossing the freshly swept boards to step onto the lawn.

His long stride, normally so purposeful, began to slow as it tended to do whenever he entered the immaculate gardens or the pathways in the woods beyond. Often when he came home, no one was there other than his parents. In the summer, when his parents left for their house in the Hamptons, there was only staff present. Addie's father, who had been the groundskeeper until he'd passed away five years ago, had been the one person he had always looked forward to seeing there.

He still missed the guy. The seclusion of the estate was Gabe's refuge when he faced decisions or needed to work a problem through. It always had been. During breaks from college and as a young man getting his feet wet in local politics, he had spent hours talking—and listening—to Tom Lowe. While the older man had tended the grounds, Gabe had followed him around the property soaking up his earthy, plain-spoken wisdom, pestering him with questions, challenging him and being challenged. Addie had been there, too, a small shadow trailing after her adored father. Because they lived in such different worlds, the man who had once owned his own farm had provided a down-to-earth candor that his own father and his uncle could not. No Kendrick knew what it was like to earn a living from the land, to suffer the whims of nature or have nothing but wit, grit and common sense to fall back on.

His mother's side of the family might be royalty, but his father's side had always been rich.

Taking another sip of much-needed caffeine, he watched Addie where she crouched by a border thick with golden-yellow chrysanthemums. Without looking behind her, she dropped dead blooms in the galvanized bucket by her knee and reached out again to check for anything faded. In the bright sunshine, her short brown hair gleamed with hints of ruby and topaz. Her shoulders and hips were as slender as a young girl's.

There was a fragility about her that seemed entirely too feminine for the denim she wore, and the work she did. A pair of clippers hung from the narrow waist of her slim jeans. The sleeves of the blue chambray shirt tucked into them were rolled up to expose her tanned and slender arms.

As if sensing his presence, or maybe realizing she was being stared at, she glanced over her shoulder. Genuine pleasure lit her delicate features. Her darkly lashed brown eyes glowed with welcome.

"I'm glad to see you're surviving my mother." Liking the way her smile always made him feel, he raised his mug to her. "I can only imagine how obsessed she's been about the grounds."

From a distance came the throaty hum of a riding lawn mower. One of the two part-time men she supervised was mowing the lawns lining the long front drive.

"I won't mind at all when this is over," she quietly confessed, checking her watch as if gauging the man's progress. "I'm already behind on fall pruning because we need everything full and green for tomorrow. I just hope no one looks underneath some of these bushes and plants," she murmured. "I've had to fill in with pots from the nursery."

Still kneeling, she pushed aside her bangs with the back of her hand. "I'm surprised to see you here so early. I wouldn't have thought you'd arrive until time for the rehearsal." The soft smile in her eyes turned to curiosity. "Did you come early to meet with your uncle Charles?"

There were times when Gabe felt she knew him as well as her father once had. Tom Lowe had been the first to recognize that he hated being idle, unless it was on his own terms. He had to be doing, seeking, accomplishing. He gave a hundred percent to whatever he needed to do once he got wherever he needed to be, but he scheduled himself so tightly that he was never ahead of schedule without a purpose.

"We met for a while last night. It's time to bring a professional strategist on board," he confided, wondering if Addie didn't actually know him even better. Tom used to warn him about burning out if he didn't learn to pace himself. Addie seemed to understand that he thrived on that pace. "Dad thinks one of the lawyers in Charles's firm might be just who we need. I'll meet with him in a couple of weeks to talk about my campaign.''

Rising, she moved with her pail to the next section of flowers, her eyes on her work, her attention on him. "Is he here, or in Washington?"

"Washington. I thought I was aggressive," he admitted, moving with her, "but this guy's got even me beat. He told Charles he thinks we should start positioning for the presidency at the start of my term as governor.''

A wrinkled leaf hit the bucket, along with a handful of browning blossoms. "What do you think?"

"It sounded good to me.''

"Shouldn't you win the election as governor first?"

He could always count on Addie's practicality to keep his ego in check.

"I suppose it might help," he conceded, thinking it wouldn't have killed her to offer just a little stroke of confidence.

"Might," she echoed with a little smile. "You always are getting ahead of yourself.''

"I think of it more as planning ahead.''

She lifted one shoulder in a faint shrug.

"What?" he asked, knowing there was something she wasn't saying.

"Oh, I don't know," she mused, curiously touching a potato bug and watching it roll into a ball. "I was just thinking that you don't seem happy unless you're dreaming huge. There's nothing wrong with that," she qualified, sounding as practical and pragmatic as her father might have, "so long as you don't overlook what needs to be done in the meantime.''

The reminder gave him pause. He did tend to set big goals. And he did sometimes fail to notice obvious details in his preoccupation to reach them. But last night's talks had been heady stuff. Rumor had it that he was a shoo-in for his party for governor. The other major party couldn't even find a candidate willing to run because no one wanted to lose to Virginia's favorite son. He had his detractors, of course, people who believed he would be nothing without his family's money or name. But he would push himself as hard as necessary to prove himself worthy of people's faith in him. Pushing himself was what he did best.

In the meantime, however, there were things that needed to be done. For one, he apparently needed to find himself a wife.

The thought had him frowning into his cup. Years ago he would have asked her father what he thought of that idea. Now he considered picking Addie's brain about that particular obligation.

He didn't know if she had learned from her dad as he had, or if she'd simply inherited his knack for knowing the right thing to do. But in the years since her father's death, she had proved herself to be as uncannily wise as her dad and surprisingly insightful where Gabe's aspirations and obligations were concerned.

He valued her insight, her honesty and the fact that he could trust her with anything. He just didn't want to think about duty or his campaign just then. He hadn't been home for a month. He'd rather just enjoy her undemanding company.

"Olivia said you have some news. Did you finish your research?"

Addie's expert eye swept the border as she moved along.

"Not yet. But I did call the president of the local historical society about what I found. She had no idea there'd been a public garden on that old property," she said, a hint of excitement sneaking into her tone. "She asked me to send her copies of what I had and offered to help get the project funded when my research is complete."

Addie had been working for years to graduate from college. While doing research for a botany class last winter, she had discovered a forgotten set of plans for an historic garden. The last time he'd been home, she had just located the property it had once occupied in Camelot.

"Funding a restoration can take forever," he warned.

"I'm learning that," she admitted, looking more excited, trying not to be. "But once the property gets an historical designation, the garden itself will be a piece of cake. I have copies of the old plans and the list of all the plants. There's reference to a water trough I still need to research, but we have nearly all of the plants right here on this property. Dad found them years ago when he laid out the colonial garden for your mother."

"Mom's going to let you dig them up?"

"Heavens, no," she murmured, still checking for anything wilted. "I asked if I could take cuttings. I've already started cultivating them."

Drawn by her enthusiasm, impressed by her thoroughness, Gabe felt himself smiling once more. "It sounds as if you have it all figured out."

"Except for the paperwork," she conceded, less enthused about that detail. "But that's what Mrs. Dewhurst said she'd help me with. She's the president of the historical society."

He knew the woman. Helene Dewhurst was an old money social maven who kept her manicured claws in everything. "Will you get class credit if she helps?"

"This isn't for school. I'm doing it because of Dad. For him, actually," she confided. "You know how he loved growing the old hybrids we don't see anymore. And you know he felt knowledge was to be shared."

Her father had loved anything with a history to it. He had also thrived on sharing in infinite detail whatever he could learn about whatever he discovered. Her father had instilled her deep respect for anything old and venerable, along with her love of the soil and the miracles that grew from it. He had also taught her more than Gabe figured any female truly wanted to know about the origins of every professional football team in New England.

Her gentle voice grew softer. "I think he'd like knowing his work helped restore something people could enjoy."

The softness in her tone was echoed in her smile. He should have known there was more to her excitement than something that would serve only her own purpose. She always seemed most animated thinking of someone else.

"How close are you to finishing your research?"

The handle of her pail landed on the rim with a metallic clink when she moved it again. "I hope to have everything together before I go back to school."

That would be in January. "See if you can get it finished before that and give it to me. I'll fast-track it for you."

Addie's eyes lit when she looked back up at him, past the heavy mug in his hand, past his broad chest and broader shoulders.

"You'd do that?"

"Of course I would."

Addie swallowed a bubble of elation over what Gabe was offering. She had been raised to be realistic. There wasn't an impractical bone in her body. And heaven knew she was always sensible. The help of Mrs. Dewhurst had already confirmed her hope that the project had merit, but with Gabe's influence, she actually had a shot at seeing it completed before she turned as ancient as the pines by the lake.

"I'll get it to you as soon as I can."

"Let my secretary know when it's coming. She'll watch for it."

"I will," she said, adding her thanks, watching him smile.

The shape of his mouth was blatantly sensual, the line of his jaw strong and as determined as the man himself. His eyes were the gray of old pewter, his dark hair thick and meticulously cut.

He was a beautiful man. He was also tall, powerful, incredibly wealthy, and he had captured the interest of every female in the country with a Cinderella fantasy. His integrity and intelligence had earned him the respect of his friends and constituents, and the envy of his opposition. Addie knew all of that. But she thought of him only as her friend. Not that she would ever share that with anyone. She had grown up fully aware of her station. Like her mother and the father she still missed, she was just an employee of the Kendricks. And staff was expected to remain on the periphery and be as unobtrusive as possible.

Addie had never found being inconspicuous a problem. She was barely five foot three, as skinny as a sapling and about as shapely, and looked more like a girl than a twenty-five-year-old woman. She'd even flunked the assertiveness test she'd found in her friend Ina's *Cosmo*. As with the group of four manicured, pedicured and coiffured women approaching Gabe now, people tended to look right past her.

"The gardens are fabulous, Aunt Katherine," she heard one of the young ladies say. "The wedding is going to be wonderful."

"You're a dear, Sydney," Gabe's golden-blond and elegant mother replied to her niece. Wearing a cream silk blouse and taupe silk slacks, Katherine Theresa Sophia of Luzandria, now a Kendrick, looked as regal as the queen she could have been, had she not married Gabe's father. Her two daughters and her niece looked just like her, fair, polished and utterly refined.

"I just hope the weather holds," Mrs. Kendrick continued. "We have the tent on the west lawn for dinner, but

I'd hate to have to move the ceremony inside. I don't know why we didn't use the cathedral downtown.''

''Because I wanted to be married at home,'' the glowing bride-to-be reminded her mother. ''And we won't have to move anything inside. There's not a cloud in the sky, and the weather report is for clear. Everything will be fine.''

'''Fine' isn't good enough.'' Mrs. Kendrick smiled at Gabe as he turned toward her. ''We want perfect. Good morning, dear,'' she said, greeting him with an affectionate peck on the cheek. ''We missed you at breakfast. Your uncle Charles wants you to meet him at the stables to go riding.''

Sydney, wearing crisp white linen, waved toward the house. ''And the kids want you to play soccer out front with them.''

''Oh, they can't play out there,'' Mrs. Kendrick said. ''The rental people will be arriving with the tent any minute to set it up. It would be best if they played down by the tennis courts.''

''Do you want me to take them riding?'' Gabe offered.

''No!'' the three younger women chimed in unison.

''We don't want anything broken,'' his little sister, Tess, explained. ''Knowing you and Uncle Charles, you'd have them out there jumping logs or hedges. A trip to the emergency room is not on the schedule.''

''Weddings are finely tuned events,'' Sydney informed him.

''What she means, brother dear,'' chimed in his other sister, Ashley, as she and another female cousin joined them, ''is that you have no idea what goes into the planning of an occasion like this. Your people could take notes.''

Silently moving another twenty feet away, Addie continued her task of inspecting the area where cocktails would be served following the ceremony and before dinner. Since the white gazebo would hold the bar, she worked her way through the profusion of red petunias bordering its base.

No one seemed to notice her as she all but disappeared behind the elegant white structure to crouch by the flowers. Just as no one had seemed to recognize that it was she and her men who had babied and nurtured every leaf and blade of grass on the palatial grounds. Any compliments about the grounds were meant for Mrs. Kendrick. Not for her. She was only the means to an end.

"So who's going to enter this madness next?" Sydney wanted to know. "Is anyone involved with someone they're not telling us about?"

"Not that I know of," replied the lovely, rather reserved Ashley. "And certainly not me. I haven't had a date in months, so that puts me at the back of the line."

"What about Cord? Is he seeing anyone since that model sued him?"

Ashley sent her tactless cousin a subtle, shushing glance. "I think my brother is laying low after that paternity suit. He's coming to the wedding alone."

"I just pray he stays out of trouble for a while," Mrs. Kendrick murmured. Her second son garnered more publicity in some years than the entire family combined. "We've had enough sensationalism for this year."

"What about you, Gabe?" the nosy Sydney ventured, undaunted. "Do you have a lady friend you're hiding from us?"

"Are you kidding?" The bride gave a little laugh. "The way the press has been digging around to find out if and when he's going to announce, they'd have come up with anything he was hiding by now. There's no woman. Trust me."

From the corner of her eye, Addie saw a good-natured

smile deepen the lines bracketing Gabe's mouth. "I think I hear a horse calling," he muttered. "I'm out of here."

"Coward," Ashley whispered.

"Smart," he countered, backing away.

He caught Addie's glance as he did, his gray eyes laughing. But he'd no sooner given her a discreet wink to indicate he would see her later, than a look of recognition swept his sister's flawlessly made up face.

"I know someone here who's getting married," Ashley announced. "Our groundskeeper," she said, stopping Gabe dead in his tracks. "I just heard it from our cook yesterday." Genuinely pleased, she shifted her attention toward the gazebo. She craned her neck, laying her hand delicately over her pearls. "Addie," she called. "Congratulations on your engagement."

Every one of the beautifully dressed women smiled at where she knelt in her serviceable denim and grass-stained boots.

With his back to everyone but her, the smile in Gabe's eyes died completely.

"My congratulations, too," Mrs. Kendrick added, sounding as sincere as she looked. "Your mother told me you haven't set a date yet, and I know we'll speak later, but I want you to know now that we're going to miss you here."

Addie wasn't accustomed to being the center of attention. More familiar with being nearly invisible in a group like this, she'd been caught completely off guard at being included in it. Even for a few moments. That had to be the reason she felt as if her cheeks were flaming.

The only thing she could think to say was "Thank you," before the women all turned their focus back to each other. She couldn't think of anything to do, either, except jerk her self-conscious glance from Gabe's when she realized it had caught on his once more.

Her cheeks were actually cool to her touch when she brushed the back of her hand over one and bent her head to her task once more. Yet, as she heard the women talking now about weddings past as they moved to where the ceremony itself would take place, she couldn't shake the feeling that Gabe had been caught off guard, too.

She just had no idea what to make of the way his brow had pinched as he walked away and headed for the stables.

Chapter Two

Gabe was panting hard when he grabbed the tail of his faded-gray Yale T-shirt, wiped the sweat from his face and planted his hands on his knees to catch his breath. The early-morning sun beat on the back of his head. The still-cool air fed his lungs.

He'd just shaved fifteen seconds off his fastest mile, and that after running his usual five.

There wasn't a muscle in his body not screaming in protest.

He glanced at the timer on his watch again, took a deeper, slower drag of air.

He'd just beaten his personal best, but the satisfaction he should have felt simply wasn't there. That disappointed him, too, considering that a quarter of a minute was the largest chunk he'd ever managed to cut off before. But he hadn't set out to indulge his competitive streak. He'd practically run himself into the ground trying to escape the restiveness that had nagged him ever since he'd walked away from Addie yesterday.

He rose slowly, wiping his face again, and started walking up the oak-lined drive from the isolated country road. He wasn't entirely sure what he'd felt when his sister had broken Addie's news. He'd wanted to think it was only surprise, that he had simply been caught off guard because she'd given no hint of being involved with anyone.

The explanation was logical, which he always was. And rational, which he tried to be, too. Considering that he had known her since she was born, he tended to think of her simply as he saw her, and not as someone with a life beyond the boundaries of his family's estate. It stood to reason that having her move outside that neat little box would jar him a little.

It bothered him that he would be so narrow in his view of someone, but the logic placated him. A little, anyway. It didn't do a thing, however, to explain his edginess. Something under that unfamiliar discontent felt a little like disbelief. Or, slight. Or, maybe, it was…disappointment.

The thoughts tightened the muscles in his jaw as he glanced toward the main house with its three stories of windows and tall, curved portico. He would have thought she would confide something so important. She talked to him about everything that mattered to her. Or so he'd thought.

The party rental truck had arrived with tables, chairs and table settings for five hundred guests. The florist was there, too. Workers darted back and forth from the boxy white vehicles pushing dollies laden with cartons or bearing bouquets and sprays of white roses and gardenias. A crew placed garlands of flowers wrapped in ribbon around the front fountain. Another ant-like procession of personnel, all bearing centerpieces, headed around back to the white tent that had been set up for dining.

Gabe knew Addie wouldn't be in the middle of all the activity. Her preparatory work was done, and it would be her nature to stay out of everyone's way. Finding her on more than a hundred acres of hedges, wind breaks, and wooded land surrounding a private lake might have been nearly impossible, too, had it not been for the sound of the riding lawn mower. Following the muffled roar, he found one of the uniformed gardeners making a final pass over the three acres of lawn down by the tennis courts and asked him where he could find his boss.

Three minutes later Gabe found her behind a boxwood hedge near the garage. Dressed in her familiar denim, she was on her knees at the sprinkler controls.

The tall wall of foliage hid both her and the six-car garage from view of the activity taking place on the opposite side of the main house.

"It wouldn't do to have the sprinklers go off and soak all the guests," she said, sensing his presence before he could say a word. "Weddings are supposed to be memorable, but I don't think that's the sort of memory your mother would appreciate."

Rising, she turned from her task, her glance moving from the V of sweat darkening the neck of his shirt to his loose gray running shorts. For the first time in memory, her smile lacked the easy welcome he had grown so accustomed to seeing.

"How was your ride yesterday?" she asked, sounding more at ease than she looked. "I hear you took out the new stallion. He's magnificent, isn't he?"

The latest addition to his father's show stable was indeed an incredible animal. Addie could probably discuss its pedigree and prizes equally as well as she could the ancestry and awards of his mother's Victorian roses. If something was alive, she was interested in it. But all he wanted to discuss was the little matter she'd failed to mention on her own.

"Why didn't you tell me you're engaged?"

The question didn't seem to surprise her. It was the accusation behind it that seemed to throw her a little.

It threw him, too.

Confusion entered her dark eyes. "Because it isn't the sort of thing we usually discuss."

"We talk about a lot of things, Addie. When I mentioned that Olivia said you had news, you only told me about your project. Something like this seems a little more important. Don't you think?"

"They're both important to me." She still couldn't identify what she'd seen in his eyes yesterday. But the intensity of it had left her with a knot in her stomach the size of an amaryllis bulb. "But you brought up the research," she reminded him, feeling that knot tighten. "There wasn't time to talk about anything else, anyway."

"You could have mentioned the other first."

"I suppose I could have," she conceded, though it wasn't something she'd felt at all compelled to bring up with him. "I was just more interested in talking to you about the project. We've never talked about my personal life."

Over the years, she and Gabe had talked about everything from pets to his political ambitions. Other than for immediate family, they'd rarely talked about their personal relationships. She had always known who he was dating, though. All she had to do was pick up the society page or listen to gossip among the staff to know who he was seeing, or if he was too busy to be seeing anyone at all. She didn't believe for a moment that he was interested in her as anything other than a friend and sounding board, but if he'd wanted to find out anything about her, the stable master or the chauffeur were as good a source as Olivia and

Ina, the downstairs maid. Gossip was practically a sport among certain members of the staff.

He must have understood her logic. The accusation slowly faded from his silver-gray eyes. The disappointment, however, remained.

"So we haven't discussed your personal life before," he admitted, sounding as if he hadn't even realized she had one. "Maybe we should now. Who's the lucky guy?"

She tipped her head, studying the lingering discontent carved in his handsome features. She had no reason not to discuss her fiancé with him. She imagined the men would even like each other, given that they shared the same strong sense of fairness, stubbornness and a consuming drive to succeed. It just felt a little awkward to talk about the man she was to marry with Gabe looking at her as if she were doing something wrong.

"Scott Baker." Her right hand closed over the pretty-but-modest diamond on her left one. She'd told Scott that she didn't need an engagement ring, that a wedding band would do just fine. But Scott was like Gabe in his sense of tradition, too. "He's a coach at Camelot High."

"How long have you known him?"

"Six months. I met him at a basketball game."

Gabe's dark eyebrows merged. "I didn't know you were into basketball."

"I'm not. Wasn't," she corrected. "I went to a game with Ina and Eddy." Eddy was the stable master. Aside from being one of the maids, Ina was also his wife. "Their son is on the team."

"Has he been at the school long?"

"Shane?" she asked, thinking of Ina's son.

"Scott," Gabe muttered, planting his hands on his hips. "Do people around here know him? Do you know him? How can you even be sure you love the guy? Six months is hardly any time at all."

The insistence in his deep voice was mirrored in his stance. He looked very big, very male and with all that muscle tense and bunched, he would have intimidated the daylights out of most men and any woman who didn't recognize the look in his narrowed eyes.

He had the same intent look he got whenever he contemplated a responsibility that threatened to get out of control.

He took his responsibilities quite seriously. All of them.

She just hadn't realized he still thought of her as one.

She could practically feel the tension radiating from his big, rather incredible body. Yet, her own anxiety suddenly began to ease.

"He's taught there for five years. And, yes," she replied, thinking of his last question. "I think I do love him.

"You know, Gabe," she continued, smiling now that she understood what was going on, "you sound just like I'd imagine my father would. I know you told him you'd look out for me, but that was years ago. I was barely nineteen. I'm twenty-five now." Affection entered her tone. "I appreciate your concern. I really do," she said, meaning it from the bottom of her heart. Except for her father, she'd never known anyone whose concern meant more to her. "But it really isn't necessary."

He didn't appear convinced.

"Scott is a nice man," she assured him. Gabe wouldn't relinquish an obligation easily. But it was long past time he let go of this one. "My friends like him, my mother is thrilled and, just between you and me, I really don't need another dad. Just be my friend and wish me well. Okay?"

For a moment Gabe said nothing. He simply studied the delicate lines of her face while the sense of calm he'd always felt around her slipped into oblivion. He hadn't even been thinking of the private promise he had made her father before he'd died, but the vow to make sure she stayed safe allowed him a handy, if not perfectly logical excuse for his behavior.

Latching on to it, he tried to ignore the strange void in his gut.

"I'm not trying to be your dad. But it sounds like you could use an older brother," he muttered, not sure that role fit, either. "Just for the record, what do you mean by you *think* you love him?"

The challenge killed her smile. "I mean just that. I doubt it's something any one of us can know for certain…"

"I would sure hope we could."

"What I mean," she continued, quietly overlooking his interruption, "is that none of us can know something like that for sure until we've been in the relationship for a few years. I don't think real love is there at first. There are feelings that can lead to it, but the real thing has to grow. It's kind of like a seed," she explained, sounding like her father now. "Some plants flourish. Others struggle. Only with time and care can you tell."

Gabe opened his mouth, and promptly shut it again. He wanted to know why she would marry someone without being as certain as she possibly could about how she felt. He wanted to know what she would do if a few years passed and she discovered that what she'd felt hadn't been love at all. When he married, he wanted the certainty. He needed to know he was entering the relationship with everything going in its favor. What he absolutely did not want was a relationship that started out with only seeds of something that *might* grow into something lasting. He wanted those seeds rooted, stemmed and blooming.

That was precisely why he hadn't felt any urgency over the advice he'd been given to find a wife. He knew that the woman he married had to be someone people could admire, and look up to. Someone the public could love. But before the public met her, he had to do all that first.

The direction of his thoughts had him backing off. So did the fact that he was about to ask Addie if she truly knew what she was doing. The wary way she watched him made it clear she no longer thought he was rowing with both oars.

His cousin's kids saved him from asking, anyway. He heard his name hollered from a distance. It was echoed a second later. The wall of leaves muffled the small, male voices, but there was no mistaking the boys' determination to find him as their shouting came closer.

"Gabe? Are you down here?"

"Gabe? Where are you?"

"Be right there!" he called back.

"Mom said to play soccer with us, and Trevor won't let me be goalie."

"I want to be goalie! And Kenny hid the ball!"

"Did not!" came a third voice. "Tyler did."

Looking far more frustrated than he sounded, Gabe shoved his fingers through his windblown hair. "Give me a minute! Okay?"

"You'd probably better go now." Addie stared at the beautifully muscled underside of his arm. Realizing what she was doing, aware that the view somehow changed the quality of the knot in her stomach, she jerked her glance to look past his broad shoulders. "It sounds as if you'll be playing referee."

The man was a state senator. He influenced the social and economic welfare of more than seven million people. He had offices in Camelot and Richmond and staff in both places. Yet, here, today, he would baby-sit.

The thought would have made Addie smile had it not been for the tension she could still feel radiating toward her. It seemed to tug at the knot, tightening it.

"I'd better go, too," she said, stepping back, motioning behind her. "I have a section of sprinklers that'll go off in a few minutes if I don't change the timer."

The boys called out again, their voices only yards away. Gabe stepped back himself—only to stop and glance to where she'd returned to the long row of gauges and digital displays.

"Where will you be tonight?"

"Helping my mom in the main house," she replied, not sure why he'd want to know, too anxious for him to leave to ask. Had she considered it before yesterday, she would have honestly thought he'd be happy for her. An engagement was special. But all she sensed in him was an inexplicable sort of displeasure.

His only response was the lift of his chin before two dark-haired future heartbreakers barreled around the end of the tall hedge. He swooped the smaller one onto his back with the ease of a man completely comfortable with children and their exuberance. A boy of about seven received a hair ruffling that had him giggling before he took off, backward, chattering to the man who could easily have passed for their dad.

Addie turned to her task once more, trying to remember which valves she'd shut off, which she hadn't. She too rarely encountered members of the extended Kendrick family to know whom the younger ones belonged to. She wasn't like certain members of the staff who followed every word written about every Kendrick, either. The only one she'd ever been interested in enough to read about was Gabe. And she couldn't begin to imagine why he would care where she would be later—unless he was still concerned about having some duty to her dad.

Maybe you need an older brother, he'd said.

She'd never had a brother, but she supposed that, in many ways, she already thought of him as one.

She hadn't always, though, she thought, opening the timer box to finish what she'd started to do ten minutes ago. When she was nine years old, and he fifteen, she'd thought of him as the smartest boy in the world. Then she'd turned ten and she had thought of him more as her knight in shining armor.

Timer buttons clicked as she turned off section after section. She could still remember the day he'd made that transition in her mind, how wet and miserable the weather had turned. And how frightened she'd been of the older kids who'd tried to take her lunch money from her at the bus stop. She could remember Gabe, too. How big and brave and commanding he'd seemed even then.

He had been enrolled in Briarwood at the time, an exclusive prep school miles in the opposite direction of the public school she'd attended. He hadn't let the fact that he'd gone so far out of his way, or that he would be seriously late, stop him from helping her, though. He'd seen what was going on, rescued her with the cool, steel-eyed glare that still had lesser males backing away and driven her to school himself. He'd pulled right up in front of Thomas Jefferson Elementary in the shiny new Jag his parents had given him for his sixteenth birthday and let her out as if he were her own private chauffeur.

She'd been in serious puppy love with him at ten, and had a wild crush on him as a teenager. As a young woman, she'd been in awe of him and all he was accomplishing, and terribly grateful for his support when her father had died.

It had been Gabe who had helped her through the deep sadness she'd felt at the loss of her dad, because Gabe had loved and respected him, too. And it had been Gabe who had prevented even more upheaval when it had appeared that she and her mom would have to move from the groundskeeper's cottage.

The cottage had been her parents' home ever since they'd lost their farm in Kentucky some twenty years before and gone to work for the Kendricks. The tidy little house just inside the woods was a benefit provided to the groundskeeper as part of his salary. It was their home when Addie had been born. But since her father no longer held that position, she and her mom weren't entitled to stay there.

Mrs. Kendrick had been terribly kind. She had waited nearly two weeks after the funeral before she'd asked Addie's mom to move up to the servants' quarters in the main house so she could hire another man. Mrs. Kendrick had assumed that at nineteen, Addie would be on her own, that she would either go back to school or get a job in town.

Everything had happened so quickly that Addie hadn't had time to consider her own plans. Her only concern had been for her mom. The thought of leaving the cottage and the memories her mom had shared there with her dad had all but devastated the grieving woman.

Addie had never known her mom to be anything less than stoic. She'd also had no idea what to do to help her until Gabe had suggested that she take over her father's job herself.

She would never have thought of approaching Mrs. Kendrick on her own. Aside from being totally intimidated by the famous woman and not at all accustomed to speaking up for herself, she hadn't felt qualified to take over such a responsible position. But Gabe had insisted there was no one better qualified, and reminded her of how she had helped her father with his chores from the time she'd been old enough to dig in the dirt. There wasn't a tree, flower or stretch of lawn on the property that she couldn't propagate, name or mow. Because her father's ailing heart had slowed him down so much, she had already dropped out of college to help him so he wouldn't work so hard.

Or lose his job. In his final weeks she'd been handling his job alone as it was.

A young woman definitely hadn't been Mrs. Kendrick's idea of a proper groundskeeper. But she hadn't wanted to take Rose from her home, either, so she had given Addie a six-month trial.

That had been five years ago. As grateful as Addie had been to the woman then, she'd been even more grateful to her son.

The problem was that now she wasn't sure what she felt toward Gabe beyond something too complicated to question.

Being her practical, pragmatic self, she didn't question it. She simply accepted that she had always cared for him, always would and headed off to make sure the florists didn't damage her topiaries with their ribbons and tiny white lights before she had to join her mother in the main house. All the rooms would need straightening while the houseguests were at the wedding.

Addie didn't usually pull housekeeping duty. On the few occasions she had, she'd truly hated it, which meant she definitely wasn't looking forward to it now. Knowing she would be in the main house that evening only added to the disquiet she couldn't quite seem to shake.

That odd unease accompanied her on her way to the house a little after six o'clock that evening. The ceremony had begun, and with everyone's attention on the couple exchanging vows by the reflecting pond, no one noticed her slip from the opening in the trees a city block away and hurry across the cobblestone drive between the main house and the garage.

The side door, or the servants' entrance as it was known by the family, led to a utility room and on into the kitchen.

Addie didn't mind being in those particular rooms. The

kitchen was Olivia's domain, and Addie had found the open space with its miles of glass-fronted cabinets, hanging pots and herbs growing on the windowsills to be as warm and inviting as the woman herself. She'd just never been comfortable in the mansion's more vast and elegant spaces. Mostly, she suspected, because she knew she didn't belong there.

As a child, she could use only the servants' door when she needed her mother. And never was she allowed beyond the doors of the kitchen and servants' areas themselves. She had been a teenager before she'd set foot in the main foyer, and then only because she'd helped her dad bring in and hang the fresh greens they'd made into holiday wreaths and garlands for the staircases and mantels.

As she headed inside now, she carried a bunch of brilliant red and gold asters she'd cut for the servants' dining table. She didn't come to the main house often, but when she did she always brought flowers for Olivia and the maids to enjoy.

The scent of something buttery and delicious drew her through the utility room with its deep sink and cabinets for boots, servants' coats and cleaning supplies. Grabbing an old china teapot for a vase from a cupboard, and scissors from a drawer, she smiled at Olivia working at the center island and stopped at the sink to arrange the flowers.

"Come on in here and do that," Olivia called, rubbing her nose with the back of her forearm since her hands were covered with flour. "As long as there's no bugs, you can use my sink.

"Oh, you brought my favorite," she observed, seeing what Addie carried when she entered the high-ceilinged room. "I just love those bright colors." As long as her arm was up, she nudged at the white headband holding back her tight salt-and-pepper curls. "So, did you see her?"

"Who?" Addie asked, bundling vase and flowers past the island.

"Tess, of course," Olivia replied, as if she couldn't imagine who else they'd be discussing. "The bride?"

"I didn't see anyone." Preoccupied, trying not to be, she set her flowers on the spotless counter and turned on the faucet. "I came up by the garages."

"Well, she looks like a vision," the loquacious cook pronounced. "I can't begin to imagine what that gown cost, but I'm sure I could feed half the county on what they're spending out there." She lifted a hand toward a golden-brown casserole on the stove, flour drifting like snow. "We're having tuna noodle as soon as we get finished up here. There's plenty if you don't feel like cooking for yourself tonight. I'm making pecan pies for lunch tomorrow, for those who aren't leaving first thing. First batch will be out in ten minutes if you want a slice."

Olivia's pies were pure sin. Addie would have loved some, too, had her appetite not disappeared on her way into the house.

"Would you mind if I take it home with me?"

"Of course I don't. I wouldn't have offered it if I didn't want you to have it," she replied with a tsk.

"I don't suppose you peeked inside the tent to see how everything looked," she continued, sprinkling ice water into her stainless steel bowl.

The ends of Addie's short, blunt-cut hair swung as she shook her head.

"Didn't think you would," Olivia concluded, adding a pinch of salt. "You're not nosy enough. Must get that from your mother. Not that she isn't nosy," she qualified. "She just doesn't talk that much about what she knows. Anyway, I didn't get down there, either. But I hear that the extra tent behind the big one is the caterer's kitchen. Your mom said they have fifty people running around down there putting the final touches on beef Wellington and salmon Oscar. Can't imagine not working in my own space.''

Her brow pleated as she gathered the ball of dough from the bowl and plopped it on the marble rolling board. ''What are you doing up here yourself? I'd have thought that after all the hours you put in the past week, you'd be taking the evening off and spending it with your fiancé.''

Addie finished filling the vase and reached for a stem of crimson red asters. ''Mom needs the help.''

There was so much to do with all the extra houseguests. More people created more laundry, more cleaning, more messes and Addie knew her mom was already exhausted. Even with Ina and the new girl working, Addie also knew her mom wouldn't quit tonight until everything was as close to perfect as she could get it. All week her mother had left the cottage an hour earlier than her usual 6:00 a.m. and returned far later than her usual eight, after dessert had been served and the dishes all done.

Her mom had always prided herself on her ability to run the Kendrick household to Mrs. Kendrick's rather exacting standards. But since Addie's dad had died, her mom had become even more obsessed with doing her job exactly right.

Addie would have felt incredibly guilty knowing she was resting and her mom was not.

''I'm sure she'll appreciate it,'' the cook confirmed on her way back from the double-wide refrigerator, cold marble rolling pin in hand. ''There's not a one of us who couldn't use an extra hand right now. Can't believe the hours we've put in to get everything ready and stay on top of everyone's needs. But that's what we're paid for,'' she murmured philosophically.

''So,'' she continued easily, putting her shoulders into

rolling out a quick neat circle of dough, "what kind of wedding are you having?"

"Something small," Addie's mom pronounced, walking in from the laundry room with an armload of freshly laundered and folded towels. Addie swore her mother had radar for hearing. She could pick up a conversation three hundred yards away. "Or maybe they should just elope. I'd be willing to pay for that myself."

Consideration joined the fatigue in Rose's eyes as she glanced toward her daughter. Even after running herself ragged all day, her dark hair and black uniform looked as painfully neat as always. "You know, Addie, if you did that," she said, setting her stack on the counter, "you and Scott could get married whenever you want. You wouldn't have to spend all that time planning and reserving and waiting for a dress to come in."

"You're not paying for my wedding, Mom."

"Do you have a date in mind?" Olivia asked.

Addie hesitated.

"No," Rose replied, speaking for her daughter as she pulled one of her ever-present lists from her pocket. "I keep telling her she needs to do that so we can reserve the church and get invitations ordered."

"You just said they should elope."

"Well, they need to do one or the other. It's not good to leave something like this hanging. Long engagements aren't necessary."

Olivia folded her circle of dough in two and expertly slipped it into a glass pie plate. "Are you waiting until after you graduate?"

Addie opened her mouth.

"I certainly hope not," Rose insisted, before Addie could say a word. "That would be over a year and a half from now. She'd be graduating sooner if she hadn't taken those extra courses Gabe talked her into," she murmured, disapproval in her tone. ''What's an elementary school teacher going to do with botany classes, anyway?''

''They did help her discover that old garden outside of town,'' Olivia reminded her.

''Well, that's taking up her time, too. She could be using the effort she's putting into that, into planning her wedding.''

While Olivia helpfully pointed out that Addie could probably do both, and the women proceeded to debate the financial merits of eloping rather than having a wedding, Addie diligently forced her attention to the stems she carefully arranged in the bright vase.

Losing herself in the simple beauty of the flowers, appreciating the colors, textures and pretty shapes, appealed far more to her than considering how little her own opinion mattered when it came to deciding her future. The cook and her mom talked as if she weren't even there, as if she were as invisible to them as she was expected to make herself as she went about her daily chores.

Being invisible was familiar. So was her mom's criticism and the guilt Addie always felt when her mom found fault with the choices she'd made. Both of her parents had wanted more for her than to tend someone else's home and land. Addie's dad had insisted on college. But her mom had never thought that four years of college was necessary. She'd considered secretarial school more practical because Addie could have a career and leave the estate that much sooner.

Addie had never felt any great need to leave the sprawling grounds. She loved working with the plants and the land and she had far more freedom being outdoors than her mother did working inside. But she hadn't wanted to disappoint either of her parents, so she had decided that she would teach because she herself loved to learn. And, being practical, there would always be a need for teachers.

Her mother had ultimately, grudgingly, been satisfied with that. But she had also made it clear that she thought the extra classes Addie had taken last winter a waste of time and money. Addie had loved the botany courses, but they couldn't be used toward her major, and taking them had kept her from taking classes that could. Her mom had thought Gabe quite cavalier for suggesting them, too, because people like the Kendricks could afford to indulge casual interests, but people like them definitely could not.

Addie swallowed past the familiar sense of defeat tightening her chest. Her mom had always insisted that setting one's sights too high resulted only in disappointment, and she wanted badly to save her from that.

Addie knew her mom meant well. But it was so hard to work for something when someone was always pulling back on your leash. She couldn't count the times her mom had remarked on how long it was taking her to get her degree. Because she needed her job to afford school, she worked full-time from spring through mid-December and attended college in Petersburg, seventy miles away, during winter term. A term a year was not exactly a land speed record.

Her mom also made a point of occasionally mentioning that she could have had an office job by now, and that at the rate she was going, she might not ever graduate. Considering that she would then have no degree and no training, she'd have no choice but to spend the rest of her life as the Kendricks' groundskeeper, a fate of which her mother definitely did not approve.

At least with her engagement, the possibility of living on the estate and serving the Kendricks for the rest of her life had been eliminated. Now, her mother's focus was simply on getting her married.

The way her mother kept pushing, it was almost as if she was afraid Scott would back out on Addie if she didn't commit to a date soon. When her mother had said before that a long engagement wasn't necessary, what she'd really meant was that a long engagement could be broken.

He has a good job, she reminded her at every opportunity. *And he's good to you. That's as good as it gets, Addie. A man like that won't wait around forever.*

It had done Addie no good to point out that her mom would have to move to the main house once Addie quit her job there. Her mom had said that after so long she was ready to move, anyway. The cottage wasn't the same without Tom, and she'd be closer to her work.

Before her mom could start in on any of her arguments again, Addie turned with the artfully arranged bouquet, set it on the table where the servants ate and grabbed the towels.

"Tell me where these go and what else you want me to do."

Oblivious to the impact of her comments, Rose headed for the cabinet- and drawer-lined hall between the kitchen and the laundry.

"You can take those up to Marie in the family wing," she continued while Olivia walked over to stick her nose into the blooms. "She's trying to make some order out of the bedrooms. I'll do the same in the guest wing after I help Ina down here."

Pulling out a plastic basket loaded with rags and furniture polish, she handed it to Addie and stuffed in a plastic bag for trash. "Ina is running the vacuum in the living room and dining room and straightening both. If you'll bring in the glasses and ashtrays from the library and straighten up in there, we should be finished well before people start trickling back in.

"And, Addie," she said, checking over the fresh jeans and long-sleeved burgundy T-shirt she'd changed into, "when you're finished, go out the front door. People will be milling around out back by then."

Addie thought nothing of the reminder to remain out of sight. She'd heard so many similar requests over the years that she simply did it automatically, slipping around like a small ghost whenever family or guests were near.

She moved that way now as she used the butler's door that led into the huge marble foyer and hurried up the nearest side of the curving, chandelier-lit double staircase to leave the towels on the antique sideboard at the top of it. She didn't know which of the rooms Marie was in, but her mom or the new maid couldn't miss seeing them there.

She barely glanced at the gilt-framed landscape hanging above the sideboard, or the brass sconces flanking the enormous work of art. Anxious to escape the nagging sense that she didn't belong there, she hurried right back down the stairs, her footsteps soundless on the thick burgundy runner, and headed across the spoke pattern in the marble tiles that radiated from beneath the foyer's round entry table.

She had no idea which rooms were whose upstairs. Except to drop off the towels just now, she'd never set foot up there before. She knew several of the rooms downstairs, though. As her dad had done before her, she brought in the garlands for the fireplace mantels every December.

The monotonous hum of the vacuum cleaner grew louder as she passed the enormous living room with its groupings of gold damask sofas and chairs and butter-colored faille walls. She kept going, the hum receding, as marble floor gave way to a Persian hall runner, and walked through a set of carved mahogany doors.

The lingering scent of expensive cigars mingled with more expensive leather, old books and lemon oil. Empty cocktail glasses and soda cans occupied end tables and the coffee table across from the open television armoire.

Intent on getting in, getting the job done and getting out, she left her basket on the round game table, opened the wide floor-to-ceiling French doors to let in some air and turned to pick up pieces of a children's game from the floor.

Applause filtered through the open doors. Moments later the lilting strains of "Ode to Joy" drifted inside.

They were playing the recessional.

Addie sat back on her heels. It wasn't just being where she didn't belong that made her feel especially uneasy tonight. It was knowing that her mom was probably right. Scott was a good man. He wouldn't want to wait forever.

He wanted to marry her now. He'd told her so when he'd proposed three weeks ago. He'd mentioned it again when she'd seen him the night before last. Though her mother didn't know, Scott definitely did not want to wait until she graduated. He wanted to help her through school himself.

She didn't know why she hesitated to set a date.

Setting a handful of plastic game pieces on the table, she stepped through the doors and onto the curved balcony. Down by the reflecting pool with its garland-wrapped Roman columns and cascades of white flowers, she could clearly see the hundreds of gowned and tuxedoed guests. They occupied row upon row of white chairs perfectly angled to have caught the sunset.

Now, in the fading twilight, the glow of hurricane candles lit the aisle, adding to the radiance of the bride as she and her groom moved down the length of white, petal-strewn carpet. A dozen attendants in as many shades of lavender followed the trailing swath of white gown and veil, along with the beaming parents and guests a few moments later.

Two dozen waiters in white dinner jackets funneled from the gazebo, bearing silver trays of champagne to carry into the elegant crowd. The string quartet continued to play, the sounds lovely and classical. The tiny white lights the florists had strung began to twinkle everywhere.

Addie stepped closer to the railing. It didn't matter that she was apparently suffering bridal jitters herself, the scene was magical.

She would never know such a wedding. Even if she'd had the means to create the fairy tale, she couldn't imagine being in front of that many people. Or having to converse with them afterward. Her knees would freeze, her tongue would tie and she would forget everything she ever knew about anything of any interest at all.

The scene absorbed her, drew her closer—and kept her from wondering why she felt more and more trapped.

She could see Gabe on the fringes of the milling assembly. He shook the hand of an older gentleman, then gallantly kissed the hand of the gray-haired matron with him. He moved on, clapping another guest on the back, buzzing a kiss across the cheek of a lady wrapped in a gold lamé stole. Two men came up to him, offering their hands as if to introduce themselves. With his back to her, she couldn't see what he did, but she knew he would have accepted their handshakes, made them feel welcome and at ease. He had a gift for that. He would draw them out, listen to what they had to say. He had a gift for that, as well. She knew, because he'd done it so very often with her.

He would have been easy to pick out of nearly any crowd. He stood taller than the rest, his presence more powerful, more commanding somehow. He definitely commanded her attention in the moments before he turned and his glance swept the empty space behind him.

As if he knew he was being watched, his glance searched the house a moment before he started to turn back. As he did, his glance moved up.

Her heart gave an odd little jerk when he seemed to

notice her. For several unnerving heartbeats, he stared at where she stood half-hidden in the shadows.

The dim lighting made it impossible to clearly see his expression. Still, remembering how unhappy he'd seemed with her, he managed to knot the nerves in her stomach once more before a woman in a strapless gown approached him with another gentleman and he turned to take two flutes of champagne from a passing waiter.

Stepping back into the shadows, she turned to do what she should have been doing all along. No good could come from being idle. Her mother had drilled that into her from the time she'd entered school. Her father had taught her that it was all right for a person to not be doing something so long as they were using that time to recharge their batteries with nature, a long walk or a good book.

All she'd been doing was wasting time.

The need to escape felt more urgent somehow. Fueled by that restlessness, she snapped on all the brass table lamps in the emphatically masculine room, emptied two heavy ashtrays into the plastic bag, and added the remains of chips from a napkin-lined wicker basket and the empty pop cans. She picked up a couple of investment magazines from the long, red leather sofa, added them to a stack by one of the matching wing chairs and gave the dark mahogany tables a quick polishing with a dust rag. The men and the kids had obviously hung out there part of the day.

She had just moved beneath the large painting of hunting dogs above the desk and was adding the last of the glasses to the tray to take to the kitchen when the squeak of a board outside the open French doors caused her head to jerk up.

Gabe stood at the threshold. In each hand he held a glass of champagne.

It wasn't until he stepped inside that she realized the champagne was for her.

Chapter Three

Addie's hand slipped from the tray as she watched Gabe cross toward her. She had never seen him in a tuxedo before. Not in person, anyway. She'd seen photos of him in one in *Newsweek* and in the newspaper, all taken at charity or political fund-raisers. She especially recalled a picture of him at an embassy reception in Washington. At the time, she remembered thinking of how sophisticated and worldly he truly must be to move in such circles.

She had often wondered since then if he simply suffered formality as part of his heritage and his job, because she saw him only at his most casual. As he stopped in front of her now, she could see for herself that he wore refinement as comfortably as he did his old college sweats. The beautifully cut black tux just made him seem a lot more imposing.

Confused by his presence, she blinked at what he held. His big body blocked her view of everything but the studs in his blinding white shirt, the blatantly sensual fullness of his mouth and the guardedness in his quicksilver eyes when he held out one of the crystal flutes of bubbling wine.

"Please," he said, when she hesitated to take what he offered. Behind him, soft strains of music and the steady drone of a hundred conversations drifted inside. "I want to apologize, Addie. I'm sorry for the way I acted this morning."

He raised the glass a little higher.

Not wanting to be rude, she cautiously took it. "You don't need to apologize to me," she murmured, her glance on the bubbles rising in the delicate glass. She felt terribly awkward standing there in her plain shirt and jeans, even if they were what she considered good clothes. When they were outside talking while she worked, the lines of social demarcation didn't seem so distinct. Here, with him radiating sophistication and surrounded by the trappings of his family's wealth, she felt as if she should shrink into the walls.

"I do need to," he insisted, his deep voice thoughtful. "I was out of line. My only excuse is that you caught me off guard.

"I've known you forever," he reminded her. "Between that and the promise I made your dad, I guess I was just feeling a little…protective."

"You have a gift for understatement," she said quietly, trying to ignore the odd tug at her heart.

"Okay. Make that a lot protective," he allowed, since he had gone a little overbearing on her. "And I really am sorry."

Looking as thoughtful as he sounded, he slowly turned the stem of his glass in his blunt-tipped fingers. "You reminded me this morning that you're perfectly capable of taking care of yourself. I'm quite aware that you're a grown woman," he assured her, repeating what she'd so calmly pointed out. "Since you hardly need looking after, I guess all that leaves me to do is hope that this Scott does right by you…and to toast the bride-to-be."

He lifted his glass, offered an apologetic smile.

"Your father wanted only the best for you, Addie. He never wanted you to have to worry or want or have to settle for anything less than what would make you happy." His broad shoulders lifted in a conceding shrug. "That's all I want for you, too."

Addie's fingers tightened on her own stem as he tapped the rim of his flute to hers. Crystal rang, the sound of celebration vibrating in the sudden quiet hanging between them.

The cheerful note seemed terribly out of place. Her father's wishes for her, Gabe's wishes, twisted hard at her heart.

He never wanted you to settle for anything less than what would make you happy.

…anything less…

The ringing died, but the words continued to echo in her head. Gabe was doing exactly what she had thought he would have done when he'd first heard her news, wishing her luck, congratulating her, wanting the best for her. She should have felt relieved that everything had gone back to normal. Yet nothing felt normal at all.

She could again feel the unfamiliar tension in him. It snaked toward her, knotting the nerves in her stomach, tugging her toward him and making her aware of him in ways she had no business considering at all.

Afraid he would see her trembling if she raised her glass, she set it on the desk and focused on one of the bubbles clinging stubbornly to the inside of the crystal. While others raced past it to burst on top, it held its own, determined to hold its ground.

Or, maybe, just afraid to break free.

She found it truly pathetic that she could relate so easily to a bubble. There were things she wanted, but there was so much more she was afraid to even consider because the dreams were so far beyond her reach. Her mother was right. Setting one's sights too high only led to disappointment. Clinging to what she had seemed so much safer.

Gabe's glass joined hers. "You're still upset with me."

"No. I…no," she repeated.

"Then, what is it?"

She shook her head, her focus on the neat pleats in his cummerbund.

"Addie," he said, and slipped his fingers under her chin. "Talk to me."

Her heart jerked wildly as he tipped her face toward his.

"I'm not really sure what to say."

"Just say you forgive me."

"I forgive you."

"Thank you."

"You're welcome," she said, and smiled because he did.

"I'm going to miss you," he admitted, that smile finally making its way into his eyes. "It's not going to be the same here without you."

"I'm not going anywhere for a while."

"Yeah, but you will. And I can't imagine that your husband would appreciate me showing up on your doorstep just because I need to vent or get advice or have you tell me my ego is getting in the way of my job."

She wanted to tell him he could come to her anytime, but she couldn't seem to find her voice. The subtle, sensual brush of his thumb over her cheek froze the words in her throat.

That touch, gentle and innocent as it was, seemed to be toying with a mental lock she'd long ago secured into place.

As a girl, she had fantasized about being in his arms. As a woman, she had long ago accepted that he was light-years out of her league and felt incredibly lucky just to have his friendship. Now, breathing in the arousing combination of aftershave and warm male, the heat of his hand seeping into her skin, she could barely think at all.

He brushed her cheek once more, the smile in his eyes slowly fading. In those smoke-gray depths, she saw what looked very much like a struggle as his glance followed the slow, mesmerizing motion of his thumb. It was almost as if he were considering the feel of her skin, savoring it, committing it to memory—and wondering the whole time if he should be touching her at all.

"Be happy, Addie," he murmured, and leaned to touch his lips to her cheek.

Gabe had felt her go still at his touch. Now he could swear she wasn't even breathing. Beneath his lips her skin felt like satin. Her scent, something fresh, light and amazingly provocative, filled his lungs. She felt impossibly soft, smelled incredible and when he drew back far enough to see the corner of her lush, unadorned mouth, his heart seemed to be beating a little faster than it had just a moment ago.

He hadn't counted on that. Or on the way her stillness invited him to stay right where he was. He was close enough to feel her breath tremble out against his cheek, close enough to see her lips part as she slowly drew in more air.

Drawn by her softness, he slipped his fingers from her chin, tracing the delicate line of her jaw. The feathery crescents of her lashes drifted down. The delicate cords of her neck convulsed as she swallowed.

She wanted his touch.

Something inside him tightened at the thought, snaring him, pulling him back down when he should have been pulling away. He touched his mouth to hers, a soft brush of contact that made his heart bump against his ribs.

He did it again, and felt her pulse race where his fingers rested against the silken skin of her neck. Sliding one arm around her, he eased her forward until her body touched his.

"Kiss me back," he whispered, and felt something molten and liquid pour through his veins when she sighed— and did.

Gabe hadn't quite known what he would do when he'd climbed the stairs to the balcony and entered the room. It wasn't like him to start anything without a game plan. He was the guy who never went into any meeting without a plan and backup and maybe a couple more contingencies for good measure. He liked to have all of his bases covered and to know as much about the other side as his own so he wouldn't be caught unprepared.

He definitely hadn't been prepared this time.

When he'd walked in, all he'd known for certain was that nothing had felt the same since he'd learned of her engagement, that he was sorry he'd acted like a jerk and that he couldn't leave in the morning without telling her he wished her well. They had known each other too long to let his knee-jerk reaction cloud their relationship.

He also knew that he had not planned on kissing her.

He most definitely hadn't planned on the impact of having her small, supple body in his arms.

She tasted like warm honey and felt like pure heaven. Slipping his hand up her side, he curved it just beneath the gentle fullness of her breasts. He wanted to feel more of her. All of her. He pulled her closer, lifted her higher against him, drank more deeply. Their breaths joined, her flavor mingled with his.

He edged his hand up, cupped the side of her small breast. She would fit his palm perfectly. He was sure of it. And would have caved in to the temptation to find out for sure if he hadn't just felt her stiffen.

The sudden stillness in her body had him going still himself. She was no more prepared for the slow meltdown of their senses than he had been. He was as certain of that as he was of the clawing heat low in his belly. He couldn't remember the last time he'd kissed a woman and felt such immediate need. More important at the moment, he couldn't remember the last time he'd kissed a woman and promptly kissed good sense goodbye.

With a ragged breath he slowly lifted his head.

Addie's grip tightened on his biceps, her fingers clutching the finely woven fabric of his jacket as she slowly lowered her head. She couldn't let go of him. Not yet. He had taken the strength from her legs. Or maybe, she thought, she had simply given it to him. There had been no demand. No insistence. Just a slow, sweet heat that had filled her, consumed her and left her burning everywhere he'd touched.

Her breathing was no steadier than his when she finally eased away, willing her knees to support her when her fingers slipped from his arms. Clasping her hands over her fluttering stomach, she felt the little diamond bite into her palm.

Gabe caught the flash of the stone the instant before it disappeared.

Guilt promptly slammed into desire. "I'm sorry," he said for what felt like the umpteenth time that night. "That was a mistake."

He shouldn't have kissed her. He should have let her go with the safe, chaste little buzz on the cheek he'd started with and left well enough alone. He had managed to explain his behavior before. He had no idea how to do it now.

Hating how distressed she looked, he reached toward

her, only to drop his hand in case she pulled away. "Are you all right?"

"You should go," she said, her voice a thready whisper. "People will be wondering where you are."

"You haven't answered me."

"I'm…I don't know what I am," she confessed, clearly rattled. "You really need to leave, Gabe. You're supposed to give a toast."

"The toast can wait."

"No, it can't. You shouldn't even be here."

Gabe couldn't argue that. Duty called, and heaven knew he always met his obligations. With her so clearly closing herself off to him, it wasn't as if staying would help, anyway. He had no idea what to do for damage control.

He took a step back, torn by the embarrassment and confusion so evident in her lovely eyes. Torn by the knowledge that he was the cause of her anxiety.

It wasn't like him not to know what to do in a situation. It wasn't like him to not know what to say. Not knowing if he should apologize again or simply say good-night, he finally decided she wanted nothing from him but his silence and said nothing before he turned and headed for the open doors.

Addie could hear his footsteps on the balcony, listened to them fade down the steps. She was shaken to the core by his kiss, the heat in it, the quiet hunger, and stunned by how shamelessly she'd melted in his arms.

Only when she could no longer hear anything but music did she release the breath she'd held and sink against the side of the desk. As she did, she turned, pushing her trembling fingers through her hair—and saw her mother in the doorway on the other side of the room.

The knot in her stomach turned to lead.

Addie had no idea how long her mom had been standing there, or just what all she'd seen. She'd obviously seen enough, though, to put the unfamiliar spots of color on her cheeks and to make her look as if she just caught her daughter kissing the devil himself.

Rose hurried in, her hands knotted, her voice a frantic whisper. "What in heaven's name do you think you're doing? Are you out of your mind?"

Unable to explain what had happened to herself, much less to anyone else, Addie added the untouched flutes of champagne to the tray, carefully because she was still shaking, and headed across the room to close the doors she wished now she'd never opened.

"Addie, answer me. What is going on?"

"Nothing is going on. I'm finished in here," she replied, her eyes on her tasks as she picked up the basket of cleaning supplies on her way back to get the tray. "What else do you need me to do?"

Her mom retrieved the tray herself. "I need for you to stay away from him," she insisted, her sensible shoes soundless on the carpet runner. Worry threaded the hushed tones of her voice. "He's only going to cause you trouble. He's wrong to pursue you. You're an engaged woman."

"He's not pursuing me."

"How long has this been going on?" she demanded, clearly not hearing.

"There isn't—"

"I know what I saw," came the truly distressed reply. "I couldn't hear you, but there's not a thing wrong with my vision. Oh, Addie," she continued, her voice falling even as her anxiety rose. "I've always been afraid you cared too much for him. You don't think I can see how you feel about him, but you've always allowed him far more influence over you than is wise. It was one thing to have a crush on him when you were a girl, but you have to forget about that man. You're going to mess up your entire life if you think you have any sort of future with him.''

Gabe was the first to leave the next morning. He'd said his goodbyes at the party that lasted long past when he'd turned in at midnight, and slipped out at the crack of dawn while there was no danger of running into anyone who might delay his escape.

Mornings were usually his favorite time of day. He especially liked it when the sun was just coming up and the whole day stretched untouched before him. It was a time of possibilities, a clean slate, another beginning. This morning, though, as he tossed his black leather suit bag into the back seat of his black Mercedes, climbed behind the wheel and headed down the long drive to where the automatic gate swung wide to let him back into the real world, it wasn't beginnings he was thinking about.

It was change.

Apparently he didn't adapt to it very well.

Addie's dad had once told him that how a man dealt with change was often the truest test of his character. Until yesterday Gabe had figured he dealt fine with it. At least he did when he instigated it himself. With something beyond his control, it was clear he'd pretty much flunked the test.

He couldn't believe he'd kissed her like that.

He couldn't believe how she'd responded to him, either. He'd tasted surrender in her, astonishingly immediate, and a hint of passion held ruthlessly in check. The surrender had nearly made him groan with need. The thought of removing the reins from that bridled passion had made for a decidedly restless night's sleep.

His hands tightened on the wheel.

Addie had never been so completely on his mind as she had in the past thirty hours. And never had she been on

his mind the way she had last night. More often than not
when he thought of her, it would be to remember her view
on some issue he needed to address—and her fervor or
sympathy when she expressed it. As restrained as she
seemed when others were around, he usually had no problem getting her to tell him exactly how she felt. All he had
to do was ask her what she thought her father would think,
and she would be the voice of reason.

During his last campaign, when his advisors had wanted
to cancel appearances because he was so far ahead in the
polls, she had made him see that by not staying out there
and encountering more of his constituents, he would miss
the opportunity to meet voters who might have needs he
didn't yet know about. And his purpose as a senator, after
all, was to serve.

When he'd been going nuts with the thought of having
to move his office because a youth center had gone into
the building behind him and the noise through the walls
was deafening, she suggested he donate soundproofing and
double-pane windows.

He'd saved a fortune in time by not having to move.
He'd also earned the undying gratitude of the youth facil-
ity's director over the unexpected savings on the center's
fuel bills.

She knew her mind, knew what she felt was right, wrong
or of no consequence.

For everyone but herself, anyway. He didn't know why
she did it, but she tended to downplay her own talents and
abilities. It was as if she didn't even realize she had them.
The only dream he'd ever known her to cling to was college. And there, he had the feeling she was doing that as
much for the memory of her father as she was herself. Tom
had wanted it for her. Therefore, she would see that it was
done.

As for anything else she might have wanted, she seemed

to settle for whatever appeared the most reasonable, or caused the least disruption for everyone else. Sometimes he thought the trait quite generous. Mostly it annoyed him that she shortchanged herself so much.

Not that he had any business being annoyed, he reminded himself. She'd apparently had dreams he'd known nothing about and was well on her way to fulfilling them.

He just hoped she wasn't shortchanging herself there, too.

Not liking the thought that she might well be, he turned on the radio, tuned to the morning news.

The thought of her no longer being around when he went home bothered him more than he would have thought possible.

The thought of how she'd felt in his arms bothered him even more.

He turned the radio up, telling himself to let it go. That bit of spontaneous combustion meant nothing. She had her life. He had his. And his did not allow for a relationship with his family's engaged groundskeeper.

He needed to find some way, though, to make sure she knew he really did want only what would make her happy.

Addie felt good. Great, actually, as she hung her serviceable brown canvas jacket on a peg inside the back door of her little house and toed off her muddy rubber boots. The gladiola corms she planted every spring had to be dug up again every fall so they wouldn't freeze over winter. She now had all eight hundred and six of them spread out on screens and would tuck them away in peat moss as soon as they were dry. She'd also separated and replanted the crowded lily of the valley crowns along the far perimeter of the property.

It had been a week since the wedding, but she was working as hard as ever.

Being her mother's daughter, she checked those tasks off the long list she'd left on the maple kitchen table and headed for the narrow white refrigerator by the stove.

The cottage consisted of only four rooms—a little L of a kitchen that occupied the back part of the cozy living area with its stone fireplace and slip-covered furniture, two tiny bedrooms and an even tinier bath. Her mom had never been much for color. What wasn't serviceable beige or brown was either pale mauve, pale rose or paler pink. Addie preferred brighter colors herself, though the only place she indulged that uncharacteristic bit of boldness was in her own room. There she'd hung yellow curtains on her window, pictures of sunflowers and lavender fields on her walls and covered her bed in bright Bristol blue.

She'd had plans to build a canopy over her bed, too. But there'd never been time.

The thought reminded her of her list—and that she needed to ask her assistants, Miguel and Jackson, if they could spare an additional day a week for her next month. The two part-time gardeners worked for other families, too, and their time would be at a premium, but she would need their help with the heavier pruning.

Although she could handle the hedges herself and had no problem keeping the bridle paths cleared and all the potted plants and borders free of anything dead or dying, an old oak by the stables needed a large limb removed before the coming winter's ice cracked it off for her. The red maples that formed a canopy on a section of the lake path needed to be pruned back, and with the autumn leaves starting to fall, there was no way she could keep the lawns cleared alone.

Her empty stomach took precedence over the list at the moment, however. Unfortunately, the fridge was nearly empty. Her mom usually ate at the main house with Olivia, and Addie rarely bothered to cook for herself. She didn't mind eating alone, but she couldn't see much point in messing up the kitchen for one person when the local grocery store stocked perfectly edible entrees in its freezer section.

The cottage freezer bore two Lean Cuisine dinners. Selecting one, reminding herself as she did that she needed to add shopping to her list, she popped it into the microwave, grabbed a handful of Oreo cookies for an appetizer and debated whether to take a shower before she ate or wait until after. Scott had a game tonight. There wouldn't be time to meet him before it started, but they would go for coffee afterward. Decaf for her, espresso for him. She had no idea how he managed to sleep with all that caffeine in his system, but he wasn't the only person she knew who seemed unaffected by what would have had her clinging to the ceiling all night. Gabe drank coffee as if it were water, too.

The thought caught her unscrewing a cookie.

Screwing it back, she set it beside the others on the counter. She had to stop thinking about him. There hadn't been a day go by in the week since the wedding that she hadn't found him creeping into her thoughts. She had thought of him often before. Frequently, in fact. But never the way she'd been thinking of him lately.

Not wanting to think of him now, not wanting to acknowledge the little ache she felt every time she did, she forced herself to concentrate on something else just as she had every time he'd entered her mind. Since she still had eight minutes left on the microwave, the shower seemed as good a distraction as any.

She made it into the little hall between the bedrooms before the ring of the phone stopped her.

Thinking it was Ina either wanting a ride to the game or offering one, or Scott, making sure she wasn't too tired to make the game, she snatched the beige receiver from its handset on the old maple end table. The amenities of the cottage hadn't quite made it into the current century. They had an answering machine, but the phone wasn't portable. Tethered to the wall by its cord, she stayed where she was between the rose-print, slip-covered sofa and matching overstuffed chair and answered with a smiling, "Hi."

A distinct pause came over the line before she heard a deep, quiet, "Hi, yourself."

Her hand tightened on the receiver. "Gabe?"

"I tried calling earlier," he said, the husky tones of his voice vibrating along her nerves, "but I guess you weren't in yet. I figured you'd have to be in by dark."

"I just got here," she said, her hand to her chest to still the erratic bump of her heart.

"Do you have a minute? I need some advice."

"Advice?"

"On a plant. I need to send one to a colleague," he explained, over what sounded like a pen or pencil tapping on a desk. "I was thinking about that conversation we had when you showed me the flowers in Mom's colonial garden. You said flowers have meanings. I just can't remember what you said they were."

She gripped the phone a little tighter.

"You've never called me for advice before." He'd never called her for any reason. Ever.

"I needed to this time," he said simply. "This colleague is important. I can't trust the choice to just anyone."

Addie slowly sank to the wide arm of the sofa. He had always had a way of making her feel as if her opinion really mattered to him, as if what she knew was of real worth. He would watch her, listen to her as if he actually relied on her to help him where he felt others could not.

She didn't honestly believe she was that big of a help to him. But she liked that he thought she was. The wisdom and knowledge she passed on had come from her father, just as the knowledge about the flowers had. If she could help him now with some of what she'd learned from him, then she would.

"What sort of message do you want to convey?"

The tapping stopped. For a moment she heard nothing but silence.

"Support, I think," he finally said.

"There's ivy. It signifies fidelity."

"What about friendship?"

"That would be rose acacia."

"Can you make a bouquet out of that?"

"Not really."

"I need something more than that, anyway," he told her, caution suddenly evident in his tone. "I need for this person to know that I hope she has forgiven me for the way I acted...and that I'll always be there for her if she ever needs anything."

This time the pause was hers.

"I don't think there's a flower that means that."

"Is there anything close?"

"Not that I know of."

"That's too bad," he murmured. "I really want this person to know that I'm behind anything she feels she needs to do." There was no mistaking the sincerity in his voice or the concern that joined it. "I just hope that marrying someone she isn't sure she loves is what she really wants."

The pretense of talking about someone else had started to die when he'd mentioned hoping he'd been forgiven. By the time he'd finished his last sentence, it was as dead as the slugs Addie had found in the snapdragons.

She didn't doubt that he meant well. She didn't question that he needed to assuage the guilt he obviously felt over the way he'd handled the weekend. She just wasn't prepared to debate her decision to marry. Especially not with him.

"I think I'd better go."

"Addie…"

"Really. I'm already late." She swallowed, feeling totally torn. "Good night, Gabe."

She didn't know what he said. Or, if he said anything at all. He wasn't the only one handling things badly. She already had the receiver back on the hook.

Staring at it as if the thing might grow horns, she stayed right where she was. She couldn't imagine why Gabe was doing this to her. In one breath he clearly intended to support her in whatever she did. In the next, he questioned if she even knew what she wanted.

At the moment, she couldn't honestly say she trusted how she felt about her decision herself. Ever since he'd kissed her, she'd been fighting dreams she had long ago suppressed. He'd resurrected them with nothing more than his touch and evoked feelings she hadn't even known she possessed until those moments she'd been in his arms. Scott had never made her go weak. He had never made her mind go blank. He had never made her feel hunger. Yet, there had been hunger in that kiss. For her and for Gabe.

Her troubled thoughts had her shoving her fingers through her short, practical hair. She didn't believe for an instant that she had any sort of a future with him. She'd been convinced of that long before her mother had taken it upon herself to drive that point home on their way out of the library. And she knew he certainly wasn't thinking in terms of anything that hinted even remotely of an intimate relationship. All he had said was that he would be there for her. Period. No more. No less. The man was being groomed for governor and beyond, and the Kendricks were all as aware of their status and position as she was of her own.

Too agitated to sit, she rose, shoved her fingers through her hair again, turned full circle and wondered what she was supposed to do now.

Deep inside she knew she was in trouble. She'd actually known it all week, but refused to consider it because she had nothing to gain by the admission. Denial was easier, neater and at least gave her a chance at a life with a good man and a home of her own. She wanted a family. She wanted children. She wanted to know the joy of having her own little boys race around the lawn, hollering and laughing the way Gabe's little second cousins did. But she knew that if she truly cared about Scott, she wouldn't have been so desperate for the feel of Gabe's hard body. And her heart wouldn't have just leaped at the sound of his voice.

She did care about Scott. Just not enough.

Because she had always been in love with Gabriel Kendrick.

Chapter Four

Leaves rustled as Addie tossed branches of lantana onto a growing stack of vegetation and attacked the fading bush once more. The metallic clip of her pruning shears melded with the brittle rustle of woody branches and drying leaves and the occasional bray of a horse. She pushed on as the sounds echoed in the crisp October air, diligently moving from one bush to the next as she took all sixty feet of the stable's border down to the ground.

Addie usually loved autumn. She appreciated all of the seasons, actually, but there was something about fall's colors, smells and the crisp air that lightened her heart. She had never regarded the season as some did, as a time when everything was drying up and dying. For her, fall was simply a time of preparation; a time when she readied the plants and flower beds to rest over the winter while she was at school. And while she was away in the rain and the snow, she looked forward to the new shoots of spring.

The only thing she appreciated that morning, however, was the constant activity as she clipped, tossed and clipped again. It was good to be busy. Being busy burned up the agitation she felt. Some of it, anyway. It didn't do a thing, however, to keep her from dwelling on why that awful distress was there.

She'd broken up with Scott two days ago, and the guilt was as fresh and raw as it had been the moment she'd done it. She just wasn't sure if the awful guilt was there because she'd accepted his ring in the first place, or because of how hurt he had been when she'd finally given it back and told him why she'd made excuses not to be alone with him for the past couple of weeks.

He'd had no problem understanding that she couldn't go to weekend tournaments with him because she had to work. And she'd gotten a lot of mileage out of claiming fatigue after his games. But she'd had no way to explain why she would quietly withdraw from his touch when he would simply try to hold her hand.

She was lousy at confrontation. She'd even considered not breaking up with him just to keep from upsetting the plans he was making. But that frightening thought had registered just about the time he'd confronted her himself. He had already sensed that something was wrong. He'd even asked if she was having second thoughts.

It had become clear in a hurry that the big jock hadn't actually expected her to admit that she was—at least not to the degree he soon discovered. She had admitted to those second thoughts, and third thoughts and fourth. She had told him she would miss him and that he was a wonderful man, but that she wasn't being fair to him. She'd acknowledged being desperately sorry for that, too, just before she'd told him that she had truly thought it would work, but she knew now that she wasn't being fair to either one of them. He deserved a woman who loved him completely. One who had no doubts about how she felt, because no one should enter a marriage with doubts.

She said nothing about Gabe. Nothing about what had prompted the apparent change in her feelings, or how she'd nearly made herself sick with worry trying to figure out how to give him back his ring. She didn't mention, either, how she felt as if she'd just kissed her future goodbye.

All Scott had said was that he should have expected something like this to happen. He claimed he should have known that a woman who'd never had a serious relationship until the age of twenty-five obviously had serious hang-ups about men and marriage. And, she was right, he didn't want to marry anyone with doubts.

Addie had no hang-ups about men. She had none about marriage. She loved the idea of a husband, home and children of her own. But she'd hurt Scott. At the very least, she'd hurt his immediate plans for his own future. She wasn't about to deprive him of taking a potshot at her if it made him feel better.

As for Gabe, she wished she'd never laid eyes on him.

Thinking about Scott was painful. Thinking about Gabe simply made her more agitated. Grabbing a handful of branches close to their roots, she freed them all with the sharp edges of her clippers. She threw them behind her, dried brown leaves falling like rain, and winced when a twig scraped her cheek on the way.

She was telling herself she needed to stop thinking about men completely before she poked out an eye, when the hum of a car engine drifted up from the long, winding drive.

She couldn't see the driveway from where she worked between the stables and the garage. She knew which car was coming, though. Over the years she'd come to recognize the sound of all the vehicles that routinely came and went from the estate. The roar and rattle of Ina and

Eddie's usually hay-filled pickup truck. The refined hum of Mrs. Kendrick's sedate little Lexus. The varying drones of Mr. Kendrick's Porsche, Ferrari and Rolls-Royce. The low, throaty purr of Gabe's Mercedes.

It was the purr that caused her to slip off her work gloves. In less than a minute Gabe would pull into the cobblestone courtyard between the garage and the house.

She didn't want to see him. Not wanting him to see her, either, which he would the minute he pulled in, she backed away from her task and headed across the lawn to a narrow opening in the thick trees.

Thanks to him, her mother was convinced that she'd lost her grip on reality. She no longer had a fiancé, and most of the plans she'd been making for her future no longer applied. As upset as she was at herself for letting her feelings for him interfere so completely with her life, she absolutely did not want to have to pretend everything was all right should he decide to wander over for small talk.

She refused to run, but she felt a certain urgency behind her pace until she stepped into the shadows of the woods. The path there led to the cottage, and the cottage was the one place on the entire property that she had never encountered him. He never went there.

The yard-wide path was dirt, beaten smooth from years of her and her parents' use. Moving deeper into the quiet, she followed it to the little storybook-like house with its willow rocker and flower boxes on the porch and lacy curtains in the windows. She'd always felt safe there, comfortable in a way a person does in the only home she has ever known. But any sense of safety she felt died minutes after going inside to wash the scratch on her cheek and down two aspirin for the tension headache brewing at the base of her skull.

She'd just opened the front door, thinking to tackle a

task farther from the house, when she caught sight of Gabe on the path.

The sunlight cut through the trees, its dappled light flashing in his dark-sable hair and catching the tasteful gold of his tie tack. His dark suit was perfectly tailored, his shoes impeccably polished. His chiseled features were handsome even with the faint frown marring his brow, and as he strode toward her, there was no mistaking the power in his long, lean body.

She rather wished he'd been built like a toad.

Mostly, she wished he wasn't there at all.

Her purpose defeated, she stepped onto the porch and closed the door behind her.

"I saw you head for the path," Gabe called, immediately aware of her reluctance. He couldn't detect so much as a trace of welcome in the gentle contours of her face. Shoving his hands into the pockets of his slacks when he stopped at the porch's single step, all he could see was strain—and a wariness he feared he'd put there himself. "You're running late."

Puzzled, she crossed her arms, shook her head. "Late for what?"

"The historical society meeting," he replied, puzzled himself as he glanced from her gray thermal shirt to her worn jeans. "I thought we could go together. Why aren't you ready? It starts in less than an hour."

Looking even more confused, or maybe it was more cautious, she picked up a pair of gloves from the seat of the willow rocker.

"I don't know anything about a meeting," she said, her tone gentle as always. "But if it starts in an hour, I'd better not keep you."

Gabe had pretty much counted on a little awkwardness with her at first. He hadn't seen her since he'd kissed her, or spoken to her since he'd blown his apology to her two weeks ago. He had not, however, considered that she would no longer be interested in his help.

"I thought you wanted my support on your project."

Tucking one glove between her arm and her side, her brow pinched. "I do."

"Then why aren't you accepting it? Look," he murmured, watching the faint creases in her brow deepen as she pulled on the other glove. "If this is about what I said before you hung up on me, let's talk about it. Okay?" He hated the guardedness about her. It didn't matter that it was his fault it was there. It didn't suit her. It robbed her of the openness he was so accustomed to from her, and denied him the warmth of her smile. She wouldn't even meet his eyes. "I really do hope everything works out for you and your fiancé."

Reaching for the other glove, she tugged it on, too. "I appreciate that," she murmured, "but there is no fiancé. And I didn't hang-up on you. I said goodbye first."

Barely, he thought, only to realize what she'd just said.

"What are you talking about?" The click of the receiver had still been ringing in his ear when he'd told himself to back off and leave her personal life alone. Aware of the distress she clearly didn't want him to see, he decided he'd backed off too soon. "What happened to Scott?"

"Nothing happened to him," she said, still avoiding his eyes as she worked her fingers into the leather and stepped off the porch. "We're just not engaged anymore."

"He broke it off?"

She shook her head, her hushed voice dropping another notch as she started past him. "I did."

His hand shot out, snagging her arm to keep her from walking away. Beneath his fingers he felt the quick tension in her strong, slender muscles.

Touching her was not good, he thought. Try as he might, he hadn't been able to get the feel of her body out of his mind. The memory had taunted his sleep, nearly destroyed his concentration.

"Why?" The memory of her response to him was just as clear, just as taunting.

"It doesn't matter."

"Of course it does." With her head bent, all he could see was the top of her dark, gleaming hair. The soft strands parted on one side, falling to hide what little he might have been able to see of her profile. "What did he do?"

"It wasn't him," she quickly defended. "It was all me."

She wasn't going to answer him beyond that. He could tell by the way she still refused to meet his eyes. It wasn't like Addie to be stubborn. He doubted she had a willful bone in her curvy little body. But there was no denying the protective wall she'd thrown up around herself.

It was almost as if saying anything more would be admitting too much.

The quick concern he'd felt for her slammed into caution as she eased away and crossed her arms. He'd been around women all his life. Between his mother, his sisters and the women who had come and gone over the years, he'd become quite adept at reading a woman's body language. Next to breathing, he considered it one of man's more basic survival skills.

Beyond her self-protectiveness, the way she avoided his eyes bothered him most. She was closing him out, pushing him back the way a woman did when she was angry, hurt or distressed—and faced with the person who had upset her.

The way she had done after she had pretty much melted in his arms.

"Addie." He spoke her name quietly, sounding as cautious as he suddenly felt. Maybe she hadn't been able to forget those moments, either. "Does this have anything to do with what happened between you and me in the library?''

She'd be lousy at poker, he thought. Her guilty glance made it as far as his chin before it fell to his chest.

"This isn't your problem, Gabe."

"It is if I caused it."

"All you did was make me see that you were right," she defended, carefully skirting his question. "I don't want to marry a man I don't love. And the best thing for you and me to do is pretend that what happened in the library...didn't." She tightened her grip on herself. "You said yourself it was a mistake."

He started to reach for her. Afraid she'd pull away again if he did, he stuffed his hands back into the pockets of his slacks instead.

He could hardly blame her for being upset. Not after the way he'd gone totally possessive at the thought of her no longer being there for him. The last thing he'd ever intended to do was cause her pain. Or to ruin the ease they'd once had. There was no doubt in his mind now that he'd done both.

"I didn't mean that the way it sounded."

She finally looked up. Disquiet clouded her dark eyes, robbed them of their light but not of their expression. The look she gave him clearly said he owed her far better than that.

"You meant it exactly that way, Gabe." There was no accusation in her tone, only conviction, and more understanding than he figured he deserved.

"I've grown up knowing every move you need to make to get where you're going," she said calmly, "and I know how careful you have to be. A man like you doesn't get involved with a woman like me. We both know that."

She had grown up listening to him unload on her father. She had been privy to discussions of how important image was and of what was expected of him long before they'd had similar conversations themselves. But Gabe was dead certain she wasn't thinking only of his career as she stood with her arms hugged around herself. She was protecting herself from being pushed aside first.

He hated that she felt the need to protect herself from him. But there was nothing he could say to restore her comfort with him. She thought he was thinking of his career when he'd said kissing her had been a mistake. His career had actually been the last thing on his mind.

He'd been thinking only of her. Of how incredibly soft her skin felt, how good her body felt flowing against his. Then he'd caught the flash of her ring and he'd remembered that she belonged to someone else.

That fact alone had prompted his remark.

"You're going to be late," she murmured.

The reminder caused him to glance at his watch, then to her jeans. His thoughts of her were dangerous enough. The knowledge that she had been affected enough by him to call off her engagement was even more so.

"I don't understand why you won't come with me." The meeting seemed infinitely safer to consider, even if her attitude toward it did baffle him. "You filed the application, everything's in motion and now you won't follow up."

Some of her guardedness slipped. Shaking her head, the confusion he'd seen earlier surfaced once more. "I didn't file an application. I haven't had time to finish the research."

"Well, someone filed it. I sent a memo to the Office of Historical Preservation to let me know when it came in. Donna got a call three weeks ago that they had the paperwork." Donna was his secretary. He would have mentioned that call the night he'd phoned Addie, too, had their conversation not been cut so short. "I wanted to add my personal recommendation, so I had her call the OHP and ask when I could tour the site. I guess they contacted the Camelot Historical Society because Helene Dewhurst called her a few days later and arranged it for today.''

"Someone filed the application? For my project?"

"You didn't know about any of this?"

Her guard continued to fall. "I don't know how I would. My only dealings with the society have been a phone call and a meeting with its president a couple of months ago. The last time I talked to Mrs. Dewhurst, she said she'd just hang on to what I had until she heard from me.''

"She has a copy of your research?"

"And the plot maps. I gave them to her when we met at the library.''

"Does anyone else have them?"

"Not that I know of. I didn't give them to anyone else.''

"Then, it looks like Helene filed it.''

At his flat conclusion, the slender slashes of Addie's eyebrows merged.

"But I told her there is information missing. Did she get it from somewhere else?''

"I have no idea. Donna summarized everything for me in a memo.'' Seeing to the details was the responsibility of the preservation office. All he was doing was putting the influence of his name and his office behind the request. "I haven't seen the application.''

"She must have misunderstood,'' Addie decided, clearly bewildered by how that had happened. "I didn't ask her to file it. I just wanted help doing it myself.''

It was Addie's nature to give people the benefit of the doubt. Gabe knew that. Commendable and generous as the trait was, he also found it decidedly naive.

"There's a lot of prestige attached to a restoration like this.''

"I don't care about the prestige.''

"But there are those who do."

"So let them have it," she insisted, totally unimpressed with any distinction she might gain for herself. "I just want to put the garden back the way it was. The way Dad would if he'd found it."

Gabe didn't care at all for the feeling he was getting. He knew what Addie's motives were. She wanted the garden restored simply because it should be, because it was something her father would have done with the Victorian plants he had propagated to preserve that small bit of beauty and heritage. She would do it *for* him, too, as a tribute to the work he'd done to preserve what many would have let fade into oblivion.

Gabe already wanted to know why she'd been excluded from the meeting. Because her purpose was so innocent, discovering that reason seemed even more necessary. "I understand that your goal is just to see it done," he assured her. "But you did the research and you deserve to be in on the planning. I know Helene," he told her, thinking of how tirelessly the middle-aged socialite had worked organizing fund-raisers during his last campaign. She was the sort of volunteer who had the right contacts, loved to entertain and loved being associated with anything or anyone that made her look good.

She also tended to steamroll over anyone she perceived as unimportant, or in her way.

"Once she gets her teeth into something, she has it organized and underway while most people are still trying to figure out what the job requires. If you want in on this, you need to come with me now."

It wasn't that he didn't trust Helene. He just didn't trust her to care what this project meant to the young woman who had discovered it. Yet Addie didn't seem nearly as impatient as he was to make sure her exclusion hadn't been intentional.

Twin lines of worry formed between her eyes. "Where is the meeting?"

"Mrs. Wright-Cunningham's home."

"Mrs. Andrew Wright-Cunningham?"

He gave a nod, glanced once more at his watch. "It's about twenty minutes from here. If you hurry, we'll just make it."

"I can't go."

His dark head came up. "Why not?"

"Do you know who they are?"

"Of course I do. Dad plays golf with Andrew at the club."

"And Olivia knows their cook. Chef," she corrected, because even among the ranks there was hierarchy. "She runs into him at the butcher. She said he studied at the Cordon Bleu. And Mrs. Wright-Cunningham had relatives that came over on the Mayflower."

"So she has a French chef and relatives who ate salt pork on a leaky boat. What's that got to do with anything?"

Addie blinked at the utter lack of comprehension in his handsome face. Aside from the fact that the hostess of the meeting had blood as blue as Olivia's varicose veins, the historical society was made up of recognized horticulture experts and ladies-who-lunch. That was a league to which Addie most definitely did not belong. The only league she had ever belonged to had to do with bowling.

"I wasn't invited," she pointed out ever so reasonably. In society, there were protocols to be followed. Even she knew that. "You don't just show up at someone's home like that without an invitation."

"So you'll go as my guest," he informed her, clearly not seeing a problem. "How long will it take you to change clothes?"

"Gabe," she said, still sounding reasonable, feeling

slightly panicked. "Can't you just tell her that I'd intended to do this project myself? I know I'll have to get the funding, and there might be others who want to get involved with the actual work, but I can oversee the restoration. Your word will have far more clout than mine."

"There's nothing I can say that your presence won't say louder. If you go, you'll show her you're committed to the project. You want her to know that, don't you?"

"Of course I do. But—"

"Being there will prove that. You can also clear up what your intentions were when you contacted her."

That's what she was afraid he meant for her to do.

"I don't have anything to wear."

"Women always say that."

"It's true! I don't own any luncheon suits."

"A dress will do fine." Frustratingly unimpressed with her dilemma, he took her by the arm and turned her toward the porch. "Come on. We have thirty minutes to find something."

It was the "we" that warned her. That and the determined grip on her arm as he escorted her across the porch and waited for her to open the door. He wasn't going to let her back down. And backing down was exactly what she wanted to do.

Mrs. Dewhurst made her nervous. She had been kind enough when Addie had met her at the city library, but the woman had also positively reeked of confidence, sophistication and status. The idea of being surrounded by a roomful of women of that same ilk put a knot in her stomach the size of a fist.

She left Gabe standing in the middle of the small, neat living room and headed for her closet. She could shower in five minutes and blow-dry her short hair in three. Makeup would take another five. Ten if she primped. That left her between twelve and seventeen minutes to decide between the flowy little pink sundress she'd bought on sale a year ago last August, a denim dress and corduroy jumper she'd nearly worn out and the navy coatdress she'd bought to wear to her dad's funeral.

Since it was barely fifty-five degrees outside and definitely fall, the sundress was pushed aside. The denim and the corduroy were far too casual.

"I really don't have anything," she called out, deliberately overlooking the fact that she could have checked her mother's closet. Not that there'd be much there other than black uniforms. Her mother's social life was nonexistent.

Hearing her claim, Gabe tossed aside the bridal magazine he'd found on the coffee table with a sticky note from her mom saying, "please reconsider."

It had been years since he'd been inside the cottage. And then he'd been there only once when he'd come looking for Tom after being unable to find him anywhere else on the property. As far as he could tell, nothing had changed. The walls were the same pale beige. The slip-covered furniture still had muted-pink cabbage roses on its tan background. The Currier & Ives prints hanging over the sofa were the same as he remembered seeing there before.

He'd never been to Addie's room, though.

After the muted colors of the rest of the cottage, walking into her private space was like stepping into sunshine.

The brilliant blues and warm yellows caught him by surprise as he stopped at the threshold. The shades were strong, bold in a way he would never have expected of her, until he considered that the colors were those of the sun and the sky, and that she would naturally choose to surround herself with brightness.

Or maybe, he thought, watching her sort through the tiny closet across from her pillow-covered bed, she was trying to surround herself with warmth.

The thought caught him off guard.

So did his presence in her room.

"If I'd known about this sooner," she said, clearly thinking he was still on the other side of the wall as she pushed aside hangers, "I could have bought something."

"Let's see what you have."

Her hands fell as she turned, her expression skeptical. "You want to see my clothes?"

"Just the dresses."

Still looking a little uncertain, she turned back and produced the pink one.

He shook his head. "That's for summer."

Putting it back, thinking this little exercise totally futile, she reached past her work shirts for the denim and the corduroy. Watching him cautiously, she held up a hanger in each hand.

"Too casual."

No surprise there. That's what she'd thought herself. That left the navy-blue coatdress.

"That has potential," he claimed. "What else do you have?"

"Nothing."

He eyed her evenly. "No woman has only three dresses."

"Well, that's all *I* have. I wear pants most of the time," she explained, wondering where he thought she went that her wardrobe would require much of anything else. Her own social life consisted of an occasional movie in town with Ina, a rare night out with the few friends from high school who hadn't left town and, until recently, dinners and games with Scott—none of which had required anything other than good jeans or slacks and a sweater.

"There has to be something else."

Frustrated, she turned to the closet again and reached into the back. "I have this," she admitted, just to prove she had nothing that would work. "But it's totally not appropriate."

Gabe's eyebrow arched. She was right, he thought. The slip of silky black fabric was definitely out of the question. From what he could tell of the strappy little number, it didn't even have a back.

"Do you mind if I ask where you wore that?"

"I haven't worn it anywhere. A friend talked me into buying it in case I had a date last New Year's Eve."

She apparently hadn't had that date. He'd had one, though. He'd attended several parties, actually. All command performances for contributors and political connections. He just couldn't remember who he'd had with him.

His glance moved back to the dress.

Doing his level best not to imagine her in it, only halfway succeeding, he indicated the coatdress. The thing would cover her practically from neck to knee and was modest to a fault.

"The navy one is fine."

"That's my funeral dress."

"Addie."

"It is," she insisted. "I've only worn it twice. Both times were to funerals. Well, one was a memorial," she quickly corrected. "It was for the guy who owned the bakery before the Brinkmeiers took it over. I didn't know him, but Olivia did and she didn't want to go alone, but the connotation isn't good. With the dress I mean."

"Maybe it's time you put a more positive spin on it." He liked what she'd done for the family's cook. It was time Addie got back some of what she gave. "Get moving, okay?"

Addie wasn't sure how she did it, but she managed to pull herself together in exactly twenty-six minutes. Even Gabe seemed impressed by that when she walked out the door. At least, he looked impressed by something as he ran a quick glance from her low-heeled navy pumps to the tailored navy wool skimming her body. She had added her only good jewelry, the pearl stud earrings her parents had given her for her eighteenth birthday, and borrowed a small black purse from her mom's closet. But even though Gabe assured her that she did not look as if she were going to a funeral, she didn't believe for a moment that anyone would mistake her for one of the beautifully dressed people clustered in the piano parlor of the Wright-Cunninghams' palatial home.

Chapter Five

"Of course I don't mind that you brought a guest. Any acquaintance of you or your family is always welcome here." Mrs. Andrew Wright-Cunningham, Essie to her close friends, pulled back from Gabe's cheek. "You know that, dear.

"Miss Lowe," the silver-haired matron continued, moving her gracious smile to where Addie stood somewhat uncertainly at Gabe's elbow, "I'm delighted to meet you. You have an interest in history?"

The question was perfectly logical, considering that history, or the preservation thereof, was why the historical society existed. It just took a moment for Addie to get past her nerves to respond as the woman in the chunky silver jewelry and pale-blue knit suit ushered them away from the maid who'd opened the door to the opulent foyer.

With her glance aimed in the general direction of the woman's second chin, she murmured, "My interest is more in historical gardens, I suppose."

"Then this particular project will be of special interest to you. We're quite excited about it ourselves. It's not often that something from the seventeen hundreds turns up undiscovered anymore."

Oblivious to Addie's connection to the project, or even to who she was, other than an acquaintance of a Kendrick, she stepped forward and touched her wrinkled and ringed fingers to Addie's arm.

"I hope you don't mind if I steal the senator for a moment. I have a houseguest from Rockport I'd like him to meet and she's leaving in a few minutes to join friends for lunch. I'm going to turn you over to our vice president.

"Tiffany," she called, her hand falling as she sought the attention of a young woman visiting with several others. "This is Miss Lowe. She's a guest of the senator and interested in historical gardens. Would you introduce her around, please?"

Addie felt the nerves in her stomach knot an instant before she turned to Gabe. He towered beside her, tall and solid as the oaks lining the drive outside. He had assured her that Mrs. Wright-Cunningham would have no problem with her presence, and Addie had to admit that the woman couldn't have seemed more kind. But he hadn't said a thing about leaving her on her own.

The hint of panic in her eyes seemed lost on him. Even as he glanced toward her, Mrs. Wright-Cunningham was threading her arm through his and chattering away as she led him off.

"Miss Lowe, is it?"

Desperately wishing Gabe hadn't just abandoned her, wishing she could just disappear until he turned up again, Addie managed a smile for the polished socialite smiling back at her. Tiffany had the same meticulously cut chin-length hair as Mrs. Wright-Cunningham, only hers was a dozen shades of blond. Her eggplant-colored suit was the same tailored knit style every other lady milling about the exquisitely appointed salon behind her appeared to be wearing.

The woman offered her beautifully manicured hand. "Tiffany Mellon."

"Addie," she replied, mindful of her own slightly ragged and unpolished nails.

"What an interesting name. Is that short for Adrienne?"

At the moment she rather wished it were. "It's just Addie," she explained, not caring to add that her middle name was May. Not with names like Tiffany and Wright-Cunningham floating around.

"Oh. Well. Would you like some tea?" she asked, skeptically eyeing Addie's perfectly presentable, but obviously not expensive ensemble.

What Addie wanted was to leave. The knot in her stomach told her she didn't belong here any more than she did in the Kendricks' main house. But she told Tiffany she would, because it seemed the polite thing to do, and followed her, adjusting the thin strap of her little shoulder bag, into the thick of the historical society members clustered around groupings of pink damask chairs and ivory silk sofas.

Addie had never been to a tea before. She knew Mrs. Kendrick hosted them because her mother would occasionally mention one in the planning stages or bring home leftover watercress sandwiches or tarts that had crumbled. She'd just never considered what went on at one until she found herself being watched over the rims of delicate china teacups by two dozen well-dressed women and six men in tweed chattering in little knots of four or five.

Two maids, both with white lace collars and aprons over their black uniform dresses, served exquisite finger sandwiches and petits fours from wheeled tea carts.

A ruddy-faced gentleman in tweed stood alone near one

of those groups of women. Approaching him, Tiffany motioned one of the carts over to her and introduced the mustached and bespectacled gentleman to Addie as Professor Williamson, a retired professor of botany.

His bushy eyebrows rose above his silver-rimmed bifocals as he extended his beefy hand. "You're a new member of the society?" he inquired, his vowels broad and Bostonian.

"Just someone interested in vintage plants," she admitted, liking him, but not so sure how she felt about the woman frowning at the scratches on her hands as she accepted his handshake.

She wore gloves when she did heavier work. Even then, she wound up with scratches and splinters. But she rarely wore them when she worked with smaller plants. It was easier to weed without the bulk, and she liked the rich, loamy feel of the earth between her fingers.

"You garden yourself, then?" he asked.

"Yes, sir," she murmured, aware of Tiffany now looking more closely at the scratch she'd covered with makeup on her cheek, and eyeing her six-year-old navy blue pumps.

"How refreshing," the gentleman said with a smile that made his rust-and-gray mustache twitch. "Someone who actually gets into the dirt when she gardens. Do you spend much time at it?"

She was about to tell him it was practically all she ever did when the tall woman in a charcoal knit behind him glanced over her shoulder.

As the woman caught her eye, Addie felt the words die in her throat.

The smile on Helene Dewhurst's perfectly oval face froze, only to magically come to life again when she turned to fully face her. Her wedge of shining brunette hair swung like a curtain with the movement, not a single strand shifting out of place. Her makeup was perfect, her gold jewelry tasteful, and there was no way for Addie to mistake the dismissal in her eyes when she gave her a quick once-over.

"Well, hello, Addie."

"Mrs. Dewhurst," Addie replied, pulling her hand back from the professor's grip.

"You know each other," Tiffany concluded, looking faintly relieved to be freed of her duty. "Why don't I leave you to visit?" she said to Helene. "I want Essie to introduce me to the senator."

"He's here?"

"He just arrived," Tiffany replied as a dark-haired maid arrived with the tea cart.

"May I offer you tea, ma'am," the maid said to Addie with a courteous smile.

It was Helene who replied with a crisp, "Perhaps later." Clearly dismissing the servant along with her inquiry, she touched Addie's arm. "Would you excuse us, Professor?" she said to the man now eagerly eyeing the glossy chocolate squares on a tiered silver serving dish. "I need to speak with this young lady alone."

"By all means," he replied, more interested in the food, anyway. "It was a pleasure, Miss Lowe."

"Perhaps we should talk over here," Helene continued, looking as polite as she sounded as she edged Addie toward a huge potted palm in an ornate oriental pot. The women occupying the pink chairs ten feet away had their backs to them. Another group stood beside a long gold credenza, remarking over its collection of Fabergé eggs and the painting of the owners' Pekingese hanging above it.

"I must admit I'm surprised to see you here." Secluded now by the plant, her voice low, Helene's smile turned patronizing. "The society's regular meetings are open to all, Addie. But this is a special tea for Senator Kendrick. It's invitation only,'' she explained, emphasizing the exclusivity of the occasion and Addie's obvious intrusion on it. ''We didn't even invite all of our regular members. Only the board and a few of our more prominent associates.''

Addie held her hands tightly in front of her, trying not to look intimidated, dead certain she did, anyway. She could identify far more easily with the maids than she could anyone else in the room. The only thing worse than simply being there was the thought of embarrassing herself or Gabe.

''I'm a guest of the senator's,'' she replied, wishing she were taller, braver, more confident.

''I beg your pardon?''

Addie cleared her throat. ''I came with Gabe…Senator Kendrick,'' she corrected, desperate to get her purpose over with. ''He thought I should,'' she explained, unashamedly throwing his weight around for him since he wasn't there to do it for her himself.

Her fingers tightened. ''Do you know who filed the application for my project?''

Sudden amusement replaced disbelief. ''*Your* project?''

''The one I came to you with,'' Addie said, suddenly even more uneasy.

''That isn't *your* project,'' Helene said, sounding as if she couldn't imagine where Addie had come by such an idea. ''And our organization filed it.''

At the blunt, completely unapologetic admission, Addie had no choice but to concede that Gabe had been right. She had even prepared herself for the rather distinct possibility that Helene had gone behind her back. She had not, however, considered that the woman would question her stake in the project itself.

''It was my research,'' she reminded her, sounding

calm, feeling a little frantic. "And I was under the impression that all the research had to be completed before the application could be filed. I never intended for you to take it over or use it without me."

It was as clear as the pea-size diamond studs in Helene's ears that she hadn't expected to be challenged. She apparently didn't care to be confronted, either. Especially by someone she so clearly regarded as an underling.

Her high cheekbones turned pink with offense as one perfectly penciled eyebrow arched. "Then you misunderstood our meeting."

The flat finality in the woman's voice had the hard edge of a door slamming shut. There had been no misunderstanding, but, faced with the certainty in Helene's cool hazel eyes, Addie couldn't think of a thing to say that would alter the woman's unexpected stance and not make the uncomfortable situation that much worse.

"There you are, Helene," came the low rumble of a male voice. "I've been looking for you."

The sound of that deep voice was blessedly familiar. Watching in uneasy fascination, Addie saw Helene's chill disappear an instant before the woman made a quick quarter turn. As she did, Helene exposed where she'd all but hidden Addie between her, the shell-pink wall and the massive palm.

Gabe's eyes darted from the society president's quick smile to Addie's pale features. "Is there a problem here?"

"Nothing we can't resolve," Helene replied, evidently thinking her social equal would understand her little dilemma. "You brought your mother's gardener as your guest?"

"This is her project," he replied easily. "I thought she should be here."

Pure indulgence swept Helene's face. "I'd hardly call this her project, Gabe. It belongs to the public."

"She knows that."

The indulgence entered her voice as she lowered her tone. "Perhaps it should be made clearer," she confided, speaking as if Addie had suddenly become transparent. "I immediately saw the potential in this project when she brought it to me. I also explained that we couldn't help her with funding ourselves and told her that would have to come from the state. I didn't realize she was under the impression that this was something she could do on her own."

"You said you'd help me file for the funds."

At Addie's quiet, decidedly unassertive claim, Helene's tone turned tolerant. "Again," she emphasized, "I believe you misunderstood."

Dismissing Addie once more, she looked back to Gabe, spreading her hands as if to say she couldn't imagine anyone being so naive. "I was about to explain to her that a girl without credentials can't seriously think she can present something of such importance without the historical society's backing. Being the earliest known public garden, it's simply too significant a piece of history to leave to the inexperienced. Obviously, you recognize the significance of it yourself to be personally endorsing it.

"I can see where you would want to bring her here to show her how we work," she quickly continued, clearly thinking him generous for wanting to teach someone like Addie how the system functioned. "But we need to make it clear who will handle this."

Gabe carefully considered every word she said. Addie just couldn't tell how he felt about what he heard as he casually pushed his hands into the pockets of his slacks and gave Helene a thoughtful nod.

"I couldn't agree more. And we'll make sure everyone understands who's in charge of what," he assured her, his tone utterly conversational. "But you know how I feel about acknowledging personal contributions, Helene. The society wouldn't have known about this if Miss Lowe hadn't come to you. By the way," he said, looking truly perplexed, "who finished the research?"

Helene hesitated. "I don't believe there was that much left to do," she replied, clearly surprised he even knew about that aspect of it. "The garden can be completed based on the information we have."

His glance cut to where Addie had tried to disappear into the palm fronds. He took a step toward her, forcing Helene to turn and face Addie herself. "Isn't there a fountain or something missing?" he asked Addie.

"A water trough," she quietly replied. "It's indicated on the drawings, but I haven't been able to find a reference to what it looked like."

"That wasn't significant enough to keep from filing the application," Helene informed him. "We had enough information without it."

"And that information is what Miss Lowe gave you?"

"Well, yes. We filed exactly what she gave me," the woman conceded, only to suddenly catch the significance of the questions.

"Oh, I see the problem," she said, light dawning. "You're talking about the little…ah…clerical error in the actual application." She sounded apologetic, looked faintly guilty. "I don't believe Miss Lowe's name was typed on the notes attached to the filing, but that can be corrected easily enough."

She seemed to think that was the recognition Gabe was talking about. But Gabe hadn't seen the application and, until that moment, he hadn't known that Addie's name hadn't appeared anywhere on it. Apparently, not even on her own research.

The audacity of the woman facing him was unbelievable. Even worse was the fact that she didn't seem to find anything wrong with what she'd done.

Gabe had long ago mastered the ability to rein in any emotion that might hamper logic, cloud his judgment or give any ammunition to the opposition. If masking what he felt served his purpose, then that was exactly what he did.

It served his purpose now.

Though he could feel the muscles in his jaw tighten, his tone remained deceptively even. "I believe it should be corrected as soon as possible."

"Of course," Helene agreed, still oblivious. "I'll have our secretary tend to it right away. So," she said, certain that she had resolved everything to everyone's satisfaction, "shall we have our tea and go look at the site? This really is an exciting project, Gabe. And your endorsement will get us the funding so much faster than if we had to wade through all that red tape ourselves."

Gabe's glance moved from Helene's confident smile to the discomfort Addie was busily trying to hide. He knew all about the value of proper support for a cause. He was also well aware that Addie's discovery was a public treasure, and not something one person could handle alone. But the woman's blatant attempt to overlook Addie and her contribution had him bridling inside.

It was one thing to omit her from a meeting. Another entirely to steal her work.

He just wished Addie would speak up for herself.

"I'll be happy to recommend it," he said as Helene started to turn, "as long as Addie heads the project committee."

He couldn't have imagined Addie and Helene sharing anything in common. In personality, attitude and experience they were at opposite ends of the human spectrum. But at the moment they wore exactly the same expression.

Both looked at him as if he'd just taken complete and total leave of his senses.

Addie's mouth was open, but she said nothing.

Helene's mouth was open, but she was already speaking her mind. "You can't be serious."

"Sure I can. Addie probably knows as much or more about horticulture as anyone here. She found the garden. She did the research. She should head the project."

"But she isn't…a member," Helene said, scrambling for a reason that wouldn't sound as overtly arrogant as all the other reasons she couldn't say aloud with Addie standing right there. *She's your mother's gardener. She isn't one of us. She's…common.*

"That's easy enough to take care of. Your membership chairperson is here, isn't she?"

"Well, yes, but…"

"Then, we'll get that detail taken care of before we leave."

Helene stiffened. "The dues are quite expensive."

"Gabe," Addie practically whispered. "I can't…"

"It's not a problem," he replied, clearly intending to take care of the money himself as he cupped her elbow to get her moving.

Helene's eyebrows arched again.

Addie's merged. "I can't let you pay for me."

"Sure you can. You want to work on the project, don't you?"

Her troubled eyes flicked toward Helene. Looking as if she didn't know whether or not she should admit it in front of the woman, she finally looked back up at him. "You know I do."

"Then let me take care of this."

She would pay him back. He had no doubt that was what she was thinking as he scanned the concern in the fragile lines of her face. He even considered telling her that she would do no such thing when he realized how protective he was feeling of her at that moment. Addie seemed to have picked that up, too. As if seeking that protection, she edged closer.

Standing as they were, his hand on her arm, their bodies nearly touching, Gabe became aware of Helene closely watching them both.

Addie seemed to notice that, too. As her suddenly self-conscious glance fell from his, she took a half step away, clasping her hands so tightly her knuckles turned white.

"Shame on you, Helene," a bright female voice admonished. "Keeping the senator all to yourself over here."

"Oh, I guess you are sharing," the woman in pearls and chocolate knit murmured, seeing Addie when Helene stepped aside. The newcomer gave Addie's petite frame a smiling once-over before her glance bounced to the man towering beside her. "I hope I'm not interrupting."

"Not at all." Slipping his hand from Addie's elbow, he splayed his fingers at the small of her back to nudge her forward. "We were just about to go find your membership chair."

"That's Mary Beth Penobscot," the woman supplied, with a helpful nod over her shoulder. "She's in the taupe Chanel right over there. Would you like me to get her for you?"

"I don't think that's necessary right now," Helene said, suddenly a little too cordial for the way she'd acted moments ago. "The senator and his…friend need some refreshment before we leave for the site." Smiling in a way that made Addie even more nervous, she motioned to the maid she'd dismissed before. "I don't believe either of them has even had tea."

"I wish you hadn't done that."

"Done what?" Gabe's hands rested loosely on the steering wheel, his expression preoccupied and his eyes on the road as they left behind the unkempt orchard that had over-taken the centuries-old garden. There had been little to see other than a few low piles of stones that had once been garden walls, but Addie had been excited all over again when she'd located them once more. Excited inside, any-way. Under the nerves.

"I wish you hadn't made the announcement that I was the one who found it."

"But you did."

"You didn't have to make a big deal of it."

He looked perfectly comfortable behind the wheel of the sedately powerful vehicle with its black leather seats and navigation system on the dashboard. Just as comfortable as he had standing in front of the society speaking about the importance of preserving history. She'd never seen him speak in public before.

She was sure she would have been impressed, too. If she hadn't been so busy trying not to hyperventilate. She was only now drawing her first relatively easy breath in more than two hours.

"I didn't make a big deal out of it. I just said that we were fortunate to have the woman with us who made this significant discovery and everyone took it from there." His narrowed glance cut toward her, concerned, measuring. "The applause made you uncomfortable," he finally con-cluded.

So had being the center of attention afterward. She had been fine with the guys in tweed and the older women who were into gardening themselves. Especially when they'd spoken one on one. But with everyone else, she'd felt the same face-burning awkwardness she'd experienced the day Ashley Kendrick had announced her engagement by the gazebo. The problem today was that she'd had no task to hide herself in. All she could think to do was point

out the old wall foundations to those who seemed interested.

Helene hadn't been one of them. Several women had
stayed back wanting to preserve their shoes from the this-
tles, but Helene and a half-dozen of her obviously closer
friends had barely spoken to her at all. They certainly
watched her, though. Her neck hairs felt permanently on
end from the speculative looks they sent in her direction.
Their heads had been together a lot when they'd watched
Gabe, too.

Addie glanced from the bucolic countryside rolling past
the passenger window to toy with a loose thread on her
skirt hem. She couldn't believe how Gabe had stood up
for her. Or, how grateful she was that he had. Having seen
the site again, she really wanted to see it blooming with
the progeny of her father's cherished plants. She just had
the awful feeling that the simple desire had somehow
ripped the lid off Pandora's box.

"I do appreciate what you did for me," she said, not
wanting him to think she didn't. "I don't do very well in
situations like that."

"I could tell. You hardly said a thing when Helene admitted she'd filed your research."

"I didn't need to. You were doing fine without me."

"Would you have called her on it if I hadn't shown
up?"

She flicked the thread. "It's a moot point."

The breath he blew sounded suspiciously like a sigh.
"You can't let people intimidate you like that, Addie. You
need to stick up for yourself."

That was easy for him to say. She doubted he'd been
intimidated by anything in his entire life. Rather than point
that out, or dwell on her myriad shortcomings, she kept
her focus on what he'd done.

"You stuck up for me just fine," she murmured. "But

I have the feeling that it's going to cost you. You're supposed to play nice with your constituents. Especially those who helped get you elected to office.''

"I don't want the vote of someone who would steal another constituent's idea.''

"But it's not just her. It's her friends. Someone like that can have a lot of influence in the community.''

"I still don't like the way she treated you. I'm sorry you were embarrassed.'' A muscle in his jaw jerked. "I knew she was a snob, but I had no idea she'd behave that way.''

Addie tucked the thread under her hem. "I'll get over it,'' she assured him, slowly smoothing the fabric. Helene's rudeness wasn't the only thing that had embarrassed her. Gabe's defense of her had, too. And his protectiveness. Especially after it had become apparent that Helene had noticed it. That unexpected protectiveness didn't seem quite so burdensome sitting alone with him now. If anything, she found reassurance in it, and a familiar sort of comfort.

"I'm used to people not seeming to notice that I'm there.'' She had never experienced that with him, though. Not ever. "I'm not so sure Helene will get over what happened today, though. She looked like you'd punched her when you said you wanted me to head the project for them.'' She could actually empathize with the woman on that one. He'd blindsided Addie there, too. She could hardly imagine being on a historical society committee, much less being in charge of one. "You're not really serious about that, are you?''

"It wouldn't be for them,'' he countered, logical as always. "You'll be a member, too.''

"But I've never done anything like that before.''

"So, expand your horizons. You're the one who told me to take advantage of the unexpected.''

"Only because Dad always said that,'' she murmured,

fiddling again with the thread. "If I said it, it was only because it was appropriate at the time."

Gabe glanced at her once more. She didn't seem to understand that knowing when to apply a philosophy was more important than knowing it in the first place. "He may have said it, but you're the one who helped me use it. It never would have occurred to me to donate insulation for the building behind me instead of moving."

"Sure it would have. Eventually."

"No," he said flatly, "it wouldn't. It didn't," he said, "until you mentioned it."

She'd mentioned something else that had struck him, too. Just a few moments ago. Only not in such a positive way. She'd said she was used to people not noticing she was there.

She was used to being overlooked.

She was used to being treated the way she'd been treated by Helene.

The realization jerked hard at the protectiveness he'd felt a while ago. He didn't even bother justifying the feeling. Or denying it. It was simply there, overriding the exasperation he'd begun to feel at how easily she underestimated herself.

There had been no mistaking Helene's lack of regard for her. The older woman had hinted at that lack of respect the moment she'd referred to Addie as his mother's gardener. She'd then proven it in spades when she'd gone on to speak to him as if Addie couldn't possibly comprehend their conversation.

She'd clearly regarded the admittedly docile young woman as being of little consequence to her. She'd even regarded the information Addie had brought to her as her due, or the historical society's, anyway. She'd acted as if Addie were a servant who'd found a bracelet in a sofa and given it to her employer. Since the bracelet didn't belong to her in the first place, the servant had no right to expect recognition for turning over something that wasn't hers anyway.

Helene's elitist attitude had said far more about her than the young woman she'd literally backed into a corner. Another point Addie's father had often made was that a person could be judged by how he treated someone who could do nothing for him. Helene obviously did not treat such people well. But his concern wasn't with her at the moment. It was with the young woman who had yet to get past the nerves that still had her fidgeting.

He'd never seen Addie this way before. But then, he'd never seen her away from the estate, either. There, he'd always sensed an air of serenity about her, a kind of peacefulness that made a person feel calmer himself simply being with her.

At least that's the way she had been—before he'd kissed her.

The road forked ahead. The one to the left was lined with fast-food restaurants and strip malls and would lead to the highway. The one to the right continued on through the country and would eventually lead to the narrow road that skirted the estate. He took the one to the right to take Addie home, but three miles down, instead of taking the road into the estate, he pulled onto the wooded service road a quarter mile before the main gate and stopped when the bend in it obscured the road behind them.

Surrounded by nothing but trees, he cut the engine. As he did, Addie's puzzled glance swung from the thread she'd wound around her finger.

Turning toward her, he draped one arm over the wheel. "I want you to answer something for me. And I want you to be honest. Not that you aren't always," he qualified. "I just don't want you holding back."

Addie gave him a nod, let go of the thread. "Okay,"

she said, figuring his mind had drifted back to his work in the silence. He looked like he always did when he hit her with a question about something he was wrestling with. Focused. Serious. A little brooding.

"Has any member of my family ever treated you like that?"

"Like Mrs. Dewhurst?"

"Call her Helene. And, yes, like her."

"No," she quickly said, swiping back her bangs as she frowned. Not a single Kendrick had ever been deliberately rude to her. "Never."

The brooding remained, setting his mouth in a grim line, drawing his brow low over his intense gray eyes.

"What about guests at the estate?"

"I'm never around them. I've seen some when I've been working on the bridle paths or something," she qualified, "but I try to leave the area before they get too close so I'm not in their way."

It was part of her job to be unobtrusive.

Gabe had no idea why he hadn't considered that before.

He'd grown up with hired help. He had a wonderful housekeeper himself in Richmond. But he'd never considered anyone who worked for him or his family differently from the way he did his secretary or his office staff. There were those he liked better than others. Those who felt more like friends than employees. But everyone had a job, and as long as everyone did it, took pride in their work and their talents weren't wasted, he paid little attention to their actual job description. Practically speaking, the security personnel his family sometimes hired were paid to maintain low profiles, too.

He'd just never considered the impact of living that way on someone as gentle and unassertive as Addie. Especially when he considered the sort of woman her mother was. Rose Lowe was as prickly as cactus, reserved to a fault and, from what Addie had confided in him, far less encouraging than a parent should be when it came to her education.

She had been sheltered by her father, held back by her mother and lived day in and day out feeling she needed to get out of everyone's way.

He'd been pushed from the day he was born to explore, thrive, conquer.

Her glance had fallen to her hem once more.

Touching his fingers to her chin, he tipped her face back toward him.

"No one should ever not notice that you're there, Addie. You should never be overlooked by anyone. You're a beautiful, intelligent woman and you have as much right to be on that committee as anyone in Camelot. I can't think of anyone more capable to head that project."

His touch was gentle. The look in his eyes was not. There was a fierceness there that warned her of anger at injustice. She'd seen that look before. She'd just never seen it because of her.

She couldn't believe he'd called her beautiful.

She couldn't believe how moved she was by his confidence in her, either. Or how badly she missed his touch when his thumb grazed her cheek a moment before he deliberately lowered his hand.

"You really think I can do it?" she asked, not at all sure he understood what he was getting her into.

"There isn't a doubt in my mind. You do all the work on these grounds. Or supervise getting it done. The garden is a hundred times smaller."

Her fingers found the thread again. "Work with the society, I mean."

"There are a lot of people there who don't think like Helene," he pointed out, tempted to touch her again, thinking better of it. They were talking easily. The way they always had. He didn't want to risk screwing that up again. "You met some of them already. But if she gives you any grief about heading the committee, call me and I'll straighten her out. It's only right that you oversee this."

His glance slipped from her eyes, grazing her face, settling on her mouth. A heartbeat later he jerked his attention to the ignition and put the car back into gear.

With everything as settled as it was going to be, Addie took a deep breath, reminded herself that she was doing this for her dad and hoped as hard as she could that she could surround herself with members like the professor and Mrs. Wright-Cunningham. It had always been Gabe's nature to overlook details in favor of the bigger picture. When he had an objective, he was like a general intent on conquering a target.

She also knew that he made his judgments based on what seemed most fair and forthright. She admired that about him. Respected him for it. When it came to fairness, he was fierce in his convictions and absolutely dedicated to following them through.

He just didn't seem to realize that in his well-intentioned effort to protect her interests, he'd thrown her in with the sharks.

It didn't take long, either, for those sharks to start circling in the water.

Chapter Six

Addie knew something was wrong the moment she saw her mother hurrying toward the cottage. There was urgency in her step, and her arms were crossed so tightly over the black sweater she'd thrown on over her uniform that a person would think she was freezing.

Her mother also never showed up before eight, and it was only five-thirty in the evening.

Watching her from where she sat on the step, pulling off her rubber boots, Addie wondered first if something had happened to someone. If maybe Olivia had forgotten to take her heart medication and suffered an attack. Or if Ina had fallen from a ladder washing windows and broken her neck. It was that kind of angst lining her mother's thin face.

"What's wrong?" Letting go of her boot, Addie wiped her damp fingers on her jeans. It had rained last night. Though the day itself had cleared, the lawns and grounds were still soaked. "Is someone hurt? Do you need me at the house?"

Reaching for the boot she'd already taken off, she snatched it up to pull back on.

"It's all over Camelot, Addie. There isn't anyone who doesn't know. Sweet mother of mercy," Rose fumed, bringing her daughter's motions to a dead stop. "Didn't you think people would find out sooner or later? Did you think at all? And you had the audacity to lie to my face! I never would have expected that of you. Ever!"

With one hand on either side of the rubber boot cuff, her sock-covered toe pointed to go in, Addie looked up at the thin, pale woman practically vibrating in front of her. She didn't know which stunned her more. Her mother's disbelieving anger or the accusations that made absolutely no sense at all.

"It's no wonder you wouldn't set a date." Her mother swept past her on the step and pushed open the front door. "Did you really break up with Scott? Or did he break up with you when he found out?"

Incredulous, Addie could only stare. "Found out what?"

"Oh, Addie, please," her mother muttered in a tone guaranteed to set Addie's teeth on edge. "About your relationship with Gabe. What else do you think I'd be this upset about?"

"My what?"

From the way her mom stood stiffly beside the open door, it was obvious that she wanted them inside where Ina's son or one of the other employees couldn't come by and overhear. Not so sure she wanted to lock herself up with all that inexplicable fury, Addie rose and stayed right where she was.

"What are you talking about?"

"Your affair," her mother frantically whispered from

where she planted herself at the threshold five feet away. "Olivia heard about it from the butcher. She hadn't been home five minutes before the Dewhursts' housekeeper called to tell her the same thing."

Addie's heart felt as if it had stopped beating.

"The Dewhursts' housekeeper?"

"She and Olivia are friends. They play bunco on Sunday evenings," her mother muttered, seeming to think Addie was questioning the woman's connection to the cook. "She overheard her employer on the phone with one of her friends. She saw the two of you together."

"The housekeeper?"

"Not her. Mrs. Dewhurst," her mother clarified, clearly exasperated with her daughter's failure to address more pertinent issues. "Apparently, so did the entire Camelot Historical Society."

Addie's mind began to race. She'd had the uncomfortable feeling yesterday when Helene and her friends had been talking that Gabe's support of her would cost him. She just hadn't counted on the nature of the talk being so completely outrageous. "It wasn't the entire society. It was only the board and some guests. All we were doing—"

"It doesn't matter if it was only one person who saw you! What were you doing going to something like that, anyway? And with him? It's bad enough that you're carrying on, but you don't do it in public!"

Her mother had barely raised her voice. Only her eyes were yelling. But there was no discounting the fervor behind her concern. Wanting desperately to calm her down, Addie held up her hands and took a step closer.

"We're *not* carrying on. There's nothing going on between Gabe and me," she insisted, trying to stay calm herself. "He's just helping me with that garden I found. Gabe thinks I should be head of the committee, but Mrs.

Dewhurst doesn't like that idea. She's making more of Gabe's helping me than there is.''

Her mother's expression didn't change. Not by so much as the twitch of an eyelash did what Addie say seem to matter.

She tried again. ''He's just looking out for my interests, Mom. Mrs. Dewhurst got the wrong idea about what she saw.''

''*I* saw you with him,'' her mother immediately reminded her. ''I saw you in his arms in the library, Addie. And what I saw was not 'nothing.' I warned you then that you'd be foolish to think you had any sort of future with him,'' she admonished before Addie could think of a way to defend what she had seen, ''but you obviously didn't listen.''

Clearly distressed by that failure, she turned toward the rocker, only to turn right back and pin her with her worried glance once more. ''Is he why you and Scott broke up?''

A sense of unreality had Addie slowly shaking her head. ''They're not saying that. Are they?''

''If they weren't before, they are by now. Olivia mentioned to Ruth that you two had called off your engagement.''

''Ruth?''

''The Dewhursts' housekeeper,'' her mother said in the same exasperated tone she'd used before. ''Is he?''

She wanted to know if Gabe was why she and Scott were no longer together, but Addie had no idea how to answer that. She couldn't deny that her feelings for Gabe had been instrumental in ending her engagement. Yet she couldn't admit that. It would only dig her in deeper.

Her few seconds of hesitation apparently admitted it for her.

''Oh, Addie,'' her mother moaned. Pleading entered her eyes. ''It will never work. Can't you see that? Gabe isn't going to be there for you. Not the way Scott would have been. Men like Gabe Kendrick have different priorities from men who aren't set on conquering the world, and his priority isn't going to be a woman he can't have beside him in front of the cameras.

"It's always the mistress who pays when she gets involved with a powerful man," Rose insisted, sounding torn between protecting her daughter and wanting to shake some sense into her. "And Gabe and his family are as powerful as they come. But it isn't just you who will pay if this goes any further," she warned, the scope of her worries compounding. "This is going to cost me, too."

The pleading turned to pure anxiety. "I have no idea how long it will be before Mrs. Kendrick hears of this, but you running around with Gabe and fueling gossip isn't going to bode well for either of us. If you don't put an end to this right now, we both could get fired."

The intimidating pronouncement was no sooner out of her mouth than her lips pinched and she crossed the porch. The rubber soles of her sensible shoes chattered like mice on the damp boards. Beneath the light knit of her sweater, her narrow shoulders looked as stiff as a plank.

A couple of uneasy heartbeats later, she had swept past, the squeaks had gone dead, and Addie was left to stare at her retreating back.

Her mother actually thought she was Gabe's mistress.

His *mistress*.

The thought had Addie sinking in disbelief against the porch post.

She wasn't sure how long she stood there after her mom had disappeared from the path. But the toes of her bootless right foot felt cold when she finally slid down the post and found herself back on the step.

Blinking numbly at the ground, she tried to think of what she could have said to convince her mother that her relationship with Gabe was innocent. But the more she thought, the more she doubted there was anything that would have made any difference. It seemed that her mother had long suspected how she felt about Gabe. And what she had seen in the library was apparently all the proof she'd needed to believe everything she'd heard.

The air felt colder when Addie pulled a deep breath of it and crossed her arms over the uneasy sensation in her stomach. She didn't know which made her feel more sick at the moment, the fact that the truth had gotten her no-where or her mother all but telling her that Gabe would sleep with her but that she wasn't good enough for him for anything else.

She shook her head as if to physically shake off the disconcerting thought. She already knew where she stood in the social scheme of things. The reinforcement hadn't been necessary. It wasn't as if she and Gabe were inti-mately involved, anyway. Their relationship didn't feel as easy as it once had, but there was nothing about their friendship for them to be ashamed of. They had nothing to hide.

The problem was what people might come to believe in the time it took for everyone to realize that.

"Uncle Charles. Leon." Gabe reached across the table in the darkened restaurant and shook the hands of his fa-ther's brother and the political advisor who would spear-head his upcoming campaign. "Sorry I'm late. The limo got stuck coming out of Kennedy."

Charles Kendrick sat back in the leather barrel chair and lifted his glass of Scotch from the gleaming mahogany table. "Airport traffic is a mess this time of evening. Don't worry about it."

Gabe had always thought his uncle could have passed for his father's twin. A year shy of his father's sixty years,

Charles had the same slashes of gray at his temples, the same heavy brows, the same distinguished features. The differences were in temperament. His father went after whatever he wanted with a passion that suffered no obstacle. Charles prided himself on quietly making obstacles disappear.

There were those who said Gabe was just like his father. Gabe himself had always aspired to be more like his uncle.

Charles motioned toward the bar with its cherry paneled walls and gentlemen's club atmosphere. "Let's get you a drink before we get started. I'll call a waiter over."

"I spoke with a waiter on the way here. I have one coming."

Gabe unbuttoned his jacket and pulled out a chair. He'd been playing catch-up ever since he'd left Camelot two days ago. The projects he'd set aside from the morning he'd spent with Addie had been shoved into yesterday. What hadn't been done yesterday had spilled over into the past twelve hours. Now, after a Rotary Club breakfast, three committee meetings, a library dedication and a short flight to Washington, D.C., he was ready to work on his future.

Gabe settled into the chair directly across from Leon Cohen. He had first met the forty-something, balding and bespectacled political strategist in his uncle's law office two weeks ago. He'd immediately liked the man's blunt, straightforward style. Leon wasn't the sort to mince words or waste time beating around the bush. He was the no-nonsense type whose job was to get the job done. Since the last thing Gabe wanted was someone to hold his hand or stroke his ego, he had hired him on the spot.

Their meeting now was to discuss potential contributors. But Leon seemed to have something else on his mind. Leaning forward with his elbows on the table, he cradled his highball glass with both hands.

"We have a problem," he announced, his tone frank and his voice low so as not to carry. Other conversations took place around them, the tones equally hushed as the movers and shakers of the nation's capital hashed out policy over paella and pork tenderloin. "Actually, we have two. The first is that I apparently failed to make myself clear when I said I need to know everything that can be used against you. If you want me on your team, you have to trust me. Completely."

"Leon needs to know about any skeletons, Gabe." Ice cubes clinked as Charles swirled the liquid in his own glass and leaned forward, too. "If you want him to map an effective campaign strategy, he needs to know anything about your personal life that can in any way influence the public's opinion of you. Or open you up to criticism by the opposition."

A motion at Gabe's side drew his attention. Masking his incomprehension over what kind of secrets they thought he had buried, he let the waiter place his martini in front of him. With a low "Thanks" he leaned forward himself when the man discreetly disappeared.

"I'm at a loss, gentlemen. I don't even have a personal life right now." He spoke half in defense, half in complaint. "I discuss bond issues while I play racquetball. I jog with my aide in the morning so we can go over the day's agenda, and I can't remember the last time I went to dinner or the theater with someone who wasn't pushing a cause or wanting me to push one. What is it you're looking for?"

Leon's glance never wavered. "The basis for the rumor that you've been hiding an affair for the past year."

Gabe had lifted his glass. Had he already drunk from it, he would have choked. "An affair?" The glass went back on its napkin. "And who would I be having this affair with?"

"Your mother's gardener," Leon supplied, looking unimpressed by Gabe's surprise. "I understand she's also the housekeeper's daughter. Word is that you're the reason she recently broke her engagement."

"She did break her engagement." Gabe mentally scrambled to figure out how anyone would have known he had anything to do with that. Or even if he truly did. Addie had said she didn't want to marry a man she didn't love, and the kiss they'd shared had weighed in there somewhere. But she hadn't broken it off for him. "She just didn't want to marry the guy."

"Then you do see her?"

"Every time I go home," he admitted without qualm. "We're friends."

"Friends?" Leon's thin eyebrows arched. "She's your mother's gardener," he pointed out, making it sound as if that somehow made true friendship implausible. "Just what kind of 'friends' are you?"

A muscle in Gabe's jaw twitched at the insinuation in the man's tone. "Good ones."

"Well, you're going to have to have higher standards than that. Or, at least better judgment about being seen with her," his advisor brusquely informed him. "I would expect this sort of carelessness from your brother, but it's exactly the kind of thing you need to avoid. Frankly, I don't care who you sleep with as long as you're discreet about it. But if you're going to sleep with the hired help, you have to keep it out of the press."

The muscles in Gabe's jaw went tight. He didn't know which goaded him more; the man's assumptions or his totally unwarranted admonitions. What he did know was that he resented his actions being compared to his charming-but-irresponsible brother's. When it came to a sense of duty, he and Cord barely even seemed to share the same genes. Cord worked hard, but he played harder. If there was a rule, he broke it. If there was an adventure, he was on it. And the women. The women alone had kept him almost constantly in the tabloids the past few years. Over those same years, Gabe had gone out of his way to keep his focus on his goals—and to keep his personal life as uncomplicated as possible.

Picking up the toothpick in his glass, he studied the olive impaled on it. As much as he'd like to, he wasn't going to draw those comparisons for Leon. In public, the Kendricks stood together, defended each other. It had always been that way. Family tradition would not stop with him.

"What press?"

He bit off the words, his quiet anger clearly surprising the man who had expected either chagrin or defense.

"There was a paragraph in the About Town section of the *Camelot Crier* this morning. It's a gossip piece that says she was seen in your company and speculates about how long you've been together. The *Richmond Times* picked it up tonight. My secretary called the reporter and what we hear is that reliable sources confirmed the broken engagement. That will appear in both papers tomorrow. He said other sources have also confirmed that they've seen the two of you in each other's company."

"We went to a meeting," Gabe said, his tone as flat as the padded-leather menu at his elbow. "Reliable sources" could be anybody. "A lot of people saw us together."

"Look." He leaned closer, his jaw working, his tone deceptively quiet. "When I say Addie is a friend, that is exactly what I mean. That's all I mean," he stressed. "There is no affair, recent or otherwise.

"You say I need to trust you," he reminded the man who had already drawn his own conclusions, "but you need to understand that when I say something, you can take it at face value. I'm hiring you to do a job and I expect you to be on my side. That means coming to me if you have a question and not assuming anything until we've talked. I'm not going to have anyone on my campaign who doesn't believe in me, and I'm not going to do anything to sabotage myself.''

''I can see where your doubts came from,'' Charles said to Leon, fully aware of the jockeying necessary in high-stakes professional relationships. Leon's excellent reputation had been hard earned and he expected it to be respected. He also wanted the prestige of Gabe's campaign. Gabe, on the other hand, had an equally excellent reputation, wanted the man's expertise and since he was paying the guy, deserved his respect unless he proved himself unworthy of it. ''But if Gabe says there's nothing going on, you can believe him. I told you this doesn't sound like him, anyway. We discussed the sort of woman he needs for a partner just last month and he's in full agreement.''

Apparently convinced, consideration replaced Leon's doubt. ''My apologies, then.''

Gabe accepted with a nod.

''So,'' Leon continued, in that easy way men have of brushing past differences as if nothing had happened at all, ''what started this?''

Charles shoved his glass aside. ''That's what we need to work on now, Gabe. I've been in law and politics for thirty-five years. If there's anything I've learned, it's that there is always a kernel of truth in a rumor. We need to know what triggered it.''

Gabe quietly contemplated his drink, took a slow sip of the biting concoction. Addie had warned him that there would be consequences for his support of her.

''I probably did,'' he admitted, proving to Leon why he could believe him. If he was at fault, he said so. ''She found a garden that our historical society is interested in, and I wanted to protect her interests in it. The president of the society practically stole her research.''

''Who's this president?'' Leon asked.

''Helene Dewhurst.'' Contemplation turned to a frown. ''She wasn't too happy when I insisted that Addie head the committee to restore the garden. She doesn't like the idea of having someone without the right connections in her circle,'' he explained, thinking Leon should have no problem identifying with the woman's mindset. Barely a minute ago, he'd questioned how friendship could possibly exist between him and someone in his family's hire. ''But Addie did the work and she deserved the recognition.''

Charles knew the Dewhursts. ''You think Helene is the source of this?''

''If the piece in the paper said something about people having seen us together, it would have to be her or her friends. Gossip runs rampant in her crowd,'' he muttered, thinking of some of the things he'd overheard her and her cronies discuss while working on his last campaign. ''And that meeting is the only place Addie and I have been together off the estate.''

Leon's mouth pursed. ''So you overrode this woman's authority within her group.'' The man was nothing if not quick. ''How insistent were you?''

''Very. I told her I'd pull my support if Addie didn't get the chair.''

''So this is just a case of someone trying to get back at you,'' Charles concluded flatly.

''I'd question if it was that overt.'' Gabe rubbed his brow, wondering if Addie had seen the article, afraid she would feel responsible if she had. ''But it could be.''

''Then, what we need to do now is stop this woman and stop the rumor.''

Leon nodded in agreement with Charles, his glasses

catching the faint glow of the single squat candle on the table.

"You have a couple options there," he said. "The most straightforward way is to counter with what you said to us about this Helene stealing her research and getting her nose out of joint because she doesn't get to play her way. The advantage you have is that it's the truth. The disadvantage is that the truth could turn into a mudslinging contest or a libel suit. Do you have enough on her to prove she did take it?"

"She admitted it," Gabe replied. "But I'm not countering with anything. She claims that Addie misunderstood their discussion. It's the word of the socially prominent wife of a bank president against a woman no one else knows anything about."

Leon nodded again, his expression more thoughtful. "Then the next option is to let the talk go away on its own. There's nothing going on, so there's no fuel. And don't say anything to the Dewhurst woman. If you come across as defensive about Addie, it'll just give her something to repeat."

"He's right," Charles concluded. "The press will be on this, and the media is what we're concerned about. They'll give the speculation a run for a week or so, but with nothing concrete to print after that, the story will die without us saying a word."

Leon's mouth pursed. "Who else knows about this garden thing?"

Gabe gave a quiet snort. "Other than the people in the Office of Historical Preservation and the Camelot Historical Society?"

"I'm looking for someone on your side who knows about this project. Someone credible and closer to you."

"There's my mother," Gabe said, remembering what Addie had told him about the cuttings she'd taken. "She's donating a lot of the plants for the restoration from the estate.''

Behind his glasses, Leon's sharp eyes gleamed.

''Perfect,'' he proclaimed, his mental wheels spinning. ''Pulling your mother's name into this will dilute all this secret affair business. Focus on the project,'' he advised. ''If your office is contacted, don't mention that you regard this woman as a friend. That would just give people something to pursue. Just say that she's been your family's gardener for however long, and that your only interest is in a project she's working on that your mother is supporting.''

Gabe hesitated. He agreed with the approach. It was simple, straightforward and his mom would handle any request for a comment from the press with her usual, inimitable grace—right after she demanded to know how in the devil such a rumor got started. It just didn't feel right to deny his friendship with Addie. She would read that quote, too.

''What do you think?'' his uncle asked him.

It wasn't like Gabe to be indecisive. Not caring to start now, he nodded. ''A shift of focus is good.''

''Excellent,'' Leon claimed, beginning to show a penchant for superlatives. ''In the meantime,'' he continued, ''either Charles or I should contact Addie and coach her on what to say if she's approached by the press. Like Charles said, they'll be on this for about a week. If the rumors persist after that, you might want to think about removing her from the picture.''

Gabe's frown was swift. ''What do you mean?''

A plate of steaming pasta drifted by on the hand of a waiter. The scents of garlic and scallops drifted behind it. Following the succulent dish with longing in his eyes, Charles reached for his menu. ''We'll find her a job someplace else. That would be the easiest thing to do with her.''

''Nothing needs to be done with her.'' Guilt caught

Gabe like a fist in his gut. He had already cost her a fiancé. There was no way he would cost her her job. "And I'll talk to her myself."

"Let Charles or me do it." Perusing his own menu, Leon missed the quick defense in Gabe's tone. "Until this goes away, the less you have to do with her the better."

"I said," Gabe repeated, "that I will talk to her."

This time Leon caught what he'd missed before. So did his uncle. Gabe chose to ignore the quick glance that darted between his advisors as he picked up his own menu and deliberately dropped the subject. Letting it go for now felt a lot safer than dwelling on the slow boiling fury he felt with Helene. He itched to confront her pettiness, but he agreed that it was best to not even let the woman know she'd gotten to him. He couldn't let go of the growing concern he felt for Addie, though.

He wasn't worried about himself. There wasn't a politician on the planet who hadn't had something controversial printed about him at some point. His work made him a target. His family name put him in the bull's-eye.

He knew how the press worked. He knew there were those among its members with integrity and a true sense of fair play. He also knew there were those who had no qualms about bending the truth for the sake of sensationalism. More importantly, he knew they were all like hounds on a bone if they thought they were on to something, and that there were those who wouldn't quit until they'd chewed off every piece of gristle.

He couldn't honestly say how Addie felt about him just now. But he didn't believe for a moment that she would ever say anything to harm him. Not deliberately, anyway. The problem was that she had no experience at all with the press. She was also as transparent as window glass. If a reporter got hold of her, it was hard to know what he or she would ask or what kind of fuel Addie's answers—or her silence—would provide.

She had no defenses against ruthlessness. That had been glaringly obvious with Helene. As he got down to the business of ordering dinner, he couldn't help but think that the last thing he wanted was for her to face an aggressive reporter unarmed.

The sun had barely risen when Gabe pulled through the estate's main gate at six-thirty the next morning. He'd flown back from his meeting at midnight and caught a few hours of sleep between two and five-thirty. During the forty-mile drive from Richmond, he'd polished off the double latte from the Starbucks near his apartment, left messages with his secretary and his aide that he had something to take care of before his 9:00 a.m. appointment and heard the morning news.

Had anyone asked him what the top three stories of the day had been, he wouldn't have been able to say. The radio was on, but nothing of what he heard registered. He was too preoccupied with hoping he could find Addie right away, and with talking to his mom so she wouldn't be blindsided by his intention to mention her name.

A thin fog wound its way through the hills on his way in. Patches of it hovered over the estate's lawns and shrubs, muting their colors even as the sunlight filtered through the trees. The sky above was clear, but that mist hung ahead of him as he pulled to a stop by the garages and climbed from his car.

The dark, slender figure of a female emerged in the distance. The size was right, but even as her head jerked up at the muffled slam of his car door, he knew the woman hurrying toward the house wasn't Addie.

Huddled into herself against the morning chill, her mother ducked her head again and continued on, her arms crossed tightly over the sweater she hugged over her uniform.

Not wanting to waste time, he headed straight for her. "Mrs. Lowe," he called. "Where's Addie?"

There was no mistaking Rose's reluctance, or her disapproval, when her head snapped up again.

He could have sworn she didn't want to answer.

"She's getting ready for work."

"What about my mother? What time will she be up?"

He had no clue why the woman's mouth thinned. Preoccupied, he didn't really care.

"I'll take her her morning coffee in half an hour."

"I have to get back to Richmond, but I need to talk to her before I go. Will you tell her that?" he asked, walking backward as he edged from her and toward the path she'd just taken. "I'll be back as soon as I can."

It seemed to him that Rose was dying to say something other than the tight "Of course" she offered. But he had already turned and was moving at a half jog into the trees. He wanted to get to Addie before she took off and he had to hunt her down. He also didn't care to waste any more time in the company of a woman who'd always iced over like a pond in winter whenever she saw him.

He hadn't bothered to tighten his tie. With it knotted loosely at the open collar of his blue dress shirt, the strips of patterned silk swung against his dark-gray suit jacket as he moved swiftly toward the cottage. He was nearly down the block-long path when he heard the dull thud of a door close. Two dozen steps later, the path opened up and he saw Addie heading away from the cottage.

He watched her head tip back as she glanced at the patch of sky visible through the flame-colored trees. A carpet of that brilliant foliage covered the ground at her feet. With the feathered ends of her shining hair swinging at the back of her head, and her gray fleece sweatshirt so big it nearly hit the knees of her jeans, she looked more like a young girl ready to spread her arms and spin than a woman inclined to lead a man astray.

She had the power to do just that, though. Or at least to cause his thoughts to wander down long and dangerous pathways. One kiss had nearly turned his blood to steam and evaporated common sense. He could only imagine what she'd do to him if he ever got her naked and moving beneath him.

The problem was that he had been imagining it. Far more frequently than he should.

"Addie."

As if a string had been pulled, she immediately came to a halt. With one hand at the base of her throat, she turned on her heel and stood staring.

He took it as a good sign that she looked more startled than uneasy. The last time he'd sought her out, the first thing he'd seen had been distress.

Her hand slid away as he walked up to her and offered a smile. "You haven't been up long."

Her dark lashes looked too silky to have yet encountered a wand of mascara, and her freshly scrubbed cheeks were already growing rosy from the morning chill. It was the faint line on her cheek that had his attention, though. "You have a sleep crease right here."

With the tip of his finger, he touched the tiny furrow in her incredibly soft skin, tracing it toward her ear and the tempting softness of her hair.

Realizing what he was doing, realizing how badly he'd wanted to touch her, he frowned at himself and let his hand fall.

"I didn't realize you went to work this early."

"I don't." Concern at his presence—or maybe concern at what he'd done—shifted through her eyes. "I was just going for a walk around the lake."

"You walk the lake? With all the miles you put on around here?"

She reached into the pouch sewn into the front of her sweatshirt. Pulling out a wadded-up bread wrapper, she held it up. "I'm going to feed the ducks."

The image of her surrounded by mallards and drakes, tranquilly tossing them bits of bread, actually eased some of the tension in his shoulders.

"Mind if I help?"

Still looking concerned, she shook her head. "Of course not. What are you doing here?"

"Damage control."

Understanding moved into the depths of her eyes. Pushing the bread and her hands back into the pouch, she turned, continuing to walk. "So how bad is it?"

"It's containable." She hadn't asked if he'd heard. Or what he'd heard. Or even if he'd figured out how everything had started. As so often with her when they started to talk, they were on the same page even as they opened the conversation. "Has anyone approached you for a comment?"

He heard her sigh.

"My mother. Olivia. Ina. Miguel. Jackson. Two women at the nursery where I was buying a Chinese maple to replace the one I had to take out. The guy at the hardware store." She paused. "Scott."

He hesitated himself. "Scott?"

"He called after a reporter phoned the school yesterday wanting to verify that we'd been engaged and asking when we'd broken up. Scott hadn't heard anything about the rumor before the reporter told him about it." She kicked at a twig, looking as if she wished it were the reporter's head. "It wasn't a good conversation."

"Let me guess." Scott had apparently been the "reliable source'' Leon had referred to. ''He wanted to know if I was the reason you broke up with him.''

The way she kept her focus on the leaf-carpeted ground made her seem as uncomfortable with the topic as she had been the first time he'd alluded to that conclusion.

''I told him the same thing I told everyone else,'' she said, still neither confirming nor denying his part in her decision. ''I told him we broke up because it wouldn't have worked.''

''What about the rest of it? The part about the affair,'' he asked, conscious of how her eyes now failed to meet his.

''I just said it wasn't true.'' She sounded conversational but looked truly uneasy. ''I said we're…friends.''

A month ago she wouldn't have hesitated over the word the way she just had. Gabe felt sure of that. The fact that she did now bothered him more than he wanted to admit. Not because of what someone looking for hidden meanings might be tempted to find, but because she apparently questioned something about that friendship herself.

He was sorely tempted to turn her around, take her face between his hands and tell her there was nothing to question. He just didn't trust himself with what he wanted to do beyond that.

''What about reporters?'' he asked, pushing his hands into his pockets. ''Have you been approached by any?''

Her head finally came up. ''Do you think I will be?''

The distress was finally there.

The need to touch her grew stronger. The need to preserve the relationship they had was stronger still.

''It's a distinct possibility if you leave the grounds again. Or if they get the phone number for the cottage.'' He curled his hands in his pockets. ''If you are questioned, just do what you've been doing. Be honest but be brief. The official line from my office will be that we're working together toward the restoration of an historical garden and that my mother is involved with it, too. She's donating the plants," he reminded her, as her glance returned to the leaves rustling with their footsteps. "I'll let her know what's happening before I go. In the meantime, we focus only on the project itself. We're not mentioning that you and I are friends. My advisors don't think it's necessary. Okay?"

What he meant was that his advisors didn't think it was a good idea. Addie was certain of that. It was what she would have told him herself, had he asked.

His voice dropped. "How are you doing with all of this?"

Not so well, she thought, wishing he didn't sound so concerned, enormously grateful that he did.

"I'm worried about Mom," she admitted, amazed at how comforting it felt to talk to someone who knew how untrue the rumors were. There wasn't a soul she could talk to who wouldn't chastise her for an affair she wasn't having, or accuse her of holding out details. No one wanted to believe the truth. "She's afraid the talk will affect her relationship with your mother. She thinks it's true."

"My mother does?"

"Mine. I have no idea what your mother thinks. All Mom said to me is that Mrs. Kendrick asked her last night if there was anything to the rumors."

That wasn't all her mom had said by a long shot. Addie just didn't care to embarrass herself by telling him how her mother had lectured her about falling for him yet again, or how humiliated Rose had been to have to answer his mother's question. She hadn't thought it necessary, either, to go into how Scott had told her she was crazy if she thought she'd ever wind up living in the main house instead of the cottage.

"So, what did your mom say?"

"That she thought there was."

"Why would she say that?"

"Because she saw us in the library."

They had reached the wide dirt path that circled the lake. The morning sun shimmered on the tree-lined water, streaking it shades of gold and pink.

Gabe barely noticed as he came to a dead stop.

It wasn't like him to miss the bigger picture. But he hadn't even considered her mother in the equation. And he definitely hadn't considered that she might have seen her daughter in his arms.

It was no wonder Mrs. Lowe had turned into the ice queen just now.

"She did?"

Addie's only response was a discouraged nod before she started walking again. She looked as if she needed the movement, needed to pace.

Feeling a little edgier himself, Gabe fell back into step beside her. He was about to ask how bad things were for her at home, when Addie spoke again.

"You know you don't need to worry about her talking to a reporter," Addie told him, since reporters were what he seemed to have on his mind. "One of the first speeches she gives new staff is never to speak to anyone about a Kendrick." Her mother would go permanently mute before she would break that rule herself. "She's not about to make things worse."

The heavy bushes rustled in the faint breeze. Squirrels chattered in the trees. The sounds followed them as they moved slowly along the water's edge.

"Has my mother talked to you?" he asked.

Praying that Mrs. Kendrick wouldn't send for her, feeling nauseous at the thought that she might, Addie shook her head. "Not yet."

"Well, don't worry about it," he told her. "You have

to deal with your mother, so I'll deal with mine. I'll take care of everything when I talk to her in a while.''

The reprieve had her releasing a long low breath. "Thank you," she murmured, wondering if he had any idea how much sleep she'd lost over that one.

"I'm really sorry this has happened, Gabe. I really am."

"It's not your fault."

"Yes, it is. If I hadn't mentioned that project to you, none of this would have happened." He had only been thinking of her when he'd defended her to Helene. He'd been thinking of what she wanted, and what he felt was right.

"Addie."

He spoke her name with patience as he pulled his hand from the safety of his pocket. Catching her arm, he stepped in front of her, holding her there with his fingers curled around her tight little bicep.

"What happened is that a spoiled socialite got her nose out of joint and decided to share her speculation about us with her buddies. People speculate about relationships all the time. I've had it happen to me before. The talk here just seems a little juicier to some people because of who I am and because of the work you do for my family. None of that was your doing."

"Who you are is why this worries me, Gabe. The last thing you need before you begin a campaign is bad publicity. I know you're still months away from announcing your candidacy, but this is exactly the kind of thing that gets resurrected when—"

"It's going to be all right. My people are on it," he insisted, looking as if he didn't want her to worry, looking touched that she did. "As for what I need," he continued, his voice turning solemn, "I just need to know I can still talk to my friend."

The man didn't play fair at all. He stood towering over

her, big, protective and looking as concerned as she was about preserving the relationship they'd always had. But that relationship wasn't what it had once been. And it seemed to change more each time she saw him.

She no longer denied the pull she felt toward him. It wouldn't have been possible, anyway. His heat burned into her arm, making her breathing shallow, causing her heart to beat in painful little lurches. She knew the only sensible thing to do was fight that pull. She knew the prince married Cinderella only in the fairy tale. Yet, something in her still needed his friendship, too.

"You can always talk to me." She'd wanted to tell him that before. The night in the library—before he'd kissed her. Before everything in her tidy little world had started to change.

A smile moved into his eyes. "Then, as a friend, tell me what you think your dad would advise about all of this."

The request turned her expression thoughtful. "Well," she murmured, thinking there was probably plenty her father would have had to say. He'd never suffered gossips well. "You know how he always preached focus," she reminded him. "So, I imagine he would tell you to do just what you're doing. Take the high road with the rumor and keep your eyes on the governor's office. And don't do anything to compromise or distract yourself from that goal."

He was already distracted. By her very real concern for him. By the lushness of her unadorned mouth. By the remembered feel of her body. Yet he knew she was right. He needed to stay focused and not think about how easy it actually would be to become intimately involved with her. Not that the woman quietly watching him seemed willing. There was still a certain uneasiness hanging between them.

"You've kept me on the straight and narrow so far."
He lifted his hand toward her cheek. The little sleep crease
was nearly gone. The need to touch remained. "I guess
I'll just keep following your advice."

He skimmed his knuckles over the cool satin of her skin
as he spoke. He would keep his eye on his goal as he
always had. Yet, as he watched awareness fight the caution
in her eyes, he couldn't help wonder if his goals were
enough, and if there might not be something he needed
even more.

The bushes rustled again. The depth of the sound spoke
of something sizable, a raccoon possibly, or maybe a stray
dog. Addie's head turned toward the thick foliage beyond
them. But even as they both looked to see what might
emerge from the bushes, the sounds stopped, leaving only
the morning silence.

As he pulled back his hand, she offered a cautious smile.
"I guess it went into the trees."

"Guess so," he agreed, as she took a step back.

"I should go find the ducks." She motioned toward the
stand of cattails a hundred yards away. "They're probably
down there."

"You probably should." He took a step away himself.
"And I should get up to the house."

"Probably," she echoed and looked back with a soft
smile.

He really didn't want to leave. Despite what she'd said,
it seemed Addie wasn't all that anxious for him to go,
either.

It had never been hard leaving her before. At least, not
as hard as it seemed to be just then. But he had to go. Yet
even though he told her to call if anything happened, and
she quietly agreed that she would, as he made himself turn
and walk away, he had the awful feeling that he was leaving her to the wolves.

Chapter Seven

"Oh, Addie. Thank heaven I caught you. I left a quiche in the oven so I only have a minute, but you really don't want to go anywhere near the main house right now. You especially don't want to go anywhere near the breakfast room windows."

Addie lowered her wheelbarrow. The hedges across from those windows were precisely where she was headed. "I don't?"

Olivia shook her head so hard her tight salt-and-pepper curls almost moved. "Definitely not. Mr. Kendrick is in the breakfast room yelling at Mrs. Kendrick about something in the morning paper. About you and Gabe," she rushed to explain, eyes wide with worry and warning. "When Marie took in the coffee he was absolutely purple with rage. Well, it was actually more of a deep pink," the loquacious cook quickly qualified, "but I caught a glimpse of him and I swear that man was about to pop a vein."

Addie slowly lowered the handles of her wheelbarrow and stared at the woman shivering in the cold morning air. Olivia hadn't bothered to throw on the hot-pink jacket she kept in the closet by the back door. From the way she'd rushed out with her news, it seemed apparent that she'd seen Addie emerge from the path with her tools and simply flown out the door.

"There's an article in the paper? What does it say?"

"I haven't seen the paper yet. I never do until Marie clears it away with the dishes when the Kendricks are finished with their meal. But whatever it is, Mr. Kendrick was in there demanding to know what's gotten into Gabe. The direct quote," she supplied, determined to be accurate, "was 'What in the bloody hell has gotten into him.' If you don't mind my asking, Addie, what's gotten into you?"

The last person to ask her that question had been her mother. That had been last night after Rose had asked her what Gabe had wanted that morning. Addie had told her the truth, that he'd wanted to know who she'd talked to about the rumor and who had talked to her. She had also reiterated that she and Gabe were just friends—not that she'd had any better luck convincing her mom of that than she'd had the first time she'd mentioned it.

Gabe had apparently told his mother the same thing.

At least, that was what Ina had overheard as she'd cleaned the room next to the atrium where Gabe had talked to Mrs. Kendrick yesterday. Ina had confided that conversation to Olivia, who'd confided it to Rose, who'd then stood outside her daughter's closed bedroom door last night for a full minute before sharing that unremarkable bit of information with her.

Addie knew her mom had hesitated that long because she'd seen the shadow of her feet beneath the door. And the information had been unremarkable. To Addie, anyway. It was the truth, after all.

Her mother had merely seen what he'd said as exactly what she expected from him.

Of course he denied the affair, she'd insisted. *It's what a man in his position does. He's not about to admit to his family that he's intimately involved with a member of their household staff. And you're not going to get anywhere by denying it, either. He'll walk in the end, Addie. He will. And you and I will be left with nothing.*

At least Olivia looked more curious that accusing.

"Nothing has gotten into me," Addie quietly defended. "I don't even know what's going on right now."

The back door slammed shut, something it seldom did because staff was always careful to not make the noise. The unfamiliar sound ricocheted like a gunshot in the morning stillness, and carried with it that same startled sense of foreboding as Ina came flying toward them.

Ina hadn't bothered with a jacket, either. As she hurried toward them with her white apron fluttering over her short-sleeved black uniform, it seemed all she'd taken time to grab was the newspaper.

The thirty-something brunette with the deep dimples had a husband, a teenaged son and what she swore was internal radar when it came to matching people. She'd worried after she'd introduced Addie to Scott that the chemistry just wasn't there and had actually been more surprised than anyone when they'd announced their engagement.

The fact that she hadn't predicted the relationship with Gabe drove her nuts.

"Deny it all you want," she said, sounding slightly out of breath as she handed the paper to Addie, "but I guarantee there isn't a soul in the state of Virginia who's going to believe there's nothing going on with you two. Not after they see this."

Ina glanced toward the house, looking guilty for being

gone, looking back just as quickly so she wouldn't miss the look on Addie's face when she saw the photograph.

It was right there on page three. Top right. Four inches by five inches in glorious black-and-white. Clear as a bell and impossible to miss.

The photographer had caught them both in full profile. They stood a foot from each other, Gabe looking down at her face, her looking up into his eyes and his knuckles on her cheek.

"Let me see that." Rather than snatching it out of Addie's hand, as Olivia looked tempted to do, she planted herself at her shoulder and tipped the paper so she could see it, too. A full five seconds passed before she murmured, "Oh, dear."

The caption under the photo read: Senator Gabriel Kendrick (R. Va.) and family gardener, Addie Lowe, rendezvous at the Kendrick estate as senator's office officially denies their involvement.

"This isn't good." Addie took a deep breath, blew it out. "This really isn't good."

"Actually," Ina said, joining her on her other side, "I think it's a great shot. It's very romantic. And you both look terrific. But, sweetie, the just-friends line is dead in the water after this. I guarantee you that no man I was ever just friends with looked at me like that."

Ina was right, Addie thought, as compelled as she was dismayed by what she saw in the photo. There was nothing platonic about the look the photographer had captured between her and Gabe. They looked like two people completely, intimately involved with each other.

Olivia obviously saw that, too. "I've known for a long time that he had a soft spot for you," she confided, sounding dismayed herself. "I knew it from the time he was a young boy. I remember how he would take extra cookies when he'd go out to watch your dad work, just so he'd have some for you. But I never suspected he'd pursue you like this.''

Her mother had used that same term. ''He's not pursuing me,'' she insisted, starting to read the article below the incriminating photo.

''You're right.'' Olivia sounded utterly convinced as she nodded toward the photograph. ''No pursuit necessary. I'd say you already look well and truly caught.''

Olivia's disheartening conclusion barely registered. Addie's heart felt as if it had just stalled.

''I don't believe this.'' Her glance flew down the six-inch long column of text. ''I don't,'' she repeated, her eyes riveted to a particularly damning quote.

Beneath her tight cap of curls, Olivia's brow slammed low. ''What is it?''

''This is worse than not good.''

''What is?'' she repeated, snatching the paper this time. Ina craned her neck past Addie.

''There.'' Addie pointed to the phrase. ''The quote from Eric Dashill.''

''Who's he?'' Ida asked.

''The chairman of the opposition party.''

Looking impressed that Addie would know that, Ina peered back to where Addie had pointed. Olivia read aloud:

''We all know that Senator Kendrick was elected on a platform of honesty, integrity and openness. Considering the official denial of his involvement with the Lowe woman issued from his office, and photographic evidence to the contrary, it now appears that he has backtracked. Since the senator apparently wants to hide his relationship with this woman, it might behoove us to question his veracity in other areas, too.''

Ida's tone filled with sympathy. "And I thought the picture would cause trouble. Rose and I didn't even read that."

The breath Olivia blew puffed her cheeks. "They're attacking Gabe's integrity. It's no wonder Mr. Kendrick went ballistic."

Addie stared back down at the paper when Olivia handed it to her. The photograph did make it look as if Gabe couldn't be taken at his word. And she could see where people, his enemies especially, would think that if he was lying about one thing, he would lie about another.

She also knew that once the seed of doubt had been planted, it could be tougher than crabgrass to kill.

Olivia must have seen her go pale. Touching her arm as if to steady her, she glanced past the damning photo to Ina. "How did you get the paper?"

"The Mr. and Mrs. left the breakfast room," she replied, looking truly concerned about Addie, too. "They knew we could hear them, so they took their discussion into the library. On their way out, I heard Mr. say to Mrs. that she needed to review the staffing situation if this is the sort of thing going on around here. Then Mrs. came back and told Mrs. Lowe to hold breakfast and said she would speak with her about the situation after Mr. left for his office." Her glance slid worriedly to Addie. "I didn't hear her mention your name, but I'd lay low for a while if I were you.

"As for the paper," she reminded herself, sounding as if she'd just mentally jerked herself back on track. "As soon as they left, I grabbed it so we could see what was going on. I knew you'd come out to warn Addie about the fireworks, so after Rose and I saw the picture, I figured she needed to see it, too."

Olivia looked from where Ina vigorously rubbed her arms against the cold to where Addie stood stock-still, staring apprehensively toward the house. It seemed heads were about to roll.

"Rose said she knew there would be trouble when Gabe came looking for you yesterday." Looking worried for them both, she tempered the accusation in her tone with sympathy. "I better get in there and make sure she's all right. She was already worried about being fired before this."

Ina stopped rubbing. "Why would she get fired? I can see where they'd let Addie go. Not that I think they should," she hurried to qualify. "She and Gabe are consenting adults and I say more power to her." She gave Addie a defiant nod. "You want him, you go for him."

"I'm not going for him." She wished someone, anyone, would listen. "All we were doing yesterday was trying to minimize the rumors."

"Well, I'd say that little exercise backfired," Olivia muttered. "And personally, I don't care who's going for whom. If it were up to me, I'd say more power to both of you, too, but that's not how things work in these circles and we all know it. Someone's going to wind up with her head on a platter," she proclaimed with a glance toward Ina. "And you and I had better get back inside before we wind up as garnish."

Olivia had a quiche to rescue and a friend to check on. Ina had sheets to change and several thousand square feet of floors to mop, wax and/or vacuum. In the prevailing atmosphere, standing around not doing any of it didn't seem a particularly wise thing to do.

Mr. Kendrick must have called for his car. Thirty yards away, one of the six garage doors suddenly rose, the mechanical groan of the automatic opener warning them all that Gabe's annoyed father was about to depart. The moment he did, that would leave Mrs. Kendrick to deal with Addie's mom and, eventually, with Addie.

Even as Ida and Olivia said they'd see her later, a sleek black car slid onto the cobblestones and turned toward the portico. Mr. Kendrick wasn't driving himself in one of his other vehicles today. Behind the wheel of a stately Rolls-Royce sat Bentley, his chauffeur's cap at a jaunty angle on his graying head.

"This is just so not fair," Addie heard Ina proclaim, as she and Olivia rushed toward the house. "There's not a reason on earth that Rose…"

Her voice faded with distance, but as Addie stared down at the paper she still held, suddenly aware that she was shaking, she didn't need to hear to know that Ina was still puzzling over why the Kendricks would consider firing her mother.

Had there been time, Addie could have told her herself. She even understood the rationale—unfair as it seemed considering how innocent her relationship with Gabe really was.

As head housekeeper, it was Rose's job to keep staff in line, to make sure that no one in the Kendricks' household hire in any way embarrassed or reflected poorly on them. There were standards of loyalty and discernment to be upheld, and, given the family's high profile, any disloyalty resulted in immediate dismissal. It was also Rose's job to bring to Mrs. Kendrick's attention any potential problem she couldn't handle herself.

Addie didn't report to her mother. Only to Mrs. Kendrick. But she could see where Mrs. Kendrick would feel that her mother was no longer qualified to insist on decorum and faithfulness among the house staff if she couldn't keep her own daughter from tarnishing her son's reputation.

For all Addie knew, Mrs. Kendrick could even think that her mom had encouraged her in the relationship. Given the trust that had been placed in Rose over the years, that could be regarded as the worst betrayal of all.

From the front of the house came the sharp slam of a car door. Moments later the shiny black vehicle became visible again and motored down the drive, two male heads visible this time and exhaust swirling behind like the smoke of an angry dragon.

The trembling in Addie's fingers worked its way to the nerves knotted in her stomach. She seldom encountered Mr. Kendrick. The house and the grounds were Mrs. Kendrick's domain. His concerns were with the fortune he had inherited from his carpetbagger relatives and turned into a family empire. On the few occasions she had been around him, she had been impressed by how closely Gabe resembled him. But she had never known Gabe to lose his temper, much less seen him furious. Not to the degree Olivia had just described his father.

It was the reason for that fury that had her abandoning her wheelbarrow and tools and heading cautiously toward the door Ina had closed far more quietly than before. She knew his father had ambitions for his oldest son. But she knew they were Gabe's ambitions, too. Gabe wasn't the sort of man to bend to another's will, to compromise his own dreams or to follow a path he didn't believe in himself. He was like a warrior born to rank. His sense of honor and duty ran as deep as his passion to protect and defend. It was in his blood, his bones and so much a part of him that for him to have chosen any other path would have been as impossible as changing the color of his eyes.

There was nothing Gabe valued more than his reputation. Now it was being called into question—because of her. And, because of her, her mother was about to be called up on Mrs. Kendrick's imported, one-of-a-kind, antique Persian carpet.

The fact that she didn't hesitate to pull open the door

and head inside would have been remarkable to her had she taken time to consider what she was doing. But time did not appear to be on her side. There was only one thing she could do to salvage the situation and she had to do it before Mrs. Kendrick fired her mother.

"You want to see Mrs. Kendrick?" Ina asked, sounding as baffled as she looked when Addie hung her heavy jacket by the back door and walked into the kitchen. "Are you nuts? She just sent for your mom, and she did not look like a happy person."

"Then go get Mom and ask Mrs. Kendrick if I can see her first. Please?" Addie begged, nervously smoothing back her hair and brushing at the beige turtleneck sweater tucked neatly into her still-clean jeans. "I don't want to just barge in there." Barging would not be dignified. Heaven knew she had nothing going for her now but her dignity. The truth certainly didn't seem to be getting her anywhere. "Where are they, anyway?"

They had gone into Mrs. Kendrick's study, a relatively small, quietly feminine room near the solarium where she tended the business of the house and her social and charitable interests. Addie had no idea what Ina said to their employer, but Mrs. Kendrick immediately agreed to see her. Before Addie could even consider what she was doing, she found herself outside the open door of that study, staring uneasily at her mother's ramrod stiff back as Rose walked away.

Her mother hadn't said a word as they'd passed. She hadn't needed to. The strain in her expression said quite enough.

Her mother disappeared though a door to the back of the house just as Addie heard Mrs. Kendrick delicately clear her throat.

Whirling around, she darted a glance from the pale-blue

sofa to an antiqued white desk. Mrs. Kendrick stood between it and a waist-high marble column supporting a white bust of a Greek goddess. Her pale platinum hair was swept back from the perfect oval of her face and held at her nape with a silk scarf the same shade of ivory as her slacks. She wore a beige turtleneck, too. Only, hers was cashmere and accented with tiny silver threads that picked up the platinum accents of her bracelet and the ring encrusted with rows of diamonds on her left hand.

Seeing that her hands were clasped loosely in front of her, Addie uncrossed her arms and did the same.

"Thank you for seeing me," she said, and promptly groaned inside because she'd just broken the first rule her mother had ever taught her about being in this house. Never speak unless first spoken to. Nerves had made her forget. That and a desperate need to get through what she had to say.

"Come in," Mrs. Kendrick replied, her tone civil, but guarded. "Please, close the door."

Addie did as requested and turned back, reclasping her hands. There was no invitation to sit. Not that she expected one. Mrs. Kendrick remained where she was, framed by the taupe drapes and the window overlooking a now barren garden. She looked as perfect as the sculpture beside her.

Refusing to consider how she must look in comparison, Addie swallowed past her reticence and took a single step forward. There was nothing more important at the moment than what she'd come to do. "I think it's best that I resign my position here," she said before the silence could thicken.

Coolly skeptical, but definitely interested, Gabe's mother studied her more closely. "Why do you think that's best?"

"Because it's the quickest way to end all of this. That picture in the paper isn't what it seems. Gabe and I are only friends,'' Addie hurried to explain, praying the woman who could have been a queen would believe what no one else wanted to hear. ''That's what we were talking about when that picture was taken. Being friends, I mean.

''I know it looks like more,'' she admitted, shaken by how quickly things had gotten out of hand, desperately needing to put on the brakes. ''But I promise you, it's not. There is nothing going on but gossip and misinterpretation. No one wants to believe that, though. And they won't as long as I'm around.

''I had no idea that a photographer had gotten onto the property yesterday,'' she continued in a rush, her concerns piling up like cars in a train wreck. ''If they did it once, they can do it again, and with the holidays coming, Gabe will be home more. If we're seen even talking, it could make matters worse, and I'd never do anything to jeopardize his chances for office. He'll announce his candidacy right after the next session, and this all needs to be dealt with long before then.

''Then, there's my mother,'' she said, needing to cover all of her bases before her nerve deserted her completely. ''She's the other reason I should go,'' she insisted, chin up and stomach quivering. ''I don't want any of this to affect her position here. None of this is her doing, and none of it should reflect on her. She has served you faithfully for thirty years and she deserves your loyalty, too.''

Addie had never in her life spoken so boldly to her employer. She didn't think she'd ever spoken so boldly to anyone for that matter.

She had no idea how her little pronouncement had been received, either. Like Gabe, his mother was too well versed in the art of control to give away much of anything.

Or so Addie was thinking when she saw the faint lines around Mrs. Kendrick's eyes deepen with what looked almost like curiosity.

As if noting her unexpected courage, or perhaps as surprised as Addie was by it, she took a step closer herself. "Both you and my son say you are only friends," she pointed out, her tone amazingly conversational. "Is that truly how you feel about him? He is nothing more to you than that?"

Addie's brow creased. "To be a friend is not 'nothing.'"

"Forgive me," the woman said graciously. "I didn't mean that the way it sounded. A true friend is a treasure," she agreed, seeming impressed by her knee-jerk response. "Perhaps I should just ask you how you feel about my son."

The query was simple. The answer was definitely not.

Addie hesitated. Caught between helping her cause and potentially harming it, she thought it wisest to focus only on his career. "I've always had the greatest respect for him," she admitted, because it was true and safe. "He's a brilliant, caring man and an excellent politician."

"I asked how you feel about him, Addie. Not if you'd vote for him."

Addie opened her mouth, closed it again.

A thoughtful look passed through his mother's eyes. "You wouldn't be here if you didn't care about him," she concluded, saving her from incriminating herself any further. "So I really didn't need to ask. Perhaps the better question would be to ask how my son feels about you."

There had been a time when Addie could easily have said that he probably regarded her as something of a little sister. She might even have mentioned the promise he'd made to her father, which only the three of them had known about. That promise had undoubtedly made him feel obligated to watch out for her, to guide her. She could have said that he thought of her as a sounding board, a confidant. But as she watched Gabe's elegant mother carefully watching her, she knew there was only one answer the woman was truly interested in.

"I can't speak for him, Mrs. Kendrick. But if you were to ask how I think he feels," she said, careful to make the distinction, "I think he regards me as friend. Nothing less. But nothing more."

"You sound rather certain of that."

"I am," she replied, thinking of how Gabe had been so careful not to touch her. Even when he had, he hadn't let his touch linger. He had made no attempt whatsoever to repeat what had happened in the library. He could have so easily, too. There had even been a time or two when she'd thought he might. Or maybe she had just wanted him to so badly that she'd imagined he'd considered it.

At the thought her glance fell to the cream-and-blue pattern in the rug.

Mrs. Kendrick said nothing. She just stood, seeming very thoughtful and not at all convinced of what she was hearing.

That skeptical silence compelled Addie to offer the only other assurance she could think of.

"Maybe it would help if you know that I have no illusions about your son," she offered quietly. "I know he needs a woman with social graces and the right background, Mrs. Kendrick. And I know I don't have either. That's why I know that all we can be is friends. But his friendship with me is costing him his credibility," she reminded her, getting back to why she was standing there quietly shaking in her work boots. "And it's hurting my mother. So I need you to accept my resignation. Please."

Mrs. Kendrick's considering silence seemed to change quality in the moments before she turned to her desk.

"So you're leaving to protect your mother and my son."

Addie frowned at the conclusion. She hadn't thought of her decision in quite those terms. "I suppose," she murmured, far more frightened over what she was doing than impressed with it.

"How soon do you wish to go?"

"As soon as possible. I can have Jackson come up to talk to you about taking over my position. He's a very dependable man and I don't want to leave you without a groundskeeper."

The reality of what she was doing sank in a little deeper. She was leaving her job. Her home. As nervous as she was suddenly becoming over what she'd done, Addie barely caught the look of approval her consideration earned her.

"Tell him I'll speak with him this afternoon." Lowering herself to the oval-back chair behind the tidy desk, Mrs. Kendrick pulled open a drawer. "What about you? Where will you go?"

Addie hadn't thought that far. She was not an impulsive person. She was practical and sensible and tended to plan out everything, usually with lists.

For the first time in her life, she was winging it.

Had she planned for such a thing, or even wanted it, she might have found the sudden freedom rather exhilarating. Instead she felt as if she'd just stepped into a deep hole and was flailing her way down in a stomach-lurching free-fall.

"Back to school," she replied, trying to ignore the sensation—and the ache she felt knowing she would never again walk the grounds' woodland paths with Gabe. She would never look up to find him watching her with his slow, easy smile. Never anticipate his coming home. "I'll move to Petersburg."

School was definitely a more logical thing to consider. She had a degree to complete. Without a job, that degree would be more important than ever.

The sinking sensation magnified itself.

"I'm supposed to attend a meeting in Camelot next

week," she said, thinking of the historical society and the project that had started this whole mess. "If I come back for it, would it be all right if I pick up what I can't take with me now? I need to find a room on campus before I can take my things."

"I don't see that as a problem," Mrs. Kendrick replied, now writing out a check from a large ledger. "You have a meeting?"

"It's the regular Camelot Historical Society meeting. I received letters from the society and the Office of Historical Preservation this week acknowledging me as the project committee chairperson."

"Then, you should attend," she pronounced, apparently having caught Addie's indecision about whether or not she would actually go. "Gabe told me yesterday that this all started because your work on the project was essentially being stolen from you. He wanted to make sure it stayed in the right hands." Light glinted off her thin gold pen as she continued to write. "Your reasons for resigning are valid," she pointed out, slipping the pen into its holder. "But the project is yours to protect as well."

With the faint sound of tearing, she removed the check she'd just written from the book. "We can't control what the press does," she continued, slipping the checkbook back into the drawer. "Or what others say or think. A person can only hold her head up and do what she knows is right." She held out the check, Addie's month's wages and the month's severance she would have paid had she fired her. A faint smile touched her mouth, part sympathy, part respect. "You're doing fine, so far."

Reaching across the desk, Addie took what she offered and quickly folded it in two. Any appreciation she might have felt about the woman's encouragement had been killed by her advice. Holding one's head up while doing the right thing sounded good, but she was getting close to her last ounce of courage. "Thank you, ma'am."

"Thank you, Addie. And, please, ask your mother to come back in."

Drawing on those last few drops of nerve, Addie swallowed, "You're not going to fire her, are you?"

Mrs. Kendrick clasped her hands on her cocoa-colored desk blotter. "We're just going to talk," she assured her, her features far more relaxed than they'd appeared when Addie had first walked in. "You don't need to worry about your mother."

The assurance released some of the tightness in her chest. "Thank you," she repeated, practically breathing out the word.

Mrs. Kendrick's only reply was a nod.

Addie knew dismissal when she saw it. More anxious than she could believe to get out of there now that her business was concluded, she turned on her heel and forced herself not to bolt from the room.

She could barely believe what she'd just done. Numb with the thought of it, the quick scramble of feet outside the door barely even registered when she turned the knob and stepped into the empty hall.

Later she could focus on all she had to do that day. At that moment all she could think about was that she had just quit her job.

She was leaving the estate.

Mrs. Kendrick hadn't hesitated by so much as the twitch of an eyelash to accept her resignation. That alone seemed to confirm just how anxious the woman was to get rid of her. But her mother still had her position. And by removing herself from potential encounters with Gabe, there could be no more photographs for the press and the public to misconstrue.

The space where nerves had knotted in her stomach suddenly felt more like a void. Leaving served another purpose, too. A far more selfish one. She wasn't leaving only to protect Gabe and help her mom. She was doing it to protect herself.

Since she'd admitted to herself how she felt about him, she no longer had denial to provide that protection. The more she was around him, the more she wanted to be with him, and the more she had to face that being with him the way she wanted simply wasn't going to happen.

There was no future in loving Gabe. With time and distance, maybe she would start getting over him.

It only took a few minutes for her to tell a speechless Ina, Olivia and her stunned, but relieved, mother what she had done and where she was going. It took the next eight hours, however, for her to go over what still needed to be done on the grounds with Jackson, finagle an appointment with her college advisor, make a reservation at an inexpensive hotel near the Virginia Commonwealth University campus and pack up her room.

Her mother would have to move to the main house in the next week or so, but Rose had been too relieved about still having her job to mind the transition. She told Addie it hadn't been the same there since Addie's dad had died, anyway, and with her gone now, she'd be happier where there were other people. She also told Addie that leaving was the best thing she could do for herself as she gave her a tight hug, then asked her to call when she got to Petersburg to let her know she'd arrived safely.

Wanting only to get leaving over with, Addie promised she would and hurried with her single suitcase to where Bentley waited for her in the driveway. Because the truck Addie had driven for the past six years belonged to the estate, Mrs. Kendrick had offered their driver to take her into Camelot where she caught a 4:40 bus for the seventy-mile ride to Petersburg.

She was halfway there when she found herself wondering if Gabe would miss her. Or if he would be relieved that she was gone.

She'd been in Petersburg three days when she found out.

Chapter Eight

"What's going on, Mom? Olivia said Addie isn't there anymore." Flanked by an American flag on one side of his desk, the state flag of Virginia on the other, Gabe sat forward in his black leather executive chair. His voice was as tight as his grip on the phone. "You didn't fire her, did you?"

"Your father wanted to," his mother replied, her voice calm despite the demand in his. "But she resigned on her own. Olivia called you?"

"I called her. I've been trying to reach Addie since Tuesday."

"That was the day she left."

"That's what I hear." Olivia had been able to tell him little else. *She left in such a rush,* the cook had said, sounding as concerned as he now felt himself. *I know she was upset about the photo and the article, but she hardly said anything at all after she talked to your mother.*

"I couldn't get an answer at the cottage until last night," he continued, rising to pace between his desk and his sweeping view of the state capitol building and umbrellas bobbing in the rain. "All Mrs. Lowe would say is that Addie is gone." The woman had also asked him to leave her daughter alone, her half-angry, half-pleading tone leaving no doubt in his mind that she blamed him for whatever it was that had happened. She'd hung up too fast for him to get details. "That's why I called Olivia this morning. I figured she'd know what had happened."

"I imagine the entire staff knows," his mother replied agreeably. "At least, they know she left. I'm not sure anyone is convinced of the innocence of your relationship, though. I overheard Marie ask Ina if she left to move in with you." Her agreeable tone turned beleaguered. "I just hope we can trust her to keep any further curiosity to herself. It's speculation like that causing all the problems."

"Mom, I swear there's nothing going on…"

"I know that," she quickly insisted. "I believe you when you say your relationship is aboveboard. And I believe Addie." A faint grating sound came over the line, the brush of a pearl, perhaps, moving back and forth along a chain. "She's actually a rather surprising young woman," she observed, sounding as thoughtful as she did intrigued. "Not quite as timid as I'd always thought." The rasp slowed, then stopped. "At least, not when it comes to people who matter to her," she qualified, and left the line dangling.

There was a hook on the end of that line. And enough bait to choke a whale. But Gabe refused to bite.

Knowing that Addie was no longer safely at the estate was infinitely more important than his mother's hint that Addie cared about him. Addie cared about everybody.

"So where is she?" That was his only concern at the

moment. "All Olivia knows is that she's staying in a hotel somewhere near VCU."

His unmasked disquiet put a significant pause on the other end of the line. For a moment Gabe thought his mother wasn't going to answer. When she did, there was a note of interest in her tone that hadn't been there only moments ago.

"I don't know. But I have the feeling that if I don't find out for you, you'll start calling hotels, and that will only tip someone off somewhere. I'll get back to you," she said, catching him a little off guard with her blunt perception. "But before I do, I want you to promise me something."

Caution brought him to a halt. "What's that?"

"I have never known you to act carelessly about anything of consequence," she prefaced, a mother's concern suddenly heavy in her voice. "But you do seem to be acting carelessly of late. At least, it seems so since our little groundskeeper broke her engagement.

"I shouldn't need to remind you that we live in a fishbowl," she continued, obviously feeling he needed reminding, anyway. "You of all my children have always had a healthy respect for that. Heaven knows, far more so than your brother," she murmured with a sigh. "Because of Cord we all know how difficult the press and the public can make our lives when we give them any reason. So, please, just promise me you'll think carefully before you do anything you might later regret."

"I'm going to call her," Gabe insisted. "I just want to make sure she's all right."

"Promise me, Gabe."

He blew an impatient breath. "Okay," he conceded. If he gave his word, he would honor it. Everyone who knew him knew that. "I promise. How soon can you get her number?"

"As soon as I talk to Rose. I'll just tell her I want to know."

* * *

The Pilgrim's Post Hotel occupied the space between a Starbucks on one corner and a bookstore on the other and made up in affordability what it lacked in charm. The front desk sported the logo of the economy hotel chain that owned it and was stacked high with tourist brochures to cover the nicks in the faux-copper countertop. That same nicked faux copper graced the room's bathrooms, whose original fixtures had probably predated the Civil War but had been sold as antiques to fund the remodel responsible for the worn red carpets and posters of various regional battles covering the cracks in the plaster.

The good news was that the place was clean and close to enough fast food restaurants and coffee shops that inexpensive meals were not a problem. But food and shelter were about the only problems Addie wasn't having as she left her cab stalled in traffic and ran the last three blocks to the hotel in the driving rain.

It had taken less than a day for her to figure out that going back to school wasn't the obvious option it had first appeared to be. She couldn't afford to be a full-time student. Not for more than one term, anyway, and if she did that, she'd have no money left at all. Not going to school meant not living on campus, which meant she'd pay more for the apartment she needed to find along with a full-time job.

After two and a half days of pounding the pavement with the want ads tucked under her coat, she'd discovered that quick employment didn't appear to be an option, either.

The good news was that she would soon be out of the rain.

Cold, wet and still upset from a remark a total stranger had made to her that morning about being a gold digger, she backed through the front door of the hotel and snapped closed her umbrella before the wind could turn it inside out. It felt odd to be recognized by strangers. The difference in their reactions to her felt even more peculiar. Yesterday the woman behind a doughnut shop counter had given her a thumbs-up and whispered, "You go, girl."

She had never understood Gabe's ease in public. Or his love of challenges. As water dripped from her beige raincoat, she considered that she would give anything to possess that ease and that passion now. He thrived on conquering obstacles. Give him a hurdle to jump and he didn't rest until he'd figured out how to go over it, around it or knock it down. He'd even once told her that he actually felt energized by the process.

With her energy sorely lagging, the only thing she felt was the damp chill that had her shivering in her wet shoes. And the only hurdle she wanted to face was finding a way to stop thinking about Gabe. There hadn't been an hour go by that she hadn't thought about calling him to ask for his advice, his guidance, or just to hear his voice.

To stop thinking about him now, she tried to focus only on how relieved she was to finally be inside. Even if she wanted to call him, she had no way to reach him. It was after five o'clock on a Friday. His office would be closed and, as she'd learned last evening, his apartment number was unlisted. Having blown far too much money in the past two days on cab fare, feeling far more discouraged than was wise to consider, all she wanted was to get to her room, get into a hot tub and figure out some way to eat without having to go back out in the rain. The hotel didn't have room service.

Thinking she might just make do with one of the complimentary apples in the basket on the bell desk, she glanced up to smile at the clerk behind it. As she did, her heart bumped her breastbone.

The clerk, a pleasant, middle-aged gentleman in a blue blazer dipped his head toward her a moment before the man he was speaking to turned around.

She recognized Gabe even before he'd faced her. The neat cut of his dark hair, his tall, leanly powerful body, the authority in his stance were all painfully familiar. His silvery gray eyes had most of her attention, though. The way they pinned hers made her heart jerk yet again, but he looked away to thank the clerk too quickly for her to catch much more than the swift tightening in his chiseled features.

That tightness remained as he pushed his hands into the pockets of his overcoat and came toward her. Droplets of rain clung to the shoulders of the gray raincoat covering his suit and the toes of his shiny black shoes.

"Hi," he said, stopping in front of her.

"Hi," she echoed, not at all sure what he was looking for as he guardedly searched her face. She wasn't sure, either, if she was relieved or distressed to find him there.

Aware that they hadn't spoken since the photo had appeared, she opted for the latter. "What's wrong?" she asked, her voice dropping to nearly a whisper. "Did something *else* happen?"

"This isn't a good place to talk." The deep tones of his voice matched hers. "Let's go to your room."

Suddenly conscious of more than his caution, her glance darted to the door as a couple rushed in, anxious to escape the deluge, their attention on each other. The clerk had already turned away to answer the ringing telephone. The man had clearly recognized Gabe, but either he respected his privacy, or was too busy to bother eavesdropping. Still, she would concede that the lobby of a hotel probably wasn't the best place to hold a conversation. Especially since she'd left solely to avoid them being seen together.

Her room was on the second floor. Rather than wait for the elevator, Gabe pushed open the door to the stairwell beside it and held it so she could slip past. She headed up without a word, conscious of the echoing silence, more conscious of him behind her, and pushed open the door at the top herself. For years, she'd felt only delight when she saw him. Now, it seemed, she felt mostly strain.

The long hallway was empty when she slid the key card into the lock and opened her door. With the flip of the switch just inside, the overhead light exposed a double bed covered in a shade of blue as faded as the red carpet and faux-cherry wood nightstands with candlestick lamps. The framed print over her bed was of the Battle of Bull Run. Or maybe that was the battle depicted in the print over the desk. The carnage looked the same to her.

Her open suitcase sat on a luggage rack by a window that would have exposed a wall of concrete had blue drapes not covered it. Closing the lid to conceal the lacy underwear that was one of her few indulgences, she dropped her purse on top and turned to see Gabe close the door.

She felt more certain than ever that something else must have happened to bring him here. She'd just looked up to ask him what that something was when she caught the full brunt of his tension. It radiated toward her like sound waves from a tuning fork, as unnerving as his glance as it slipped from her damp, windblown hair to where her lipstick had long since faded.

"Are you all right?"

The defense in his tone surprised her as much as the question.

"I'm fine," she replied, lying through her teeth as she stepped out of the wet-and-ruined two-inch heels that were killing her feet. "But that's not why you're here." His silence made her hesitate, disbelief tugging hard. "Is it?"

She was not doing okay. Knowing her as he did, Gabe felt dead certain of that as he watched her shiver. She looked wet, tired and lost—and absolutely determined to hide the latter from him.

"Pretty much," he admitted. He could have helped her. Had he known what she was doing, that's exactly what he would have done, too. "When I heard what you'd done, I wanted to make sure you were okay. And to find out why you left." That was just as important to him now. "Why didn't you call me? Didn't you think I'd be worried about you?"

There was no mistaking the concern beneath his odd guardedness, or the accusation in his voice.

Thrown by both, she picked up her shoes and set them by the radiator. It had never occurred to her that he would be worried. At least, not worried enough to be upset with her for not calling him. She couldn't let herself believe that she mattered to him that much. It was far too dangerous, far too seductive. More than anything, she desperately needed to keep how she felt about him in perspective.

"I didn't call because I didn't think I should." She wouldn't tell him about how badly she'd wanted to call him, of how she'd sat in that very bed last night trying to get his number because she desperately needed to talk about everything that had happened. But even if she'd managed to get his number, she doubted that she would have called. The person she needed to talk to was also the person she needed to talk about, so it seemed she was left to cope on her own.

"And I left because I thought it would be better if we didn't have any contact. That way there's nothing anyone can misinterpret or misread."

"You should have told me what you were doing. We might have found another way to handle it."

"They're questioning your integrity," she reminded him, determined to be the friend he'd always known. "That's not something you want to mess with."

She started working at the buttons on her coat. "I read in the paper this morning that you refused comment on both the photo and the attack on your honesty. I understand not wanting to justify an accusation with a response. But you know how much damage speculation about a person's honor can cause. I hate that I'm the reason you're having to defend yourself," she confessed, wishing her fingers weren't so cold, "and I don't want things to get worse. Leaving seemed to be the best thing I could do for you and for my mom."

Gabe watched her turn away once more, her motions agitated as she pulled off her coat and hung it to drip from the clothes rod by the bathroom door. Everyone from his advisors to her mother wanted him to stay away from her. Even his own mother felt that Addie had made a wise decision in removing herself from his world. Or so she'd admitted before she'd given him the name of the hotel and reminded him again of his promise.

From the way Addie moved across the close quarters of the room, rubbing the arms of the navy-blue coatdress she'd worn to the meeting that had now become something of a millstone around their respective necks, it seemed even she was intent on putting distance between them.

He couldn't deny her wisdom about the situation. Her instincts were dead-on when it came to how people perceived what they read and heard. His refusal to comment on the photograph was only fueling speculation. Even his own people had seemed hard-pressed to hide their doubt when he'd explained the innocence of what had taken place.

Those were his problems, though. And he would handle them. He was more concerned right now with doing what he could to make sure the woman media had labeled "mysterious" and "gamine" would be all right. He truly had intended only to call her. But after four tries and no answer, he'd needed to see for himself that she was okay.

He felt a muscle in his jaw jerk as he glanced around her bargain-priced room. It wasn't unlike some he'd stayed in himself while visiting the poorer hollows and hamlets in the eastern part of the state. Still, he wasn't all that thrilled with her accommodations. He would let that go, though. The place was clean and she was in a safe part of town. It would do until she could get settled somewhere more permanent.

Making sure she had a plan to get settled was all he intended to do as he shrugged out of his own coat and hung it next to hers.

As he did, he noticed a folded, and damp, section of newspaper sticking from the top of her purse.

"Olivia said you're going back to school," he said, tipping his head sideways to see what she'd circled. "Are you going to live on campus?"

"I was. But I can't now. You need to be a full-time student to get into the co-op I usually stay in, and I can only afford night school. I'm looking for an apartment. At least, I will once I get a job," she qualified, relieved by the change of subject. As relieved as she could be, anyway, considering her present prospects. "Landlords don't want to talk to you unless you have one."

Gabe didn't seem terribly pleased with her response. He didn't comment on it, though. Reaching toward her purse, he pulled out the section of newspaper sprouting from it and frowned at the ads she'd circled. "What sort of work are you looking for?"

"Anything I think I can do."

"Any luck with any of these?"

"I'm not sure yet." With her back to him, she sank to the far edge of the bed. "I had a couple of people say they'd call me back."

"What about this position at Uptown Floral?" he asked, apparently thinking it the most likely candidate for someone who loved flowers.

It would have felt like heaven to take off her wet, rain-splattered stockings. Preferring not to carry on their conversation while she stripped them off in the bathroom, she held her feet toward the radiator instead. "I waited for two hours for the owner to show up, but he'd already filled the job."

From the corner of her eye, she saw Gabe move to the desk a few feet away.

Loosening his tie, he frowned and rested a hip on the dark wood, one Italian-shod foot dangling. "What about this one taking care of plants in businesses?"

She'd actually had an appointment for that interview. The establishment had also been in a suburb on the opposite side of town from the florist, which meant she'd had to grab a cab rather than take the bus to make it on time. "When I got there the person I was to interview with had gone home sick."

"Wasn't there anyone else you could talk to?"

"Apparently not," she said, not feeling anywhere near as philosophical at the time as she sounded now. "I did fill out applications at two fast-food places, though," she said, not wanting him to think the day had been a total loss. "And I filled out an application for seasonal help at a department store." Along with about a hundred other people, she thought, but didn't mention. "Since I don't have sales experience, the woman I talked with said I'd be considered for gift wrap or stock room first, but any position I get there would end after the holidays."

Her chances of getting anything other than minimum-wage employment until after she graduated looked as slim as a sapling. And graduating had just been shoved even further into her future. Working for the Kendricks, she'd been able to save most of her modest salary for her term-a-year of school because her living expenses had been next to nothing. Now living expenses would eat up anything she could earn. Completing her courses at night, if she could even afford them, would now take just shy of forever.

Studying her cold toes, she curled her hands together to warm them, too.

"What about an apartment?" Gabe asked, apparently sensing the same dead ends she did on the job discussion.

"I stopped at a rental search office yesterday." The job search was merely disheartening. What she had to look forward to in the way of a roof over her head threatened to be downright depressing. "The lady there pointed out that I'd have to have a source of income before I can rent anything, but she showed me listings in what we figured would be my price range."

After the comment about needing a job first, it had been clear that the woman had thought she was straight off the farm. Having lived her life on the estate with occasional stays on a campus, Addie pretty much felt like she was. It was one thing to read about, study and discuss life beyond those relatively cloistered boundaries. But life on her own was like taking off rose-colored glasses and walking straight into thorns.

"She suggested I rent a room in a house if I can find one," she continued, giving up any hope of finding a place that held even a hint of the peace and security she'd left. The prices of even semidecent apartments were light-years beyond her budget. "Or check the ads for people looking for a roommate." She frowned at her toes. "I'm not sure

I like that idea though. What do you think of living with a total stranger?''

"That it's a bad idea. You never know what you're walking into.''

"That's kind of what I thought.''

Paper rustled, the sound impatient as he tossed the want ads onto the desk.

"This isn't right.''

Her pensive expression moved to where he frowned back at her. "What isn't?''

"Any of this. You shouldn't have to start over this way. You had a good job and a decent place to live and now you're…here.''

The muscles in his big body seemed as tight as a trip wire as he rose and jammed his hands into the front pockets of his slacks. With the sides of his jacket pulled back, the gold buckle on his belt flashed when he turned. "You need to finish school,'' he informed her, starting to pace. "That needs to be your first priority. Forget about the job and enroll full-time. That'll take care of being able to live on campus, too,'' he said, his brow low in concentration. "I'll pay your tuition and housing.''

He spoke with utter certainty, as if his conclusion was the only acceptable alternative. Just like that, he'd weighed, measured and decided. Being accustomed to having his conclusions acted upon, he undoubtedly expected she would agree.

He certainly looked as if he expected her to do just that when he turned back to face her. "You can enroll first thing Monday.''

As insecure as Addie now felt about her future, his totally unexpected pronouncement held enormous appeal. It would solve all of her immediate problems.

"It's too late in the term,'' she replied, knowing she was going to be stuck with those problems, anyway.

"Even if it weren't, I wouldn't borrow any more money from you. I still owe you the membership fee for joining the historical society."

"You don't owe me anything," he countered flatly. "And it wouldn't be a loan. Consider it a gift."

"I can't accept it."

"Why not?"

"Because I can pay my own way." Eventually, she mentally qualified, appreciating his desire to help but totally uncomfortable with the direction of their conversation. "And because of what people would think if they found out that you'd paid out thousands of dollars for me. Who knows what the media would make of it? Or my mother, for that matter."

He'd opened his mouth to counter her at the mention of media involvement. He'd promptly shut it at the mention of her mom.

The room was too small to pace. Four strides and he'd gone from the desk to the door. Four more and he was back, reminding her of a caged panther with his restlessness.

"Then find a decent apartment and let me take care of your rent."

From her perch by the heat, she stared up at him, incredulous. She didn't always agree with the broad-stroke method of problem solving he tended to utilize, but the man's decisions were invariably reasoned and rational. Now he didn't seem to be thinking at all.

"That would be worse than paying my tuition. If anyone discovered that you were covering my rent, I'd go from being someone you're lying about sleeping with to your kept woman." She read the tabloids. She watched *Extra*. She'd now also experienced firsthand the way an innocent incident could escalate, so she knew exactly how these things worked. "The press would be all over it."

"They don't have to find out."

"If you tried to cover it up, it would only give them more headlines."

"It wouldn't be a cover-up," he insisted, frustration fairly leaking from his pores. "I'd never do anything illegal."

"I know that."

"There would be nothing wrong with—"

"I won't take money from you."

The absolute conviction in her voice had him turning away, pacing again. She absolutely did not want to secretly take funds from him. They had nothing to hide and he would only be helping a friend. But no one would see it that way. Just thinking of having to conceal where her rent came from made her feel guilty and she'd yet to do anything wrong.

"Having to do this is good for me," she said, lightening her tone, evading the subject entirely. She was afraid he was feeling guilty, too, and guilt was the last thing she wanted him to feel toward her. "I had no idea how sheltered I'd been," she admitted gamely. "I'm twenty-five years old. I can name the genus of every plant in the city. But I'd never filled out a job application before nine o'clock yesterday morning." She forced herself to smile, wishing he would, too. "Since my marketable skills are obviously lacking, it's about time I acquired some."

Her smile looked tired, revealing the strain of the day that she clearly preferred he didn't see. Aware of it anyway, profoundly touched by what she'd done, Gabe pulled his hands from his pockets and crouched in front of her.

He wanted to help her, but he was now at a total loss about what to do. He'd never in his life been in such a position. He was the one people came to for answers. If there was a problem, people looked to him for a solution. At the moment he had none. Her logic was irrefutable.

Even his advisors would have insisted he listen to her. Yet what struck him most was that every reason she'd just given to not take his assistance had been to protect him. Because she was protecting him, she was faced with the total restructuring of her life.

He couldn't begin to imagine how something like that would feel. He knew only that he felt humbled by what she'd given up and how she had asked for absolutely nothing in return.

He knew how badly he wanted to touch her. He'd ached to do it since he saw her in the lobby. But he wasn't thinking of what he wanted when he reached up and nudged back her bangs. He was thinking only of her and how small and alone she looked trying to be brave.

"I'm so sorry I put you in this position, Addie."

He didn't question how responsible he felt for her as he offered the apology. Or how badly he wished he could make the uncertainty shadowing her eyes go away. "You don't belong here. And you definitely don't belong in some stranger's house renting a room while you work at a job that pays next to nothing and go to school at night.

"If we can't get you into school somehow, then you belong back in the cottage," he insisted, letting his fingers slip to the side of her neck. "You should be working with your plants and doing what makes you happy. If I hadn't—"

She shook her head, cutting him off even before she murmured, "Don't." Something like pain flashed through her eyes an instant before she lowered them. "Please, Gabe. I told you why I had to leave. And they're not my plants. They belong to your family. All I did was take care of them."

It was hard enough to be missing the grounds she'd so lovingly tended without having him make it sound as if she had any particular claim to them. It was even harder knowing that by not being in the very place he said she belonged, he would no longer be part of her life. "If you were going to apologize again for what happened in the library, I'd really rather you didn't."

She didn't think she could handle him telling her again that it should never have happened. It would just hurt to hear it and she already hurt because she already missed him—something that didn't make a whole lot of sense at the moment because he was right there, touching her.

That contact was hard to handle, too. As gentle and soothing as it was, all it did was make her want more.

Knowing she would soon be alone again, feeling utterly empty because of it, the wish for him to hold her, to shelter her, became as strong as her need for distance.

Fearing he could sense that struggle, she started to move away.

The weight of his hand on her shoulder stopped her. The feel of his free hand on her thigh stalled her breath.

He remained crouched at her knees, his face even with hers.

"I was going to say that if I hadn't gone home to talk to you and Mom the other day, there would have been no photo. I should have just called and this wouldn't have gotten so out of hand." His thumb moved lightly against her collarbone. "But I wanted to see you," he confessed, sounding as if he'd just reduced all his other motivations to that single fact.

His gray eyes narrowed, searching. "Do you think I wish I'd never touched you?"

Addie hesitated, her glance falling to where the heat of his splayed fingers penetrated her dress, her slip, her skin. "It would be the sensible way to think."

"That isn't what I asked." He wasn't sure the word *sensible* applied where she was concerned anymore. When it came to the surprisingly strong, surprisingly stubborn woman in front of him, he simply reacted. "Do you think I regret kissing you?"

That wasn't what he'd asked, either. But it was probably more to the point. That kiss seemed to have changed everything.

The delicate cords of her neck convulsed as she swallowed. "Yes."

Beside them the window creaked as the wind tested the panes. Air leaked around them, fluttering the edges of the closed drapes that muffled the beat of the rain. "In some ways I do," he murmured, hating that she would believe that. "But not the way you think."

He watched her lashes lift. Doubt clouded her lovely eyes.

"I mean it," he insisted, surprised by how badly he needed to erase that uncertainty. He could handle doubt from anyone but her. "I regret the publicity and the trouble with your mom and that you felt you had to leave. And there have been times when I wish I'd never touched you." He offered the admission quietly, his deep voice falling as his fingers gently caressed the side of her neck. "But only because touching you makes me want you more."

His thumb slipped to stroke the sensitive hollow at the base of her throat. Beneath that light caress, Addie's pulse skittered wildly. He was just being honest with her, wanting her to understand. "I just don't want any of this to ruin what we have."

She shook her head, slowly so she wouldn't disturb the comforting motion of his fingers. What she understood was that she wanted more, too. She needed his touch as much as he needed to touch her. "I don't, either."

"So, you don't hate me, then?"

She shook her head again, her glance falling along with her voice. "I could never hate you," she murmured. "What happened was as much my fault as yours."

"How do you figure that?"

The weight of his hand on her thigh shifted slightly, the faint friction of his fingers increasing the warmth. That heat shimmered up. The heat of his hand at the curve of her shoulder shimmered down. She swallowed. Hard.

"Because I always wanted you to do what you did."

With her focus on her lap, her eyes were hidden from him. There was something there she didn't want him to see. Needing to know what it was, he slipped his thumb along her jaw and nudged up her chin.

The instant he did, his gut tightened.

Conflict and yearning struggled in the depths of her eyes.

Snared by that struggle, torn by it himself, he edged closer. "Hey," he murmured when her glance shied from his. "Look at me."

The conflict remained as his glance moved over her face, but the longing drew him as he slid his fingers into her hair. "Aw, Addie," he whispered, and covered her mouth with his.

He had wanted her from the first moment their lips had touched. In that instant a barrier had disintegrated, crumbled right at his feet. Or maybe that pile of rubble had been his guard. Once that guard had fallen, he had found himself completely susceptible to everything he hadn't let himself consider about her before. He had always been drawn by her gentleness and the sense of tranquility that had surrounded her. The tranquility was gone. He'd all but destroyed it. Yet the gentleness remained. Beneath it he'd discovered a quietly simmering passion that fairly begged to be explored.

She opened to him, allowing the gentle intrusion of his tongue, playing havoc with his heart rate, heating his blood. Now, as before, she slowly leaned into him, inviting him nearer. A faint moan bubbled deep in her throat.

Aroused by that small helpless sound, by the feel of her, he drank it in, kissed her more deeply.

Addie cupped his cheek. Beneath her palm, the late-afternoon stubble of his beard felt deliciously rough, the skin of his temples amazingly smooth. She framed his face as he did hers, needing to be closer. That need felt as necessary to her as air. Each breath increased that need. Each breath drew his masculine scent deeper inside her, tightening her breasts, softening her low in her belly. But it was more than the shockingly quick physical desire he elicited that slowly drew her arms around his neck. It was simply that need to be close, and to know for a few precious moments how it felt to be wanted by the only man she'd ever loved.

Heaven help her, she would always be in love with him, too.

He knew he should let her go. The thought registered vaguely through the red haze of desire slowly fogging Gabe's brain. He should ignore the way her scent filled his lungs, the softness of her skin, the supple strength in the slender muscles of her arms. He ached to feel her against him, under him. He wanted to know the shape of her body, her breasts. He wanted to know the taste of the nipples he could feel harden beneath the fabric under his palm. She was becoming like a drug in his blood, making him crave, making him need. The rational part of him knew that if he didn't pull back, he would only complicate a situation that was growing more complicated by the second. And he would pull away. The very second she told him to stop.

His mouth never left hers as he rose forward, easing her back, sliding her up with him on the bed. Covering her body with his, he slid his fingers through the silk of her hair. She mimicked the motion, slipping her hands through his, drawing him deeper still.

He wanted more. He'd told her that. The knowledge

made common sense fade, turned rationality inside out, trashed sensibility. Addie knew that she needed to be sensible about him, too. But the world around them had faded. All that was left was the darkness beyond the window and the heavy beat of the rain on the glass. Even the corners of the room seemed to dim, closing them in, cocooning them in each other. She had a lifetime to be sensible. Now nothing mattered as much as the quiet hunger that built between them while the rain continued to fall.

His hand slipped beneath her hip, aligning her more intimately, pressing her into his hardness. Heat jolted through her as his breath caught. Her own stalled, too, leaving her heart racing as she arched against him, fisting his jacket in her hand, aching to be closer still.

"Addie."

Gabe groaned her name. The guttural sound of it tore from his chest as he lifted his head. With his heart beating like a trip-hammer, he smoothed her hair from her face. His eyes glittered darkly on hers. She was beautiful. Delicate. Exquisite. She had him ready to bay at the moon. And if they didn't slow down, he was going to undo every one of the buttons on her dress, strip off everything under it and do what he'd wanted to do since he'd walked into the room.

The thought alone would have made him moan had she not just touched her fingers to his mouth. With her glance searching his face, he completely forgot what he'd been about to say. Or if he'd intended to say anything at all.

Naked desire shimmered in her eyes, as raw as the hunger that ripped through him when his mouth covered hers once more. His hand slipped over the tight mound of her breast, seeking buttons, easing aside her dress, freeing her from slippery satin and lace.

She moved with him, pushing her small hands under his jacket, sliding it back from his shoulders. His jacket hit the floor, along with his shirt and tie, her dress and her stockings. Slacks, shoes and socks were peeled away. Filmy lace and practical white cotton landed somewhere beyond the bed. His mouth never left hers unless it was to follow his hands to kiss the skin he exposed. And once the barriers were gone, his hands never left her body except to fumble for the little foil packet in his wallet and pull her under the sheets to warm the gooseflesh pebbling her skin.

Their legs tangled, hard and rough over shapely and smooth. His mouth became more demanding. Addie encouraged that demand, looping her arms around his neck, stretching herself against him while his seeking hands roamed her back, her hips. The hard wall of his chest crushed her aching breasts, making her press closer. The corded muscles of his stomach, the hard length of him, his heavy thighs, she could feel all of him now. It just wasn't enough.

She whispered his name.

He whispered hers back, feathering kisses along her ear, the side of her neck, dipping to catch one turgid nipple.

She stroked his hair, feathered kisses of her own along the corded muscles of his shoulders.

Gabe eased her to her back, need clawing at his gut. He wanted to lose himself in her. He wanted her lost in him.

That need was like a living thing inside him as he rolled on their protection. For one totally insane instant he considered not using it. He wanted nothing between them. The need to be in her without that barrier felt primitive, basic. But the need to protect her, to protect them both from an even greater complication banished the thought in the moments before he lifted himself over her.

She reached up, seeming as desperate for him as he felt for her when he eased himself inside her, robbing her of her breath, stalling his own. He gritted his teeth against the exquisite feel of her, wanting to take it slow, wanting to savor. But what he wanted no longer mattered. Conscious thought became impossible. He wasn't even sure where his body ended and hers began. He knew only the blinding, white-hot heat that seemed to fuse their very souls.

Chapter Nine

The beat of rain on the window filtered into Gabe's consciousness. The drumming sound of it lulled him, inviting him to remain suspended in the twilight between total awareness and the half-conscious, sated sensation that relaxed his body and his mind.

His breathing slowed as he lifted himself to his elbows. Addie lay beneath him, her eyes closed, her lashes curved against her flushed cheeks. Edging a damp tendril of hair from her face, he rested his forehead on hers. He figured they had a minute, maybe two, before reality hit. He planned to savor every second before it did.

They had less than thirty seconds.

From the floor came the muffled ring of his cell phone.

He lifted his head, watched Addie's eyes open. The skin of one cheek had pinked where his face had rubbed it. Her lush mouth looked ripe and swollen from his kisses. Possessiveness swept through him, swift and undeniable. She was totally vulnerable to him, had been for far longer than he would ever have suspected.

Marveling at that knowledge, he drew his fingers over a faint line in her brow. ''It'll go to voice mail.''

''Are you sure you shouldn't answer it?''

''Do you want me to?''

''No.''

''Then I won't,'' he murmured, and watched her feathery lashes drift down once more.

She was avoiding his eyes. Or, maybe, he thought, she was just avoiding the moment when they would leave the bed. As long as they remained in each other's arms, they didn't have to face what came next.

Not certain himself what that was, not wanting to consider it now, he sifted his fingers through the softness of her hair once more.

''Are you all right?'' he asked, aware that the ringing had stopped.

He felt her take a deep breath, lifted himself a little more so she could get more air.

Addie didn't know if she was all right or not. She didn't want to think about it. All she wanted was to prolong the warm lethargy filling her, to soak up the feeling of being held by Gabe, to memorize the weight of his body, the feeling of him stroking her.

The ringing started again, the sound more insistent and intrusive than it had been only moments ago.

Gabe's fingers stilled on her brow.

''Maybe you'd better get it,'' she murmured, the protection of that lethargy slipping further away. ''It sounds as if someone really wants to talk to you.''

Gabe hesitated long enough to plow his fingers through his hair before his weight shifted. With their legs still tangled, he reached over the side of the bed and pulled the offending instrument from the clothes scattered there.

Moving back over her, he glanced at the number displayed on the caller ID. "It's my secretary," he muttered, and flipped open the phone.

"Hi, Donna," he said, his tone preoccupied. "Is there a problem?"

Addie immediately suspected there was. Even as her glance strayed over his beautifully carved shoulders, she felt the tension in his heavy muscles change quality.

Rolling away from her, Gabe reached for the nightstand and grabbed the watch he'd taken off so the band wouldn't tangle in her hair.

"I'd appreciate it if you would," he said, scowling at the time. "Just leave them with the doorman." His deep voice dropped. "You, too. Thanks."

The phone closed with a snap.

"I'm speaking at a civic thing at eight," he said before Addie could ask what was wrong. It wasn't that he'd forgotten about it. He'd had it in the back of his mind when he'd arrived at the hotel. And when he'd arrived, he'd had plenty of time.

He didn't now. He had exactly an hour and a half to get back to Richmond, change into a tux and finish the speech he hadn't been able to concentrate on because he'd been preoccupied with finding the woman pulling the sheet with her as she sat up.

"I left my speech notes at the office. Donna is dropping them off."

"You have an engagement at eight? Tonight?" Grabbing his watch, Addie frowned at the time, too. "Where?"

"The Press Club in Richmond." He pulled a breath, his glance searching the concern masking her face. "I have to go, Addie. I can't cancel at the last minute."

She held the sheet up with one fist. Her grip on it tightened as her eyes shied from his. "Of course you can't."

She understood. He knew she did. Canceling would just

give his opposition more to criticize. Now that questions about his integrity had been raised, his failure to show would probably wind up in the paper as shirking his duty.

Duty. Until that moment he'd never thought of it as a four-letter word.

His conscience jerked hard as he looked from the vulnerability she couldn't hide and handed her the little scraps of lace that had landed at the far edge of the bed. He had an obligation to Addie, too. He couldn't just walk out on her. And he wouldn't.

"Come to my place with me." He could figure out later how to deal with what had just happened. Right now there was simply no time. "I could use your help with my speech on the way. It's barely half written."

It wasn't like Gabe not to be prepared. Addie didn't think it was, anyway. He'd always struck her as the sort of man who anticipated everything and rarely put off anything until the last minute.

Fifty minutes later, however, sitting on the end of his king-size bed in the jeans and blue sweater she'd pulled on before they'd left her hotel and practically run to his car, it was clear that he was down to the wire on his speech. He obviously hadn't anticipated her interrupting his afternoon. She would be willing to bet her first job offer that he hadn't anticipated what had happened during that interruption, either.

Heaven knew she hadn't.

"Then I want to talk about the importance of each citizen contributing to the community," she heard him say over the splash of water against tile in his bathroom. "What can I say that every speaker at every civic award function hasn't already said a couple hundred times?"

The rich tones of his voice filtered toward her, along with scents of soap and shampoo from his steamy shower. He'd shaved off his five-o'clock shadow while they'd integrated the notes they'd made in his car with those he'd picked up from the doorman less than ten minutes ago. Now, with him grabbing one of the faster showers on record, they were in the refining stages.

"I have no idea what every speaker has said," she admitted, trying not to think of him naked and wet on the other side of the steamed-up glass. There was no door between the bathroom and spacious bedroom with its wall of taupe curtains covering what she was sure must be a spectacular view of the city. Through the arched opening straight ahead, she could clearly see a long black marble vanity, the mirror rising to the ceiling above it and a corner of the glass-block shower stall.

The splash of water ended abruptly.

"Maybe you could talk about the pebble in the pond effect," she suggested, wondering at how normal their conversation seemed, unbelievably grateful that it did. "How one person's action spreads out to affect everyone else? Or about how the only people who have a right to complain are those willing to work on a solution to the problem? Have those been used to death?"

The door to the shower opened. As steam billowed out, Gabe's arm appeared to snatch a black towel from the silver rack next to it. A moment later, he emerged, tucking the towel low on his hips. Water sluiced over his magnificent chest, over the hard six-pack of his abdomen and disappeared into the low-slung terry cloth.

Swallowing hard at the memory of his hard body covering hers, she watched him grab another towel and start drying his hair.

"Probably. But I like them," he said, his voice muffled by the thick ebony fabric. "I can talk a minute around both of them. Where will that put me timewise?"

A legal pad he'd pulled from his briefcase in the car rested on her lap. The sheet of notes and white index cards his secretary had dropped off were spread beside Addie on the heavily quilted taupe-and-black-striped comforter. By the time she'd picked up the card marked "service" to note both thoughts, Gabe had disappeared behind the wall of black enamel cabinets and electronic equipment to the left of the arch.

"Seventeen minutes."

"I have three more to go," he called from the hidden side of the bathroom.

"Could you use what Dad used to say about how we can't escape the responsibility of tomorrow by evading it today? You could tie that in with people who actually do something instead of just complaining about it."

"It was actually Abraham Lincoln who said that."

"It was?"

"Yeah. It's good, though," he said, his voice growing more muffled. "Put that on the card, will you? That'll work with what your dad said about not being able to enjoy a harvest unless you first labor in the fields."

Addie dutifully wrote out the quote. Her dad had also said that a person who prays for rain shouldn't complain about the mud. Heaven knew she'd wanted those incredible moments in Gabe's arms. In another few minutes, though, she was going to have to face the messy reality of having pretty much kissed rationality goodbye. "How do you want to close?" she asked, intent on ignoring those looming doubts for now.

"I'll just say the usual about how fortunate we are to have people like these in our community. I can wing that part. Do me a favor, will you?" he asked, sounding as if he'd just stuck his head in a closet. Or, walked into it, more likely. "Number those cards. If I drop them, they'll be easier to put back in order."

She could hear rustling, the thump of something solid;

the brush of wood against wood as drawers opened and closed.

The sounds of his movements continued as she neatly numbered the cards, stacked them and set them carefully beside her. With nothing else to do, she drew a very long, very deep breath and let it slowly slither out.

As long as she'd been busy, she'd been fine. Relatively speaking. She just wasn't sure now what she should do next.

If Gabe didn't leave in the next five minutes, he was going to be late. Since there was no way he could get her back to her hotel, she wondered if she should ask for his phone book and call herself a cab.

She hadn't hesitated to come with him, or given any thought to how she would get back. The need to hurry had simply taken precedence, and allowed her to feel nothing but relief that he wasn't simply bolting from her bed and walking out the door.

She could only imagine the humiliation she would have felt if he had.

The relief that had saved her from facing such embarrassment was fading, though.

Gabe walked in fastening the cuffs of his starched white formal shirt. He had his tuxedo jacket slung over one arm, and his dark, freshly combed hair was still damp. The tiny piece of tissue stuck to the side of his lean jaw testified to how rushed he'd been when he scraped the razor over it.

He seemed just as rushed now. Cuff links fastened, he whipped on his jacket, glancing at his left arm as it emerged through the sleeve. Checking his watch, he winced at the time and turned, flipping back his collar.

Addie had already risen. Not wanting to slow him down, she picked up the cards from the bed and handed them to him as they left the bedroom.

"I'll call a cab from downstairs," she said, following

him through his spacious living room. "What's the address here?"

He didn't seem to care for her idea as he tucked the cards into his pocket. Beneath the dark slashes of his eyebrows, his gray eyes narrowed. "There's no need to do that. This thing won't last more than a few hours," he insisted, overlooking her question as he reached his semicircular foyer with its gleaming gray marble floor and modern silver chandelier. Reaching into the closet by the door, he pulled out a black overcoat. The gray one he'd worn earlier hung next to hers on a brass coatrack, still drying. "Stay. Please," he asked, turning back to catch her by the chin.

Without waiting for a response, his dark head descended, blocking her view, her world, of everything but him as his mouth settled on hers. In the space of seconds, he altered her heart rate, her breathing and seriously tested the strength in her knees before he set her back to seek her eyes.

"Wait for me?" he asked, his eyes a little darker than they'd been only moments ago. "Will you?"

Breathless, she could only nod.

"Good," he pronounced flatly. "It wouldn't look good for you to take a cab from here, anyway." Patting his pocket to make sure he had his notes, he reached for the handle and pulled open the door. "And don't answer the telephone," he instructed with a glance back at her. "Or the door. Okay?"

At his hasty request, something inside her seemed to go still. But as hurried as he was she forced herself past that quick sense of warning.

"Okay," she agreed, and even managed a fairly credible smile when she touched her finger to the spot of tissue. "Don't forget to take that off."

"Thanks," he murmured, and still rushing, practically slammed the door behind him.

Addie stared at the door's carved panels, listening to the beat of his footsteps. The refined ping of the elevator bell came seconds later.

In the sudden silence, the stillness inside her slowly turned to a chill.

She hadn't been prepared for him to jerk her heart around the way he just had. One moment, it had leaped at the thought that he wanted her to stay. The next, he'd asked her to remain out of sight, and her heart felt as if it had simply stopped beating.

It was one thing to make the decision herself to stay out of public view. It felt like another entirely to have him ask her himself to make sure no one knew of her presence.

Crossing her arms over the sudden knot in her stomach, she turned in the small entry hall. She knew Gabe had to be cautious, particularly since the press was actively looking for things to exploit. He needed to be especially cautious now that they had done exactly what everyone thought they were doing anyway.

His priority isn't going to be a woman he can't have beside him in front of the cameras.

It's always the mistress who pays....

Her mother's words destroyed the attempt to be rational. They also fanned the disquiet that had her feeling an urgent and definite need to move.

She was not his mistress, she insisted to herself, tucking her arms tighter as she paced past the back of the black leather sectional couch defining the living area of the spacious apartment. They had slept together once. A mistress was more...long-term. Or so it seemed to her as the electronic ring of a telephone stalled her footsteps.

His open living area, with its sleek, masculine touches of glass, leather and stone, flowed into a dining room and around a corner in an L to the kitchen. His bedroom and a guest bath were through the doors on the opposite side. From where she stood, she could see the telephone, the portable kind, on the black granite counter dividing an ultramodern kitchen from the rest of the space. It rang three more times before she heard a click and Gabe's straightforward recording to leave a message.

Whoever it was apparently didn't want to. All she heard was a dial tone before the machine clicked off.

She started pacing again, slower this time, because time was something she had in abundance at the moment, and headed for the wall of windows.

She was right, his penthouse view was indeed impressive. Or would be if the weather were clearer. Even through the rain, she could see the ribbons of car lights, streaks of red and white against pitch-black, winding the wet street below. The lights of the city wavered in the distance.

If he'd wanted only to hide her, he wouldn't have brought her there in the first place. He wouldn't have kissed her the way he had, either.

Rationalization took the sharper edges from the anxiety gripping her as she turned from the window. Clinging to those thoughts, she paced to the wall of books surrounding a huge television screen no thicker than a framed picture.

He had books on art and athletes, tomes written by nearly every former president, technical thrillers and mysteries. A bust of Thomas Jefferson occupied a shelf near one holding a large replica of a clipper ship. Tucked among them were little bits of memorabilia. A picture of his family. A rock that looked painted by a child.

The rock captured most of her attention. Running a finger over the bright colors, she wondered if he wanted children.

They'd never talked about it. But she knew he was good

with them. Better than good. He seemed to truly enjoy being with them.

She shook her head, shaking off the errant thoughts as she drew back her hand and wandered to the sofa by the long glass coffee table. Tall crystal obelisks rose beside a pewter bowl of marble and malachite balls. Next to them was a stack of magazines and a copy of the *Washington Post.*

She lasted thirty seconds with the *Post,* before she stood again and walked into the dining room. The table for ten held a thick, polished-marble sculpture of a figure eight. Or maybe it was supposed to be infinity.

She was wondering if Gabe had picked it out or if a decorator had done it, when the phone rang again.

This time the caller did as instructed.

"You're not answering your cell," a male voice immediately complained. "It's Leon. Call me when you get this. We have a situation."

A minute later the phone rang again.

It was his secretary this time.

"Gabe. Leon's trying to reach you. Call him as soon as you can. I'll be home this weekend if you need me."

Ten minutes later trying to occupy herself with a copy of *Richmond* magazine, the phone rang once more.

Whoever it was hung up.

She set the magazine back on the stack, carefully aligning the edges with those beneath it, just as she'd found it. Each ring brought the reminder that she wasn't to answer. Not that she would have, anyway. Not unless Gabe had asked her to. But the electronic sound grated along nerves that already felt a little too raw, and tugged a little harder at the uneasy certainty that she should never have come with Gabe.

She didn't belong here.

All she had to do was look around to know that. The

marble sculpture on his dining table probably cost more than she'd made last year. His view was of the entire city. His ambitions ran to running the country. Her needs were simple. His could never be. So what was he doing with a woman with no social credentials who planned to be a teacher, if she could ever graduate, but who really wanted nothing more than to work with shrubs and flowers and to have a family of her own?

Growing more agitated by the minute, she headed for Gabe's bedroom. By now he had undoubtedly had a spare minute to ask himself those same questions. And she was driving herself crazy here. The best place for her was back at her hotel.

She'd left the yellow notepad on the comforter. Taking it back into the living room with her, she left a note telling him where she'd gone, grabbed her coat from the rack, her purse from the entry table and headed for the elevator in the private vestibule outside his door. She didn't call for a cab. She didn't know the building's address and she wasn't about to go digging through Gabe's mail looking for it. Not that she knew where it was. The overflowing basket near his shiny chrome coffeemaker was probably a good bet, but all she wanted now was to go.

The ride to the lobby took less than half a minute. It took another ten seconds for her to realize she wasn't at all accustomed to deference. The moment the elevator doors opened to the building's lobby, the doorman looked up from his chair behind the small U-shaped desk. Remembering her from when she'd come up from the parking garage with Gabe, the short, squat gentleman in the burgundy uniform and cap immediately rose to open the locked lobby door.

"I'm sorry," she murmured, stopping him before he could. His cheeks were ruddy, his pale-blue eyes kind. Had his hair been white rather than thin anemic blond, he might have reminded her of Santa Claus. "Do you have a phone down here?"

"Of course, ma'am. Is there something I can do for you?"

"I just need to call a cab."

"I'd be happy to take care of that. I can flag one for you. May I ask where you'd like to go?"

She had no sooner told him than he disappeared out the heavy glass doors and bounced down the steps. From just inside the doors, she could see him under the burgundy awning that stretched to the street, protecting him from the rain. With one arm outstretched, the fingers of his free hand at his mouth, he gave a piercing whistle she could hear even through the inch-thick glass.

Within seconds a cab slid to a stop in front of him. After speaking with the driver, he turned back to open the building door for her.

Thinking to save him the trip, unaccustomed to having doors opened for her anyway, Addie started out herself.

She'd reached the first of the three steps to the sidewalk when she saw the doorman turn to open the cab's back door. An instant later, a flash of brilliant white light nearly blinded her.

Caught midstep, no longer able to see where she was going, she grabbed for the handrail as her other hand automatically rose in defense of the unexpected brightness. Another flash met the voice of the doorman shouting, "Hey! Get out of here!" an instant before one more burst of light preceded a faint click and whir and the sudden double beat of feet on pavement.

One set of feet raced off, another moved closer.

Around a corona of white she saw the burgundy serge-covered arms of the doorman reach to where she'd come to rest on the bottom step. Having caught the rail, she'd half swung, half fallen to the hard concrete step.

"Ma'am, are you all right?"

"I'm...I think I am," she murmured, letting go of the rail as she blinked toward his voice. The flash spot began to fade, turning dark a moment before kind but worried eyes came into view.

"Are you hurt?"

Startled and shaken, but otherwise unscathed, she shook her head. She hadn't noticed anyone standing on the sidewalk. But then, she hadn't been looking for anyone, either. With the neat hedges flanking the doors, a news kiosk on the corner and all the cars lining the narrow street, whoever had just taken her picture could have been lying in wait anywhere.

"Do you want to go inside, ma'am? Or to the cab?"

Inside seemed safer. She had no idea who the hit-and-run photographer was. She didn't know if she would be followed. All she knew at the moment was that going back in would reduce the opportunity for more photographs. More important, it would eliminate the possibility of someone following her into her hotel with questions that were only bound to create a bigger mess no matter how she answered.

"Inside, please."

She brushed off her hands, wincing a little when the motion revealed a scrape where one palm had skidded on the step. She could still feel her palm stinging when the doorman took her elbow, helped her to her feet and escorted her into the lobby.

Leaving her protected from view in a little utility room behind his desk, he dismissed the cab, then hurried back in to where he'd left her between a coffeemaker and a mop bucket. One of the two upholstered visitor's chairs near the doors would have been more comfortable, but with all that glass, she would have been very visible, too.

Other than wanting to be sure she hadn't broken anything, the man whose name tag identified him as Reginald didn't seem to think that what had just happened was at all unusual. As she assured him that she truly was all right, she realized it probably wasn't extraordinary to him in the least. Working where Gabe lived, he had undoubtedly seen press and photographers hanging around before. With a Kendrick, it was simply par for the course.

"If you're sure you're all right…"

"I'm positive. Really."

Lifting his cap with one hand, he scratched his head and settled the cap back into place. "Can I get anything for you, then?"

All she wanted at that moment was the film from the camera that had just been used. Since there wasn't a snow-ball's chance in the Sahara of that happening, she offered her rescuer a strained smile. "No, but thank you."

He smiled back, looking a little uncertain. Or maybe it was uncomfortable. She was in his little closet and she'd just declined any further help. He didn't seem to know what to do with her now.

"I'll wait for Gabe upstairs," she said, feeling more than a little uncomfortable herself.

Relieved, he walked with her to the elevator and pushed the call button so she wouldn't have to do it herself.

"Thank you," she said again, his obvious solicitude adding another layer of discomfort. She wasn't sure why it was there. If he treated everyone that way, or if it was because she had been with Gabe. There was now the pos-sibility, too, that he had recognized her from the papers.

The door opened with a whisper. Stepping inside, she reached for the button for the top floor.

The door closed, but the button wouldn't light.

After three more tries, she closed her eyes against the certainty that this was definitely not her night, opened them again and pushed the circle marked open. When she had come in with Gabe earlier, he had used a key when he'd pushed the button.

The bellman was back at his desk. Apparently, he knew what the problem was. He had just as apparently thought she might have a key herself.

He didn't say that, though. The man was the epitome of discretion. Without a word, he walked over to the elevator, extracted a wad of keys the size of a baseball from his pocket and unlocked the penthouse floor.

"Thank you," she said for what felt like the dozenth time.

"You're welcome, Miss Lowe."

His use of her name pretty much answered her question about his deference. He had recognized her from all the publicity.

The elevator door closed on his polite smile. Eighteen stories later, she stepped back into the private lobby outside Gabe's apartment. Once she reached Gabe's door, though, there was nowhere else for her to go.

She wasn't entirely sure what it was she felt at that moment. Or if she was feeling at all.

Turning her back to the mural of Roman columns, she slowly slid down to the marble-tiled floor.

She was still there when Gabe stepped off the elevator two hours later.

Chapter Ten

Gabe saw Addie lift her head the moment he stepped off the elevator. She sat with her back to the wall, her arms wrapped around her raised knees. Pulled into herself as she was, she looked very small, very fragile and more than a little worried.

She also looked as if she wasn't quite sure what to say about why she was sitting outside his door instead of inside where he'd left her.

Feeling decidedly cautious himself, he watched her tip back her head as he walked over and held out his hand. "The doorman told me what happened," he said, relieved that she was all right, furious that she could have been hurt when she fell. "Come on."

There was no mistaking her unease as he helped her to her feet. He just wasn't sure if that uncertainty existed because of the incident outside his apartment building, or because she'd now had time to consider what had happened back at her hotel.

He could cheerfully strangle whoever had been lying in wait with the camera. His own feelings about having caved in to his physical desire for her weren't so immediately clear.

Unlocking his door, he motioned her inside. Her glance made it as far as his jaw before she crossed her arms over her long raincoat and slipped past him. Her uneasy silence followed her in, crowding around them as he closed the door and making the rattle of his keys sound unusually harsh when he dropped them on the narrow entry table.

The strain snaked between them, thickening as she took a step back.

He knew she wasn't accustomed to living in a fishbowl. And she definitely wasn't privy to the protocols of eluding those who lived off invading other people's lives. Her naiveté would cost him, too. Just how much, he couldn't be certain. But as unhappy as he was with her encounter with the camera outside, he was far more concerned with why she'd felt so compelled to leave in the first place.

"You said you would stay."

He'd spoken the reminder quietly. Still, Addie swore she heard accusation behind it as he uncrossed her arms and took her hands in his. Turning her palms up, he frowned at the dried scrape that reddened the pad below one thumb.

Apparently, the doorman also had told him about the little fall she'd taken.

She had suffered far worse scrapes simply doing her job. The little abrasion would be gone in a matter of days. Watching his jaw tighten when he gently ran his finger below the faintly sore spot, she had the strange and certain feeling that the damage done in her few moments outside would take far longer to heal.

There wasn't a doubt in her mind what he was thinking at that moment. That, now, everyone would know she had been to his apartment. It was even possible that they had been followed from her hotel. The clerk there might not have been as discreet as he'd seemed and tipped off the press to the famous senator's presence there with her.

She had contemplated those disconcerting possibilities herself ever since her backside had hit the shiny tiles in his lobby.

"I didn't know a photographer was out there," she quietly defended. "If I had, I wouldn't have left."

That wasn't the explanation he was after. "You can never know where they are."

"I'm beginning to realize that."

So why did you go? he started to ask, only to have his own doubts stop him cold.

He felt the tension crawling through his body as he let go of her hands to smooth back a strand of hair from her cheek. He had never intended for their relationship to get as complicated as it had become. Heaven knew he'd never intended to make love with her. He'd thought about it. Nearly driven himself to climbing walls as he'd lie in bed wondering how it would feel to slip inside her. But he'd never actually thought he would cross that line. At least, he hadn't until he'd realized that she wanted him, too.

Letting his fingers slip away, he watched a little more uncertainty creep into her eyes. He understood that ambivalence completely. Addie was not a one-night stand. Walking away from her as if nothing had happened was out of the question. The problem was that going back to the way things had been before didn't seem possible, either.

Her arms snaked around herself again. "You're angry with me."

"No." That much he could address without question. It wasn't anger he felt. Not with her. Confused and unnerved, maybe. Neither of which were terribly comfortable. Or familiar. But not angry. "If I'm upset with anyone, it's whoever was hanging around down there. None of this is your fault.''

''I didn't listen,'' she murmured, taking blame anyway. ''You asked me to stay out of sight.''

''That wasn't what I said.'' He'd asked that she not answer the phone or the door. But before he could remind her of that, he realized that no matter how he'd phrased it, staying out of sight was exactly what he'd wanted her to do.

He met the disquiet in her eyes. He knew that she as much as anyone understood the need for absolute discretion, but the request had clearly stung. It didn't help that, as badly as he wanted to, he couldn't think of a thing to say to soften that unintended hurt.

''So,'' she murmured, graciously sparing him the struggle. ''How did your speech go?''

''It went fine.'' He hated the position he was in with her. He hated having to be so careful, so certain of what he was doing. Mostly, he hated what he was doing to her.

The temptation to reach for her was strong. The need to do nothing that might make things worse felt even stronger. He needed time, and the best thing he could do right now was get her back to her hotel. ''Thanks for your help with it, by the way. The points you suggested got the best applause.''

Skepticism merged with her obvious disquiet. ''Really?''

He couldn't help the faint smile her disbelief brought. There didn't seem to be an ounce of ego in her delicious little body. ''Really,'' he confirmed, and would have told her he'd tell her about it on the way down to his car—had the phone not rung.

He considered ignoring it until the quality of her discomfort shifted.

''You might want to answer that. Leon called right after

you left." She stepped aside so he could pass. "You have a 'situation.' Don't worry," she murmured, when he hesitated. "I heard the message when he was leaving it on your machine. I didn't talk to him."

The note of defense in her assurance nudged hard at Gabe's conscience.

"What kind of situation?"

"He didn't say. He just said he'd left a message on your cell phone."

"I had it turned off."

"Well, that one's been ringing about every ten minutes ever since."

Gabe glanced at the caller ID as he picked up the receiver. "Leon," he said by way of greeting. "What's going on?"

"Where have you been?" came his strategist's quick demand. "I've left messages for you everywhere. Word is out that Addie Lowe is attending a meeting of that historical society in Camelot on Monday," he continued, apparently deciding that where Gabe had been didn't matter now that he had him on the line. "My source at the *Richmond Times* said they're sending a camera and reporter. The *Times-Dispatch* is, too. Donna said one of the local network affiliates called your office wanting to know if you're scheduled to show. You're not going anywhere near it, are you?"

"Hadn't planned on it," Gabe replied, since he hadn't even known about it. "Can't this—"

"Well, don't, okay?" Leon asked, completely overriding Gabe's attempt to put the call off until later. "On *Extra* tonight, they showed the picture of you two at the estate, and her senior photo from a high school yearbook. They called her your 'mystery woman.' Reporters will be like sharks on live bait trying to get a scoop on her now," he predicted with utter certainty. "That meeting will be their first opportunity to get footage and public comments. The sound bites that come out of it will only put her out there even more.

"We need to tell her not to go," Leon pronounced, still operating under the assumption that the rumors were just that. "Then we need to figure out how to kill this whole Addie issue before it goes any further. I think the best thing to do will be to have her call a press conference herself later in the week. We'll have her dump everything back on the media. She can tell them she didn't show at the meeting because their pursuit of a story that isn't there was making it impossible for the society to do their work. That ought to help put an end to this," he concluded, sounding as confident as he did pleased with his solution. "What do you think?"

What Gabe thought was that the whole thing could wait. They could figure out later what to do about the meeting. At the moment he was far more concerned with the tension between him and the woman who could hear his every word as she paced the confines of his entryway.

Biting back impatience, not sure he succeeded, Gabe started pacing himself. "This isn't a good time to talk, Leon. We'll deal with this in the morning."

"We need to start looking for her in the morning," Leon emphasized. "I called the estate in Camelot and whoever answered the phone said she quit her job and moved away. The woman said she had no idea where she'd gone, either."

More than likely that had been Addie's mother. Mrs. Lowe almost always answered the phone at the estate to screen calls for his mom. "I'm sure we can find her."

"That's the other thing I want to talk to you about. Did you know that she'd left?"

"Yes."

"When?"

"When what?"

"When did she leave?"

"Monday."

"Where did she go?"

"What difference does it make? Look, Leon," he said, feeling his grip on his patience slip. The line beeped, indicating he had another call. The number in the ID display was his mother's private line at the estate. She never called this late. "We might have another photo to deal with before Monday. We need to talk about that first. Just not now," he insisted over another beep. "I have to go. I'll call you in the morning."

It wasn't like him to hang up on someone, but Leon was wanting to know what photo he was talking about when Gabe cut the connection.

He'd just taken a deep breath when the phone rang again.

"Oh, Gabe. You're home," his mother said, sounding as if she might have been responsible for a few of those earlier calls. "Were you able to talk to Addie?"

The urgency in his mom's tone had his glance cutting toward the entry.

"Why?" he asked, caution heavy in his tone.

"Because she told her mother she'd call her tonight at eight, but Rose hasn't heard from her. She needs to talk to her and she's worried."

Turning his back to the entry, he lowered his voice and paced the other way. "She's fine."

"You talked to her, then?"

There had been talking involved. "Yes."

"Did she say if she was going out tonight? Or when she'd be back?"

"Not exactly," he hedged. "Is something wrong?"

"Not with her mother. But there's a problem with this historical society you have her involved in. Addie told me she was coming for a meeting on Monday. Actually, I encouraged her to attend,'' she confessed, her concern growing more apparent. "I think it's going to be a little more than she bargained for.''

"I heard about the press, Mom.''

"The press?''

"Isn't that what you want to warn her about?''

"I want to warn her about Helene. What about the press?''

"What about Helene?''

"I asked first.''

"What about her?'' he insisted, no longer pacing.

"She's not being at all gracious about Addie being head of that committee,'' she accused. "She told her hairdresser that she won't have to worry about working with her after that meeting. She said she had an easy way to get rid of her, and that she wouldn't miss that meeting for a year's worth of pedicures.

"I have no idea what sort of loophole she's discovered,'' his mom continued, a hint of disgust in her well-modulated tones, "but it wouldn't be fair for Addie to walk into that meeting unprepared. Her mother was going to tell her about it when she called. But the more I thought about it, the more I think perhaps I should speak with her myself and suggest a way or two for her to handle the likes of Helene.'' A worry entered her voice. "You're saying that the press is now involved?''

Closing his eyes, Gabe pinched the bridge of his nose. The night just kept getting worse. "It looks that way.''

A considered silence filtered over the line. "In that case, perhaps she shouldn't go to that meeting. It might be in everyone's best interests that she not appear in public at all right now.''

The "everyone" his mother referred to was him—and their family. He had learned to deal with media and the public at her knee. And no one was a better judge of character. Or people's motives. His mother knew Helene's actions could cause Addie embarrassment. With the press connecting him with Addie, he was also fairly certain his mother was thinking about how anything her housekeeper's daughter said or did would now reflect on him and his reputation.

His mom's concerns were valid, and she wasn't even fully aware of how extensive the press coverage could be.

The thought prompted another nudge at his conscience. He'd considered before that his actions with Addie had jarred the lid on Pandora's box. It seemed now that it had been ripped off completely. Helene could make Addie uncomfortable even without the press. But the press could totally invade Addie's life and leave her with no privacy at all. With the "mystery woman" label, reporters would excavate every scrap of information they could find on her. They would interview old schoolmates, teachers, shopkeepers she associated with, dig up her birth certificate, search her driving record, all in an effort to figure out who she was, what made her tick, what she was after.

He had opened her up to the scrutiny and criticism he'd lived with since the day he was born—and she was no more prepared for that than she was to build herself a rocket and fly to Mars.

"Gabe? Are you there?"

Plowing his fingers through his hair, he muttered, "Yeah. I'm here."

"Were you going to talk to Addie again?"

That was pretty much unavoidable. "Yes."

"When?"

"As soon as we hang up."

"But she's not at her hotel. I just tried."

"She's…here."

Gabe could practically see his mother's eyebrow slowly

arch as he waited for her response. The longer he had to wait, the more he would know she disapproved. Katherine Kendrick was known for her pregnant silences.

It wasn't disapproval in her tone. When she finally spoke, what he heard was more like frank concern.

"Do you think that's wise?" she asked. "What if someone saw her enter your building? Or sees her leave?"

"That's pretty much already happened."

The silence this time seemed considerably longer.

"Was it necessary to take her there?"

He blew a breath. "Yes."

The rushing sound on the other end of the line made it sound as if his mom had released a disappointed breath of her own.

In her considering silence, her tone grew heavy with caution.

"Is it possible," she began, as if she were bracing herself, "that you're more involved with her than you've led everyone to believe?"

"It's…complicated," was all he could think to say.

"I realize that, dear. That's why I'm asking."

"Now really isn't a good time to talk."

"If she's right there, I don't imagine it is. Just do something for me, Gabe. Remember the promise you made to me. And while you're at it, please ask yourself why you're risking your reputation for her. That is what you're doing, you know."

He had promised before to think carefully before he did anything he might regret. But it was a little late now to consider that. As for why he was willing to risk his reputation for her, he'd never considered that he was doing such a thing. At least, he hadn't until now.

"I have to go," he said. "I'll talk to her about the meeting."

He told his mom that he would talk to her later, and

said goodbye with the weight of family expectation adding itself to his shoulders.

He'd just broken the connection when his eyes met Addie's.

"I'm the 'situation,'" she concluded.

His voice dropped. He felt responsibility toward her, too. "It seems so."

"What happened?"

She had tried not to eavesdrop. She really had—for about ten seconds, anyway. She had heard only his side of the conversations, but she'd caught enough of Gabe's terse responses to know that there was a problem, and that she was at the root of it.

"What are you supposed to do at the historical society meeting Monday?"

Thrown by the question, she mirrored his faint frown. "I'm just supposed to report on where we are with funding, I think. And talk to whoever wants to be on the committee. I got a letter from the Office of Historical Preservation last week that said our request for funding will only be partially approved, so we'll need to get more money from someplace else. I'm hoping that whoever wants to work on the project will have some ideas for that." She tipped her head, searching his face. "Why?"

"Because it could turn into a media circus," he muttered, "and Helene is apparently gunning for you."

"Gunning for me?"

"Mom said she heard that Helene has a way to get you off the committee. I don't know what she has in mind," he confessed, looking as if he'd rather not be telling her this at all. "I don't think it will be anything overt. Helene is too conscious of her own image to do anything that will make her look bad in front of her peers. And she definitely wouldn't do anything to look that way in front of the press."

CHRISTINE FLYNN   197

"She invited the press?"

"I don't know that anyone invited them," he admitted.
"I think things are just starting to snowball. Reporters
were probably digging around for information on you and
stumbled onto the meeting." His tone went flat. "We were
a clip on *Extra* tonight."

Addie's own voice rose an octave. "*Extra?* The television show?"

"Leon said they showed the picture from Tuesday's paper and a class picture of you." He pushed back the sides
of his overcoat, shoved his hands into his slack's pockets.
"I'm really sorry I got you into this, Addie."

He had mentioned that before. From the way his jaw
worked, she had the feeling he was sorry he'd gotten himself into it, too. It seemed safe to assume from what she'd
caught of his conversation with his mother, that Mrs. Kendrick wasn't very happy about it, either.

All evening long she had felt as if she were floundering.
Now she felt as if she'd finally sunk in over her head.
"Just tell me what I should do," she said, forcing a calm
into her voice that didn't want to be there. "I don't want
to do anything that will embarrass you," she told him,
fairly certain that preventing that had been the purpose
behind his mother's call. "I should definitely stay away
from that meeting, shouldn't I?"

Gabe's first thought was that it would be easiest if she
didn't go. If she didn't, he wouldn't have to worry about
what might show up on television that night, or in the
newspapers the next day. His mother felt that would be
best, too. But this wasn't only about him. As his glance
slid over the unmasked anxiety in Addie's sweet face, he
knew this was also about a woman who never thought
twice about giving up what she wanted for the people she
cared about.

He could easily accept that she had left everything familiar to save her mother's job. After all, she'd quit college to help her father, then stayed on so her mother wouldn't have to leave the cottage. But when she'd left the estate a few days ago, she hadn't just given up her job and her home for her mother. She'd given up all her security to make things easier for him.

The thought squeezed hard at his heart. But her fear that she might somehow embarrass him took precedence at the moment. He knew there were those who felt she wasn't good enough for him. As much as he hated that, what he hated more was that she bought into that mind-set herself.

"How much does that project mean to you?"

"It doesn't make any difference what it—"

"Yes, it does. Forget about me. I want to know what you'd do if I weren't part of the equation. Would you let Helene push you out, or would you stand up to her and protect your position on the project?"

The tension radiating from Gabe's big body already had most of her nerves in knots. The thought of facing the polished and obviously prejudiced socialite only tightened them more.

She would have done it, though. For her father's memory.

"If you weren't involved, I would go." Without Gabe being connected to the project, the prospect wouldn't have been nearly as daunting. There would be no press. "But you are," she hurried to qualify, "so that doesn't matter."

"It matters," he insisted. "I've cost you enough. I'm not going to cost you this, too. Just let me make a phone call.

"Don't," he murmured, silencing any protest she might have made with the touch of his knuckles to her cheek. His irritation seemed to ease with the contact. It did nothing to alter his determination. "You need to do this."

She might have debated whether or not need had anything to do with it had he not already headed to where he'd left the receiver on the dining table. He'd barely picked it up when it rang again.

Beneath the shoulders of his black overcoat, his shoulders rose with his deeply drawn breath. "Kendrick," he said, a second after he'd punched the talk button. "He's here now?" she heard him ask. "Yeah, it's okay. Send him on up."

"Leon's here," he muttered, even as he punched the buttons to end that call and place another.

The man obviously hadn't wanted to wait until morning to take care of their "situation." Thinking Gabe didn't look terribly pleased about that, not thrilled about it herself since she seemed to be the problem, she watched him lift the receiver to his ear.

"I'm calling my assistant to have him take you to the estate tonight," he told her while the line connected. "It's possible press is still hanging around here, so he can take you out the back way. You'll need preparation for that meeting." He lifted the receiver closer to his mouth. "Mom knows those people. She can help you."

"Your mother?"

Someone must have come on the other end of the line. Gabe held up a finger, silently asking her to wait a moment as he turned away.

"You need a life, Mike. I had a feeling I should try the office first. Forget the rewrite on that bill," he said, sounding as if he knew exactly what the young lawyer would be doing at nearly eleven o'clock on a Friday night. "I need you to swing by here, then run out to Camelot. And come in through the garage," he instructed, after a moment's pause. "Don't park on the street."

Addie had no idea what his assistant said in the long moments before Gabe told him he'd see him in a while, then headed for the door to answer the knock that sounded on the other side. She simply watched Gabe, mindful of his air of quiet control while she struggled to feel as if she had any control at all.

She was certain that putting herself anywhere near microphones and cameras at that meeting would be a huge mistake. Facing his mother right now didn't feel like such a good idea, either. Especially when she considered that Mrs. Kendrick probably regarded her as her least favorite person at the moment. But going back to the estate was truly the only practical thing to do. If the press was following her, the last place she wanted to go was back to the hotel.

"You didn't tell me you were in town," she heard Gabe accuse as a slightly rounded, balding and bespectacled man in khakis and a brown bomber jacket walked in.

"You didn't give me a chance," the shorter man replied, then went still the moment he saw her standing beside the sofa.

His expression turned suddenly, openly cautious. "Miss Lowe," he said, acknowledging her with a slight nod. "I'm sorry to interrupt."

"Addie, this is Leon Cohen." Gabe closed the door, finally shrugged off his coat and left it on the coatrack. "You've heard me mention him before."

"You're going to manage his campaign," she said, reaching for Leon's hand since he'd walked over and held out his. It felt strange to have people know her on sight. At least with this man she had the advantage of being familiar with his name. "You've been with Gabe for over a month now, haven't you?"

"Right at that." Caution turned considering. "I'm a little surprised to see you here," he admitted, with a significant glance toward the man now at her side. That glance slid from Gabe's tuxedo to the hem of her jeans and athletic shoes visible beneath her nondescript beige raincoat.

"But it might be a good thing that you are," he continued, as if he hadn't even noticed the incongruity in their dress. "Did Gabe tell you about the situation we have on Monday?"

Half the people she knew would have answered for her. Gabe didn't say a word.

"He did."

"And he asked you to cancel?"

Hesitating, Addie glanced toward Gabe, then looked a little uncertainly back at the man he paid to know what was best for his career. "Gabe feels I should go."

"Excuse me?"

Leon's thin eyebrows rose in disbelieving arches as his glance swung to his high-profile client.

Gabe's expression became unusually closed. "It's her project, Leon. I'm not going to ask her to jeopardize it."

"Then, I will. Due respect, ma'am," he said, looking back to her. "But there's a lot more at stake here than some—"

"She knows what's at stake," Gabe insisted. "We'll talk about this later."

"But she can't handle a roomful of—" Leon cut himself off, looked back to her. Despite his obvious disagreement with Gabe's decision, he had the manners not to talk about her as if she weren't even there. "There will be television cameras and reporters at that meeting, Miss Lowe. Everything you say and do will be caught on tape and film. Gabe told me that the two of you are just good friends, but that isn't what the public is believing at the moment.

"Depending on the slant the editorial department at a paper or a news station decides to take," he continued, seeming to look at her more closely, now that he'd gotten past her slightly messy, finger-combed hair and the coat that hid all but the bottom of her jeans and athletic shoes, "what winds up in print or in a film clip may not be flattering. Or even a true representation of what you said. The problem with sound bites is that they're presented out of context. Same goes with quotes. You can bet your petunias that no one's going to ask about that garden you're working on, but they will want to know about your relationship with Gabe.''

''Leon,'' Gabe growled.

Addie held up her hand, silently asking him to let the man speak. The more she knew, the less chance she had of making a fool of herself. Or him. ''Go on.''

''If you tell them you're good friends, they're going to want to know how good. I don't want to embarrass you,'' he hurried to say, not looking totally comfortable himself, ''but that picture of the two of you is all over the country. I wouldn't put it past any one of them to come right out and ask if the two of you are or are not sleeping together. How will you answer that?''

Addie knew what he was doing. He wasn't looking for confirmation or denial himself. He just wanted to know how she would handle such an intrusive question. If she would get annoyed, or flustered or provide a calm, rational response.

The fact that her glance shied from them both had him sighing.

''That's what I'm talking about. No offense, but you're not up to this. I can see I did embarrass you, and I'm sorry about that, but you look as guilty as—''

''Leon.''

''She does, Gabe. I can see the shot now, and it's only going—''

''Enough.''

The edge in the clearly enunciated word had Leon closing his mouth. The two men held each other's glances: Gabe's steely and daring him to push; Leon's turning from pleading to slowly dawning comprehension. It seemed there was nothing more that needed to be said, anyway.

Addie wasn't sure, but she thought Leon swore. The word was too low and too terse to distinguish.

A sudden, heavy silence between the three of them ended with a jarring knock on the door. Since the doorman hadn't called, it seemed safe to assume that Gabe's assistant had an elevator key. At least Addie assumed it was his assistant who rescued her from the unnerving way Gabe and Leon looked at each other in pure challenge before Gabe walked to the door and let his assistant in.

Mike Walsh was a thin, angular young man, with close-cropped curly brown hair, round wire-rimmed glasses and the air of a perpetual student. He also had a nervous energy about him that made Addie wonder if he didn't consume copious quantities of caffeine.

Mike tossed a file onto the credenza, said he'd leave it there for Gabe in case he needed something to read tonight, then turned to shake Leon's hand even as he glanced toward her.

"Miss Lowe?"

"Addie, this is Mike Walsh," Gabe said. "Mike, I need you to take her to the Pilgrim's Post Hotel over by VCU to pick up her bags, then out to the estate. She tried to leave tonight and a camera caught her, so watch for press.

"When you get to the estate, Addie," he continued, putting himself between her and the balding man who'd closed his eyes and run his hand over his face at mention of the camera, "just go to the cottage. I'll call Mom after you leave and tell her you're coming. She'll call you in the morning."

"Excuse me, Miss Lowe." Leon, hands on his hips now, stepped into view. "Gabe," he said, his tone respectful but decidedly flat, "I really don't think this is a good idea."

Gabe ignored him. "Okay?" he asked her.

It was clear enough from Leon's tense expression that he considered her and her actions something he and Gabe must deal with. Now.

She feared Gabe felt the same way—that she was something he had to deal with, only for an entirely different and far more distressing reason. "Okay," she murmured, and waited for him to give her some indication that he didn't totally regret that she existed.

All she got was a bigger knot in her stomach. He held her glance long enough to make it clear he really didn't know how he felt, then stepped aside because he was blocking her path to the door.

"I'll call you later." He spoke the assurance quietly, the touch of his hand to her back feeling vaguely protective as he handed her over to Mike.

Feeling as if she were being pulled along by forces far beyond her own power, she picked up her purse from beside the file on the entry credenza and felt his aide touch her elbow to get her moving through the door.

She didn't know which unsettled her more as Gabe's aide punched the button for the elevator that would whisk them to his waiting car: not having any idea where she stood with Gabe, or the fact that she once again had to face his mother. And her own.

Chapter Eleven

"I don't get you, Senator." Leon stood by the sofa, accusing and frustrated as he shook his balding head. "When a candidate pays for my advice, he usually takes it. So far, I don't think you've listened to a word I've said."

"Of course I have." Striding past him, Gabe loosened his black bow tie and jerked open the button beneath it. "I agreed to make the circuit of talk shows and political roundtables. And I'm hiring one of the speech writers you recommended. I did that just last week."

"I'm talking about her." Leon's arm swung toward the closed front door. "I don't appreciate that you wouldn't level with me," he grumbled, following Gabe around the sofa to make sure he had his attention. "I'm the last man on earth anyone would ever accuse of being sensitive, but a person would have to be deaf, dumb and blind not to see that there's something between the two of you. If I can see it, how in the hell did you expect to convince everyone else you're not involved with her?"

"Because I wasn't involved with her," Gabe retorted. Stripping off his tie, he flipped it onto the coffee table and glared at the man glaring back at him. "Not the way you mean." His voice dropped to a growl. "Not until now."

Gabe watched the man's mouth open and promptly shut again. He would bet his seat in the Senate that Leon had been fully prepared to launch into his speech about trust and skeletons and how he wouldn't work for a candidate who wouldn't level with him. Between the unpredicted admission and the vein he could no doubt see throbbing in Gabe's temple, he seemed to think better of it.

Leon's eyebrows nearly merged over the bridge of his silver-rimmed glasses. "You mean the situation changed," he said in a voice flat with conclusion. "As in, you weren't involved before but you are now?"

A level glance was Gabe's only response.

It appeared to be enough.

Gabe expected Leon to swear. Instead, apparently more sensitive than he believed himself to be, or at least more judicious, he said nothing. He just stood, apparently weighing the tension that had locked Gabe's jaw tight enough to shatter teeth, and considered how the change affected the handling of his job. He was not a man to waste time on what could have been. He dealt with what was.

"So," he began, his strategist's mind plugging the new information into the equation. "Do you want her in the picture or out?"

Gabe snorted air through his nose. "It's not that simple."

"It's never simple when a woman's involved. That why I have two ex-wives. You said before that you and Addie had been friends," he reminded him, making it sound as if being a friend and being romantically involved were mutually exclusive. "But is she someone you can trust?"

That he could answer without a doubt. ''Yes,'' Gabe murmured.

''You're sure? She's not going to sell her story to the tabloids or a publisher if this doesn't work out? The house-keeper's daughter and the crown prince of Camelot has too much potential to let go. The Kendrick name alone will sell, and inside info on one could almost guarantee she'd be on the talk-show circuit.''

Worst-case scenarios. A politician had to ferret them out, be prepared for their effects. Leon had a gift for hom-ing in on the most damaging. Putting out fires before they started was one of the reasons Gabe had hired him.

''I can't imagine her doing that.'' He'd known other women who might have, had they been around longer—which was precisely why they hadn't lasted past the second date. ''Not Addie.''

''Is it possible she's after your money? Your status?''

''No way.'' Status was the last thing she would ever seek. ''She's not like that at all.''

''I've got to admit she doesn't look the part,'' Leon muttered.

''I've known her all her life, Leon. Addie isn't after anything.''

''I'm just looking out for your interests here,'' the man defended, having the good sense to keep any other obser-vations about her lack of polish to himself. He'd made the mistake once of being critical of Addie and who she was. He clearly wasn't about to exercise that error in judgment again.

Clasping his hands behind his back, he started to pace. ''What about you? How far are you willing to go with this? You obviously care about her, but is she someone who can fit into the governor's office? The White House? We can probably make the struggling working girl angle work in your favor with the middle class, but how will it play with your peers?''

Gabe knew that Leon was only doing what he was being paid good money to do. He was playing devil's advocate. He was also buffering his usual bluntness with his subtle reminder that Addie did not appear to be the ideal partner for someone with his ambitions. But he was getting way ahead of himself. And discussing Addie as if she were a campaign issue hit Gabe all wrong.

Or maybe it was just the pressure of yet another person wanting answers that made him turn his back on Leon and the questions piling up and pressing down on his shoulders.

He stared toward the night-blackened window, his reflection staring back at him.

He understood the responsibility he felt toward Addie— but not the possessiveness that had blindsided him weeks ago. He understood the need to make sure she was all right and that she would have a way to take care of herself now that she was no longer in his family's employ—but not the restlessness that had wrecked his concentration until he had seen for himself that she was okay. And he definitely understood raw need. There was nothing especially complicated about sex. The taste of her had entered his blood like a forbidden drug the first time he'd kissed her, and he'd been like an addict fighting the need for a fix ever since.

''We're going to need something soon here,'' Leon prodded, apparently taking Gabe's silence for consideration. ''You can't put any more denials out there. Not now. You're credibility has already taken a shot with this, and that was before—''

The muscles in Gabe's jaw started to work as he slowly shook his head. ''I'm not doing this now.''

''You need a strategy, Gabe.''

"I said, I'm not doing this now." He fairly bit off the words as he turned around. "I'm not going to talk to you about her. I'm not going to talk to anyone else, either. No advisors. No reporters. No press. This is between Addie and me."

"And anyone who watches television or reads a paper," Leon reminded, looking concerned that he would overlook that. "You don't have the luxury of keeping this between yourselves. It isn't like she's someone you just met. It's already out there. The question is, where do you go from here?"

Gabe wasn't prepared to answer that question. In the space of hours, his relationship with Addie had been altered—and every decision he made now had a direct impact on his relationship with her and his future.

He needed breathing room. He needed time.

He shoved his fingers through his hair. As soon as Leon left, he would throw an overnight bag in the car and head for the solitude of the estate.

Or so he thought before he remembered that the estate was the last place he could go. Addie would be there, and he needed distance from her right now as much as he did from the man waiting for him to decide his fate.

He'd just have to find that distance some other way.

The sudden determination in his expression only deepened Leon's concern. "What are you going to do?" he asked, watching skeptically as Gabe headed for the door.

"I'm going to kill the rumors and buy myself some time."

"How are you going to do that?"

Gabe opened the door. "As soon as I figure it out, I'll be sure to let you know." Not wanting to block the path to the elevator, he stepped aside. "Good night, Leon."

It was well after midnight when Addie found her mother waiting for her in the cottage. She had used Mike's cell phone to call from his car and let her know she was coming so she wouldn't scare her to death waking her from a sound sleep. Not that her mother ever slept that soundly. Not anymore. Ever since the evening in the library, there had been many nights when Addie had heard her trying to be quiet in the kitchen while she made herself a cup of herbal tea, or while she'd watched whatever she could find on late-night television to keep her mind off whatever it was keeping her awake.

Tonight she had both the tea and television, but the volume on the TV was down so low that her mother had apparently heard the faint creak of a porch board and pulled the door open before Addie could even reach for the knob. Addie could see the tea, untouched, on the coffee table.

Stepping inside, she saw her mother push her hands into the pockets of the long pink robe cinched tightly at her waist. Her face had been creamed free of makeup, and her graying hair hung in a dark braid over one shoulder.

"Why wouldn't you tell me why you were coming back when you called?" she asked as Addie closed the door.

In the warm glow of the table lamps, Addie watched her mother study the strain in her face.

"Because I didn't want to go into it in front of a stranger."

"What stranger?"

"Gabe's assistant," she replied, bracing herself for her mother's reaction as she set her bag by the television with its black-and-white images flickering on the screen. The movie was one of her mother's favorites, an old romance from the middle of the last century. "He drove me from Richmond."

Her mom's response seemed as predictable as rain in winter. The mention of Gabe caused her mouth to pinch.

The mention of Richmond had her brow lowering in confusion. "What were you doing in Richmond? You were supposed to be in Petersburg. I tried calling your hotel at least a dozen times," she informed her, looking worried, sounding frustrated. "Were you with Gabe?"

Hating the uncertainty she was dealing with, weary from worrying about it, Addie turned to the closet beside her.

"You were." A discouraged sigh escaped her mother's lips. "I thought your leaving here was to end the rumors about you. How can you hope to do that if you're seen with him in a place like Richmond? And in the company of his staff, too?"

Slipping off her coat, Addie carefully hung it on a hanger and placed the hanger on the rod. She had no answers. She couldn't even fall back on the argument that her relationship with Gabe wasn't what her mother thought it was.

"It's late, Mom." The weariness she felt dragged at her, colored her tone, drained the energy from her movements. "Can we talk in the morning?"

The quiet request met with a moment of troubled silence. "I think you should leave in the morning," her mother said, making it clear she thought there would be no time then to talk. "The reason I tried to call tonight is because of that meeting of yours on Monday. There are rumors that it's not going to be pleasant for you, Addie. I wanted to warn you so you wouldn't come." Distressed by what she'd heard, and clearly questioning Mrs. Kendrick's reaction to her return, she glanced in the direction of the main house. "You shouldn't be here at all."

"I heard about the meeting," Addie murmured. "And thanks for wanting to warn me." She offered a faint smile as she closed the closet door. She knew her mother worried about her. That was apparent even through her almost perpetual disapproval. "But Gabe thinks I should go. He's the one who sent me back."

The faint lines in Rose's brow turned to furrows.

"He sent you back because of the meeting?" she asked, as Addie picked up her bag and headed for her room. "Or, he sent you back so you would be here for him?"

The sudden flatness in her mother's tone caught Addie two steps from the hall. The question itself had her spinning back around.

"Why won't you listen to me about him?" Distress turned to demand as her mom crossed her arms like shackles around her middle. "You're an intelligent young woman, Addie. Yet all that man has to do is suggest something and it's as if you have no sense at all. You could have had a good job by now and been out on your own if you hadn't let him encourage you all these years about college. I thought when you left here, you'd finally be able to make a life for yourself and escape the hold he's always had on you. But you only made it seventy miles before he reeled you back in."

Bewildered by her mother's perceptions, Addie felt her bag slip from her fingers. It hit the floor with a thud. "Reeled me back in?"

"He doesn't care about your interests in that meeting," Rose insisted, her agitation growing. "He just wants you here so you'll be available for him. I know how men like him think. And I know that you're going to wind up with nothing but a lot of broken dreams and a reputation it could take years to live down. I've told you before that he won't be there for you. He's going to find himself a woman like his mother and sisters. Or one of those lady attorneys with a high-profile career and a list of connections as long as his own. Once he does, you'll never see him again."

Addie had never in her life challenged her mother.

Heaven knew she had silently disagreed with her, become exasperated with her, wished she could make her listen. But she was already battling the awful insecurities of no longer *having* any security, of not knowing how Gabe felt about her anymore and of possibly losing the best friend she'd ever had. Despite her mother's insistence, she didn't believe for a moment that Gabe didn't care about her interest in the project. He'd gone against the counsel of his highly qualified advisor and probably his own mother to see that she protected her stake in it. But he was fully capable of leaving her without his friendship and with a badly broken heart.

Hearing her mother throw her worst fear in her face was simply more than she could handle.

Her stance mirrored her mother's—self-protective, defensive.

"You know something, Mom?" A faint tremble entered her quiet voice. "I've lived a lifetime with your low expectations of me. No matter what I've done or what I want, you're always there to remind me that I'll only be disappointed if I try to reach any further than you think I should. Why have you always had so little faith in my abilities?" she asked, her eyes pleading. "And why is it that you think all he wants is to use me? What is it that makes me so unworthy of the friendship of a man like Gabe?"

The sudden tightness in her throat robbed much of the strength from her last words. The unwanted stinging in her eyes had her blinking hard as she waited for the woman staring at her with her mouth open to speak.

When her mother did nothing but stand there looking stricken, Addie swallowed hard and reached to pick up her bag.

Her mother's hand on her arm stopped her.

"Oh, Addie," she began, her tone as anguished as she looked. "I don't think you're unworthy. I've never thought that. You're a good person. A good daughter. And I do have faith in you,'' she insisted, tightening her grip as if she feared Addie would pull away. ''I've just tried to protect you from building impossible dreams. I understand those dreams. I do,'' she frantically assured, ducking her head to catch Addie's eyes, to make her listen. ''I just don't want you to suffer because of them. And you will. I just know it.''

Addie's reply was no less distressed, no less adamant. ''How do you know that?''

''Because I once had them myself. I know how easy it is to love a man like that,'' she admitted, her voice now barely more than a whisper. ''I know how seductive their power can be.''

Addie felt herself go still. For a moment she didn't say a word. She just watched her mother's still-pretty face go pale as the insistence drained from her and her glance fell away.

With her hand at her throat, her mom stepped back. ''I just don't want you hurt like I was.''

Addie could only stare as what her mother had just admitted slowly sank in. In that single-minded way children have of regarding their parents, she had seldom thought of her mom having had a life beyond the one she had shared herself. And she'd definitely never considered her in a relationship with any man other than her father.

''What about Dad?''

''It happened before your father. I knew your dad then. We'd gone to school together. But we'd never dated. We actually never dated at all before he married me.''

''I don't understand.''

''I'm sure you don't,'' her mother murmured. ''It doesn't make much sense to me when I put it that way.''

Addie took a step closer. ''Who was he?''

''His name was Peter McGraw. I was twenty when I

went to work as a secretary in his campaign office," she said, rubbing her arms as if to ward off an internal chill. "Unless his wife has strangled him in his sleep, he's probably still involved in Kentucky politics. I know he was house majority leader for a while.

"He was just a councilman when I met him," she continued, still rubbing. "But I fell madly in love with him, and I thought he loved me. Just like I'm sure you think Gabe loves you," she contended, clearly thinking her daughter felt more secure in the relationship than she truly was. "I was so crazy about him that I didn't even question why he never took me out in public. I just wanted to be with him, so I didn't even think about it. At least, I didn't until he dumped me for the daughter of his legal counsel.

"It didn't take long for me to figure out that she was more socially acceptable in his circles than I was, Addie. I was nobody and he kept me hidden. But he took her to fund-raisers and his country club. He'd never had any intention of marrying me. But they were engaged in a little over a month." Her hands went still, her grip on her arms tightening. "That was about the time I realized I was pregnant.

"He wouldn't take my calls." She spoke quickly, as if she needed to get the telling over with, as if going into greater detail would be too painful or too humiliating. "So I finally went to his office. He told me that if I told anyone the child was his, he would deny it."

"Oh, Mom." Unprepared for what her mother revealed, Addie reached out, only to pull back when she saw her mother's hold on herself tighten more. "What did you do?"

"There wasn't much I could do. At least, there wasn't anything I thought I could do," she quietly confessed. "Your dad used to say that a good offense is better than a good defense. That's what Peter did. He went on the offensive and started a rumor that I was sleeping around. When it became apparent that I was pregnant, everyone assumed that I was loose and no one would believe the child was his. Things were different then. We didn't do DNA testing. Not the way they do now. And an unwed mother in a small town wasn't something any girl wanted to be.''

Slowly shaking her head, she took a deep breath. ''I don't know what I would have done without your father,'' she confided, the long strands of silver in her hair glinting in the lamplight. ''Tom and I had known each other since our freshman year. I think he'd had a bit of a crush on me even back then,'' she mused, her tone softening. ''But he told me he wanted to take care of me, and I was desperate to be taken care of. We didn't lose the farm the way we said we had. He married me then sold it so we could get away from all the talk and the shame.'' Her voice fell. ''I lost the baby a few months after that, and we came to Camelot when the money ran out.''

''That's when you and dad went to work here?''

Her mother nodded. ''You were born four years later.''

She took a deep breath, finally lifted her head. ''He gave up everything for me, Addie. He made it so I could hold my head up again. You have your father's huge heart,'' she told her, ''and I simply can't bear for you to be hurt the way I was. That's the only reason I'm telling you any of this. Please. Please,'' she pleaded. ''Don't make the mistakes I did.''

Addie had the feeling her mother would have taken her past with her to her grave had she not felt that recounting the experience would save her daughter from the same fate. She felt utterly certain of that as her mom finally turned away.

Her mother had lost a child. She had been betrayed and abandoned by a man she'd thought had loved her. She had married a man she didn't love because she had been frightened and alone. Addie didn't doubt for a moment that her mother had learned to love her father, but it had never occurred to her that her mom had harbored such scars all those years.

It was no wonder she had always discouraged her friendship with Gabe. It was no wonder, too, that she was so worried about her now.

The floorboards creaked beneath the beige carpet as Addie walked over to where her mom stood staring down at the cold cup of tea.

"I'm sorry," she murmured. She touched her hand to her shoulder. "I really am."

Her mother's fingers settled over hers. "I'm sorry for you, too," she said, giving her hand a pat. "I'm sorry for you, too."

Chapter Twelve

"Remember that you don't have to answer a question just because it's asked," Mrs. Kendrick said. "Silence and a level look will often let a person know they're being intrusive and out of line. Pretending you didn't hear and going on to someone else's query can be effective, too. But humor is helpful, if you can think of something clever and noncommittal."

"I'm not feeling terribly clever." Looking from the floor-length mirror in one of the mansion's six guest bedrooms, Addie covered her stomach with her hand. "I think all I'm feeling is nauseous."

"Then, remember what I said about breathing." Mrs. Kendrick stepped back to check the fit of Addie's jacket. She had borrowed it from her youngest daughter's closet, along with its matching deep-burgundy skirt. The suit was one Tess had left behind after her wedding, together with an armoire full of clothes she hadn't worn in a couple of years and had asked her mom to donate to a charitable cause.

The chic little ensemble fit only because Marie had taken it in and hemmed it. The burgundy kidskin pumps Addie wore fit only because tissue had been stuffed into the toes.

Gabe's mother smoothed the back of the collar, then ran her glance to the back pleat of the narrow skirt. "If you feel yourself getting more nervous, breathe in long and deep to the count of seven. Slowly release to the count of ten. That will keep you from hyperventilating," she claimed, stepping around Addie to see how the lapels lay now that the short, trim jacket was buttoned. "And don't fidget with your hands or brush at your hair or your face. No one needs to know you're nervous. Especially Helene. Keep your hands loosely clasped in front of you when you're standing, or folded in your lap when seated.

"When you are seated," she stressed, reaching to the dressing table and the pile of scarves she'd brought from her own wardrobe, "keep your knees together and cross your ankles off slightly to one side. Never cross your legs in public. Especially if there could be cameras around. There's nothing more unflattering than a shot of the back-side of a thigh."

Choosing a navy scarf with gold threads woven through it, she whipped it around Addie's neck. With a frown she promptly pulled it away and reached for one of pink-and-burgundy silk. "When you give your report in front of the group, seek friendly faces and talk to those people. If you'd like, you can talk to me. I'll try to sit in the middle of the room."

"You're going with me?"

Mrs. Kendrick didn't seem to like that scarf, either. "Gabe asked me to," she replied, and turned back with a simple narrow gold necklace.

Her attention remained on the necklace as she moved behind Addie to clasp it, but Addie could easily see the elegant woman's beautifully made-up face in the mirror of the tastefully appointed bedroom. Nothing in Mrs. Kendrick's refined features betrayed her feelings about what her son had requested of her. She didn't reveal another word of what Gabe had said, either.

In the three days since Addie had been back, she hadn't heard from Gabe at all. Not even yesterday after the photo of her outside his apartment Friday night appeared in the Sunday society section. The photo hadn't proved nearly as troublesome as it could have. A reporter had obviously contacted Reginald the doorman to confirm her presence there, but Reginald had omitted a few pertinent details.

Addie didn't know if Gabe had spoken with him or if the man was simply being respectful of Gabe's privacy, but he had said only that he remembered seeing her with papers for Senator Kendrick. The papers he'd referred to would have been the envelope of speech notes Gabe's secretary had dropped off, and which Addie had held for Gabe because he'd already been dealing with his briefcase and the key for the elevator. From the way the quote read, since Reginald had been careful to mention that Gabe hadn't even been home at the time the picture was taken, it sounded as if she'd simply dropped those papers off. The photo was apparently of interest only because there were so few of her.

"I think simplicity suits you," his mother decided, moving around again to check her handiwork. "As petite as you are, scarves and large pins are too fussy. What do you think?"

A sinking feeling joined the nervous knots in Addie's stomach as she looked from the woman with the black-and-camel scarf draped at the throat of her black turtleneck dress. Gabe had spoken with his mother about her, about the meeting. But he hadn't bothered to call her, even though he'd said he would.

"Addie?"

"Oh, it's fine," she murmured. "Thank you."

"You didn't even look, dear."

With a touch of chagrin, Addie skimmed the reflection in the mirror. The image there was definitely her, only far more...polished. At Mrs. Kendrick's suggestion, she had smoothed her hair behind her ears to hug her head and reveal the gold button earrings she had loaned her to match the gold-colored rims on the covered buttons on the jacket. Her eyes were darkened with smoky shadow and a bit more mascara than she usually wore, and the foundation and colored lip gloss she wore made her skin glow.

Her nails, however, were hopeless. She had spent the weekend helping Jackson with the last of the pruning and had done what she could with a nail file, cream and clear polish, but no one who saw her hands would ever mistake her for a lady of leisure.

Still, thanks to Gabe's mother, she didn't have to feel self-conscious about her appearance. And that, the woman had kindly told her, would free her to focus on how she handled Helene and the press.

When Mrs. Kendrick had sent for her Saturday morning, her sole focus had been on helping Addie present an air of poise and self-confidence at the meeting. She hadn't said a word about how anything Addie said or did at that meeting could reflect on her son. Nor had she asked a single question about their relationship. It had almost seemed to Addie as if the lady was helping her simply because of her own interest in the project and because she didn't care for the way Helene was treating a former member of the Kendrick staff. Mrs. Kendrick did, however, say she felt it wisest not to mention just yet that she had resigned her position at the estate. There was no sense offering anything else for people to speculate about.

Only once had she mentioned Gabe that day, and that had been to recommend that Addie deflect any questions about him by focusing on the reason she was attending the meeting and describing the project. She made it clear that Addie needed to be the one in control of her responses to the press and her handling of Helene.

As for Helene, Mrs. Kendrick seemed to feel that anything the woman came up with to remove Addie from her chairmanship—or the society itself, if that was her goal—could be countered simply by reminding her in front of the members that it was her research that allowed the society to file the application, and that she, through Mrs. Kendrick, had the plants they needed for the project.

"You will remind her kindly, of course," she'd said. "The goal isn't to embarrass her, no matter how much she might deserve it. If you treat her graciously, you will have the upper hand and set the tone for future dealings with her. I'm sure when more people are made aware of your contributions, most of the society's members and the locals who read about it in the paper will supply all the pressure you will need to get Helene to back down."

Mrs. Kendrick gathered up the accessories they hadn't used. "I'll get my coat and meet you in the foyer. Bentley will drive us. Do you have your report?"

"It's downstairs in the kitchen."

"I'll have Ina bring it to the foyer. I'd ask your mother to come see how nice you look, but she will have left to see the florist about arrangements for a luncheon I'm having next week."

She took a step toward the door, only to turn right back. "One more thing, Addie. I can tell you not to let Helene and her little circle intimidate you," she said, sounding as if Gabe might have mentioned how the woman had cowed her before, "but I know that a person can't simply turn off the way she feels. Maybe it will help if you know that true class has nothing to do with money or social station. It's all about behavior. And you," she said with an approving smile, "have class. All you need to do now is show them your strength."

Breathe.

Addie repeated the word like a mantra as she sat with her knees together in the back of the sedately luxurious silver Rolls-Royce. Mrs. Kendrick occupied the seat next to her, deep in conversation on her cell phone with her daughter Ashley about a ball they were organizing for one of Mrs. Kendrick's favorite charities.

Addie barely heard a word. With their destination getting closer by the second, her sole concern was on surviving the next couple of hours. According to the woman beside her, confidence could be faked. All she had to do was stay in control and focus on the project.

The approach had an uncomfortable ring of familiarity. Keeping attention focused only on the project had been what Gabe's advisors had recommended as a way of handling the rumors when they'd first begun. No one wanted either of them to mention any sort of relationship beyond the project, and her being a family employee. There was to be no mention that they were friends.

It seemed he and his family were still opting for the same approach. But since Gabe hadn't bothered to speak to her himself since he sent her back, she couldn't help but wonder if they soon would be friends at all.

Not knowing where she stood with Gabe did nothing for the nerves jumping in her stomach. Suspecting that his mother did know, but afraid to ask for fear of what she might hear, she silently begged their driver to keep going when the car slid to the curb in front of the stately old

Camelot Public Library. A WRIZ news van from Richmond was parked next to one from a CBS affiliate in Washington, D.C. The sedans parked near the no-parking zone looked suspiciously as if they might belong to newspaper reporters. But other than the four reporters hovering like vultures over carrion outside the building's double doors, the only other people about were a few onlookers curious about why the news trucks where there.

"Take a deep breath, Addie," Mrs. Kendrick said, as the gray-haired Bentley opened her door for her. "And don't stop to answer any questions. Just keep walking and answer on the way to the meeting room."

It soon became apparent that Mrs. Kendrick's presence had not been anticipated. The moment the regal-looking woman stepped from the car, the people on the street started pointing, whispering or calling her name. Instantly recognizing the international celebrity, and the unexpected bonus to her story, a female reporter in a red turtleneck and a tan trench coat made a beeline for her.

Her competition, with their respective photographers in tow, was right on her heels, inches from knocking her down to get there first.

"Mrs. Kendrick," the woman in the trench coat asked, frantically waving her own cameraman closer as Addie thanked Bentley for helping her out, too, "what do you think about your son's relationship with Miss Lowe?"

Making sure Addie stayed with her, Katherine Kendrick walked up the building's short flight of steps. Her smile remained gracious even with microphones shoved toward her face, a video camera rolling and newspaper cameras flashing.

"I'm pleased he is as interested as I am in her project," she replied, expertly evading the root of the question. "He has always been interested in history, and I have always loved plants. Thanks to Miss Lowe, we can work together on something we both enjoy.''

''But what about their personal relationship?'' another female reporter asked, this one in turquoise and black. ''Does your presence here mean you approve of it?''

A man in a baseball jacket with a *Richmond Times* press pass dangling around his neck spoke at the same time. ''Miss Lowe. We're told by Senator Kendrick's office that he is on vacation for the next several days. Are you joining him?''

The members of the press had their microphones thrust out as they all took the last few steps in a single, mobile mass. Mrs. Kendrick completely ignored the question posed to her to thank the bystander who opened the door so she could pass. Caught off guard by what the other reporter had said about Gabe being away, Addie felt her step falter an instant before she followed Mrs. Kendrick's lead and bought herself a moment by thanking the bystander, too.

''I didn't know the senator was on vacation,'' she finally, politely, said, and hurried into the quiet lobby that reminded her more of the vestibule of a church than the entrance to a public building.

The reporters were right behind.

''You didn't know he's in Vermont?''

''How many engagements have you had, Miss Lowe?''

''Mrs. Kendrick. Is it true that Miss Lowe's parents both work for you?''

''You did say the Robert Browning Room, didn't you?'' Mrs. Kendrick asked Addie over the clamor of questions.

Gabe is in Vermont? Addie thought. Heels tapping on the marble floor, she gave his mother a nod. ''There's a sign to the meeting rooms over there.''

''Miss Lowe—''

''Mrs. Kendrick—''

"Will you excuse us?" Katherine asked, as they turned down a long hall. "We're late for our meeting. There it is, Addie," she murmured, and headed for the open door halfway down with all the voices spilling out.

Those voices began to hush the moment they stepped into the crowded little room with its American flag in one corner and literacy posters lining the pale-blue walls.

Normally, a regular meeting of the Camelot Historical Society wouldn't garner the attention of anyone beyond the sixty or so of the more devoted members actually interested in preserving history. Today it seemed as if its entire membership and their nosier friends were present. Every row of folding chairs was filled, leaving those who had arrived too late to find a seat to stand along the walls.

Like a giant wave in the ocean, the silence that began in the back of the room rolled its way toward the front as the crowd parted to let Mrs. Kendrick and Addie pass. As the din died, the board members occupying the long table in front looked up from their conversation with one another. Addie recognized the blond Tiffany immediately, along with three other women who'd had their heads together at the garden site.

Helene Dewhurst, looking quite fashionable in navy knit, didn't appear at all curious about the silence. Seeming to think that it only meant that Addie had arrived, she looked up from her seat in the middle of the table with a tolerant smile on her perfectly made-up face.

That smile faltered briefly when her glance moved over Addie.

Addie wasn't sure if Helene hadn't expected her to show up, or if she simply hadn't expected her to show up looking as if she belonged there. Either way, as she found a place along the wall to stand, she saw that smile die completely when Helene noticed Gabe's mother.

She recovered even as she rose, smiling hesitantly as

she skirted the table to greet the woman taking a chair a few rows back that a younger woman had vacated for her.

Helene held out her hand, totally ignoring Addie, who stood ten feet away.

"Mrs. Kendrick," she cooed, "what an unexpected pleasure. I haven't seen you since the senator's last fundraiser. I didn't know you were joining us."

"I should more often. After all, I am a member," Katherine reminded the woman, her tone utterly conversational. "But you know how busy we all get with our various commitments."

"Oh, my, yes," Helene replied, pleased to have that in common with her. "That's why I'm a bit surprised that you're taking the time to join us."

"I'm actually doing double duty," Addie heard Mrs. Kendrick confide. "Gabe couldn't make it himself today, so I told him I'd represent both of us. This project is important to him, you know. The early 1700s were his favorite period. And I'm especially interested in the garden restoration because so many of the plantings were the same as those used at our home." Smiling at a reporter who'd slid along the wall to stop near Addie, she murmured, "I do so love gardens."

Mrs. Kendrick withdrew her hand to take her seat, and turned to two women she obviously knew. Breathing deeply, Addie watched her return their greetings. Helene, having lost her attention, turned away herself to take the podium beside the head table.

Helene didn't say a word to her. Apparently feeling she still held an ace despite the senator's famous mother's presence, she didn't even make eye contact. It was as if Addie weren't there at all.

Wishing she wasn't, wishing Gabe would walk through the door right now and prove that he wasn't seeking even more distance from her than she'd already begun to suspect, Addie crossed her arms tightly over the manila file folder. She had tried to stand with the folder clasped between her hands in front of her the way Mrs. Kendrick had instructed, but her hands were shaking. If the goal was to keep Helene from seeing she was nervous, she would just have to keep them wrapped around herself.

The moment the society's president stepped behind the podium, she rapped her gavel against the wooden block it had rested on. The low buzz of conversation faded as a single flash from one of the cameras at the back of the room captured her on film.

Obviously aware of the television cameras already recording so nothing would be missed, and the newspaper photographers jammed at the back of the room, she spoke into the small array of microphones the various media had clamped to the chest-high pedestal.

"I would like to welcome all our visitors," she began, looking completely at ease with the little room jammed to capacity. "It's wonderful to know so many of us are interested in the preservation of Virginia history, particularly in the area around Camelot.

"As you know," she continued, sounding as if she were doing nothing more than conducting a normal meeting, "we have a very special guest speaker today, Dr. Richard Albright from the National Arboretum in Washington, D.C."

A smattering of polite applause greeted the neatly bearded, middle-aged gentleman in the front row. "But before I introduce him, we need to address our regular business with our officers and committee reports."

With the other four members of the board looking on, Helene called each officer and chairman to the podium in turn—which meant everyone present had to sit through the minutes of the last regular meeting, the treasurer's report, the membership report, the report of the education com-

mittee and reports on the upcoming annual dinner and a
tour of Monticello for underprivileged children, which the
society sponsored every May.

With those reports out of the way, and the membership
listening courteously, Helene took the podium one more
time. The only committee that hadn't been called was Addie's. But instead of calling her for her report, she sent an
apologetic glance in her direction.

"As many of you know, we had greatly anticipated re-
storing one of New England's oldest public gardens. Our
chairperson was to be Miss Addie Lowe," she said, with
a nod to where Addie stood hugging her file. "Miss Lowe
did the research that allowed us to file our application,"
she said easily, neatly removing the possibility of Addie
using the one defense Mrs. Kendrick was sure would work
in her favor.

"Regretfully," Helene continued, while people craned
their necks to get a better look at Addie glued to the wall
between an easel and a lady who seemed to have bathed
in perfume, "we have received a letter from the state Office of Historical Preservation stating that it can only partially fund the project." She arched an eyebrow toward
Addie. "You received a copy of that letter, didn't you,
Miss Lowe?"

Addie glanced to her file. The letter Helene referred to
was the very one she had been prepared to tell the membership about herself; the one lying neat and flat in her
little folder that showed a copy had been sent to Helene
as the society's president.

She cleared her throat, loath to have her voice tremble
when she spoke.

"I have it right here," she said, mentally scrambling for
a new argument now that Helene had taken the only one
she'd had.

"Then you know how large our deficit will be. We are

at least fifty thousand dollars short on the asking price to purchase the land, and our little organization can't afford to make up that sort of difference in funding next year. Since the project has stalled,'' she concluded with just the right mix of disappointment and authority, "we'll dissolve this committee and possibly take the matter up at some future date.''

As if she expected no discussion whatsoever, she removed a sheet of paper from her own folder and turned her smile to their guest speaker.

"Dr. Albright was invited to speak before this unfortunate turn of events,'' she began, "but I'm sure we'll all be fascinated to learn the role native plants played in the lives of our early ancestors...''

Addie swallowed hard and stepped forward. Nearly everything Mrs. Kendrick had told her about control had flown out of her head. Addie's only thoughts now were of her dad and of Gabe.

The woman had cost her too much to cost her this, too.

"Excuse, me,'' she said, hating the attention she called to herself by so blatantly interrupting.

Helene's eyebrow arched as she glanced toward her.

"I don't see where funding needs to be a problem.''

Helene clearly hadn't anticipated the interruption. Or the challenge. She didn't appreciate either. Still, pure indulgence entered her voice.

"I'm sorry, Miss Lowe, but you're out of order. We follow Robert's Rules in our meetings. Since you may not be familiar with those procedures,'' she continued, apparently not willing to be totally discourteous with so many people watching, "I will allow that funding *is* a problem. It's fifty thousand dollars we simply don't have. Our board talked it over and it just isn't feasible now. There is no point in taking up everyone's time discussing it.''

In addition to herself, the other members of the board

CHRISTINE FLYNN   231

were four of her friends, two of whom were looking rather uncomfortably in Mrs. Kendrick's direction. The other two seemed to be uncomfortably aware of the flashing cameras.

"It's fifty thousand dollars we could have if you would lend your expertise to a fund-raising effort," Addie countered, grasping at the only thing she could come up with to salvage her position. Her father had once said that the proudest people had the greatest weaknesses. Since Helene's greatest weakness seemed to be her rather high opinion of herself, her pride seemed to be as vulnerable a place as any to prod. "I obviously don't have the experience myself to do something like that, but I've heard that your functions are extraordinary."

"Oh. Well," she murmured, caught off guard by the compliment.

"You said yourself that this garden was too significant for one person to handle alone," she reminded her as a cameraman worked his way forward to crouch by the easel. "As important as it is, I can't imagine that you would deny the society and the public your talent to make the restoration possible."

Gabe himself had told her of Helene's organizational accomplishments, but Helene didn't appear at all interested in the source of her information. She simply looked at a loss for a way to respond to the unexpected logic and flattery and totally perplexed by any possible way to gracefully refuse her help in front of a roomful of people and the national press.

The guest speaker, thoughtfully stroking his Van Dyke beard, saved her from taxing herself too hard.

"My apologies to you and Mr. Robert and his rules for the interruption," he said, "but may I speak?"

"Of course," Helene replied, looking rather grateful for the reprieve.

"I was visiting with one of your members before the

meeting. Professor Williamson," he said, with a nod toward the ruddy-faced gentleman that Addie had met at Mrs. Wright-Cunningham's tea. "He mentioned that the original notes for the garden indicate several species of rose that have nearly faded from existence in this area due to cross pollination and hybridization. He also indicated that you have access to those roses. If that's true, there could be funding available from any number of horticultural organizations. Which species is it?"

For a moment Helene simply stared at the man. She'd already looked a bit flustered. Now her mind appeared totally blank.

"I appreciate your hesitation," he offered, clearly crediting her with more knowledge than she possessed. "Without confirmation from a university or recognized arboretum, I would hesitate to say for certain myself. But what is it you suspect you have? Quite often something as common as *rosa setigera* is mistaken for a find."

Helene's glance fell to her notes a moment before she smiled uneasily at the crowd.

Suspecting that the woman didn't know crabgrass from hay, Addie offered to help her save face. "May I answer that?" she asked, making it sound as if Helene knew the answer, but that Addie was simply more anxious to respond.

"Please," Helene mumbled.

"It's nothing as common as the Prairie Rose," Addie said, easily identifying the flower the doctor had just referred to by its Latin name. "What we have more resembles *robusta*. We have two varieties growing. A climbing and a bush, along with an old variety of iris, tansy and the more common plants and herbs used in colonial gardens. With Mrs. Kendrick's permission, I would be happy to send you specimens."

Looking genuinely pleased, and now far more interested

in her than the woman at the podium, the gentleman nodded. "I would be happy to receive them. I'll give you the address after the meeting."

"Yes. Well." Helene cleared her throat. "We need to move along now. Since that committee has been dissolved, this discussion no longer falls under the business of the society."

"Madam President." From her chair at the end of the head table, Tiffany leaned forward. "Perhaps we shouldn't dissolve this committee so quickly. The doctor did just say there might be other funding available. And Miss Lowe does have a point about a fund-raiser."

"I concur," came a rusty male voice from the middle of the room. Professor Williamson stood up to be recognized, resplendent in his three-piece tweed suit and his graying red hair looking electrified. "I don't think this is something the board should have handled on its own, either. The membership needs to vote on this."

"I agree with the professor." A beautifully groomed middle-aged woman rose on the other side of the room. Addie recalled having seen her at the tea. She just couldn't recall all of her name. As nervous as she was, all she could remember was Andrea Smyth-Something-or-Other. "This is too important a project to sacrifice to personal agenda."

Tiffany cleared her throat as murmurs rumbled from front row to back, heads bobbing in agreement.

"Madam President," she repeated hurriedly. She sent a discomfited glance toward Addie. Looking as if she might have underestimated her dedication to the project, or perhaps just guilty at having so quickly judged her, Tiffany looked back to the woman at the podium. "Professor Williamson has a point, too. The membership needs to decide this. Therefore, I move that we keep the committee with Miss Lowe as chair and explore our funding opportunities for the restoration project."

A multiringed hand instantly shot up from the middle of the third row. "I second," called Mrs. Wright-Cunningham.

Assenting murmurs from the membership drifted forward.

Now that Helene had mentioned following a certain protocol for the meeting, she had trapped herself into following it. Addie just couldn't decide if she looked embarrassed, annoyed or betrayed as she reluctantly turned back to her microphones.

"We have a motion on the floor," she said, repeating what that motion was. "Discussion?"

No one said a word. Not even the ladies she'd apparently thought she could count on to back her. Not a single one of the beautifully dressed women at the table seemed willing to state her position against Addie with cameras rolling.

Seeing wisdom in silence herself, all Helene said was, "All those in favor?"

Everyone eligible to vote raised their hands, Mrs. Kendrick included. Seeing Mrs. Kendrick arch her eyebrow at her, and realizing she also had a vote, Addie poked her hand into the air, too.

"Opposed?"

All the arms came down.

Recognizing defeat when it surrounded her, Helene did her best to regroup. "Motion passed," she said with an amazingly bright smile. "So, Miss Lowe, you will speak with Dr. Albright about additional funding?"

With the photographer still on his knees in front of her, his camera flashing, and the news camera zeroing in on her from across the room, Addie murmured, "Whenever he's willing."

"Good. And if nothing materializes there, then I will be more than happy to organize an event. Thank you for suggesting it. Now,'' Helene continued, most anxious to be done with the matter, ''that concludes the business—''

''Madam President.'' Tiffany interrupted again, her perfectly cut hair swinging as she leaned forward once more. Her voice dropped to nearly a whisper. ''You need to ask for volunteers for her committee.''

Helene was obviously not accustomed to overlooking such details. She was also obviously not accustomed to needing reminders of such details in front of large groups.

An extra hint of color crept beneath the blusher artfully applied to her cheekbones. ''May I have a show of hands of those interested in serving on the garden restoration committee?''

Thirty hands went up. Seeing Mrs. Kendrick's hand in the air, another dozen rose.

The immediate show of support for the young woman she had once so easily dismissed clearly wasn't what Helene had anticipated. She had obviously come into the meeting confident that no one would care if one little groundskeeper got pushed aside because she wasn't in the proper social league. She hadn't counted on Mrs. Kendrick's obvious approval of Addie, either. Or on the effect the prominent woman's presence had on the members of her board. Three of those volunteering were seated at the table beside her.

Overwhelmed by the members' response, all Addie could do was offer a hesitant smile before she stepped back against the wall.

Helene nervously cleared her throat. Glancing at the door as if she fully expected to see the senator walk in and further undermine her rapidly slipping prestige within the group, she struggled for the surprising graciousness Addie had shown her.

''Madam Secretary, if you will prepare a sign-up sheet,'' Helene asked the woman beside her, ''perhaps it will be best if those interested would leave their names and telephone numbers after the meeting. Will that be all right, Miss Lowe?''

The condescension when she'd addressed Addie before had slipped from her tone. What replaced it sounded more like grudging respect. Or, perhaps, grudging wariness.

With a nod, Addie indicated that would be fine.

''Now,'' Helene began again, only to stop and glance with uncharacteristic uncertainty toward her vice president.

Thinking of nothing else she had overlooked, Tiffany nodded.

A moment later, looking desperate to be out of the spotlight before she did anything else to embarrass herself, Helene did what she'd been trying to do for the past ten minutes and introduced the guest speaker.

Addie was certain she would have found Dr. Albright's lecture quite interesting. Unfortunately, she couldn't concentrate on a word he said. Now that she had survived Helene, all she could think about was that Gabe had left— and turned the handling of her over to his mother.

By leaving her under Katherine Kendrick's watchful eye, he had put Kendrick support behind her, which had ensured that her interest in the project would remain protected. She knew he couldn't have done it himself without fueling the rumors. She just didn't know if he'd wanted that support there because he cared about her, or because leaving her with her project intact would leave him with one less thing to feel guilty about if and when he ever got around to telling her that what had happened between them had been a mistake.

That uncertainty robbed her of the relief she might have felt when the meeting met a merciful end an hour later. As soon as Helene thanked everyone for coming and people began to stand to the scrape of chair legs on pine flooring and the din of conversation, Dr. Albright headed straight for her. Cornering her by the easel, he spared her from the press, who didn't seem interested in her at the moment, anyway. They had all headed for Helene and Andrea Smyth-What's-Her-Name to grill them and anyone else around about the personal agenda remark.

Addie only caught bits and pieces of the questions being thrown at them. She was too busy answering the queries of the man who soon proved to be interested in more than her father's old roses. Because of her own interest in horticulture, he was interested in her, her background—and, because she happened to mention that she wasn't exactly working with the roses anymore because she no longer had that job—in her future.

Five minutes and a few more questions later, he made her an offer she could hardly believe. Or refuse.

She still couldn't believe what he'd offered when, twenty minutes after that, she sat in the car with Mrs. Kendrick, telling her of the offer she had received and wondering how something could be so exciting and so depressing at the very same time.

Mrs. Kendrick's only response was a smile of congratulations and the comment that she must come into the house when they got there and tell her mother her news. She felt certain that Rose would be thrilled for her.

Addie was sure she would. A job in Washington, D.C., would put a lot of miles between her and Gabe.

That discouraging thought lingered in her mind as they finally pulled into the drive. Trying to shake it off, she wondered aloud if her mother would be back from the florist yet. Even as Mrs. Kendrick said she thought she should be, Addie couldn't help but think it might be better if she wasn't.

Gabe's car was there.

Chapter Thirteen

Addie wasn't sure if it was her usual unease at being in the main house that accompanied her through its front door, or if it was knowing that Gabe was somewhere on the property that had her feeling thoroughly unsettled. All she knew for certain was that it felt quite odd to have one of the staff hold the door for her as she entered the opulent foyer behind Mrs. Kendrick.

Ina's polite smile for her employer dissolved to a look of anxious concern the instant she caught Addie's eye. Because Mrs. Kendrick was only a few feet ahead of them, Ina couldn't explain why that concern was there. The best she could do was give Addie a surreptitious nod toward the hall before she closed out the chill air.

"I see Gabe is home," Mrs. Kendrick observed, referring to the presence of his car. "Where is he?"

"In the library, ma'am."

"I was going to make some calls, but I think I'll go see him first. Do you know if he's staying for lunch?"

"No, ma'am."

Looking curious about her son's obviously unexpected appearance, Katherine handed her gloves and purse to Ina to take upstairs, and hung up her coat herself. "Is Rose back?"

"She returned about an hour ago."

"Addie needs to see her. Where is she?"

Clutching purse and gloves to the front of her uniform, Ina cast another glance toward the hall. "She's in the library, ma'am." Hesitation marked her tone. "With the senator."

There was no doubt from the uneasy look in the maid's wide blue eyes that Addie's mom wasn't simply in there making sure the room had been properly cleaned and polished. The only question was what Ina had seen or overheard that had her looking as if she were trying to warn Addie of trouble in the making.

With her mother and Gabe alone together, there was only one thing Addie could think of that would cause such concern. Knowing what she now did about her mom, and understanding how protective her mother really was of her, it seemed entirely possible that Rose had decided to warn Gabe away from her herself.

Desperate to believe that her mother hadn't just made the situation worse, Addie held her breath at the muffled sound of a door opening and hurried footsteps in the hall.

Within seconds Rose appeared in the archway near the sweeping arm of the left staircase. With her hand covering her mouth and her eyes suspiciously bright, she hurried toward the butler's door under the staircase balcony.

She'd made it halfway across the back of the foyer before she even noticed the three of them watching her. But all she did was give a quick shake of her head as if she were either too overwrought or too overwhelmed to speak before she disappeared through the narrow little portal.

The door had barely closed when the sound of heavier footsteps drew Addie's anxious glance back to the hall. Gabe was walking toward the foyer, his dark head lowered and his hands jammed into the pockets of the slacks he wore with a blue sweater that did incredible things for his shoulders. Totally preoccupied, looking faintly brooding, he didn't even notice he was being watched—until he looked up.

Brooding turned to hesitation when he saw the three women on the other side of the round entry table. Glancing past the tall vase of fresh flowers centered on it, he looked from his mother and Ina to Addie.

Fifteen feet of mosaic marble tile separated them. Still, Addie could feel the tension in his big body as he skimmed a glance over her hair, her face and down the length of the neat, stylish suit.

A faint smile tugged at his mouth.

"How did it go?" he asked.

"Okay," she replied, worried about what her mother had said, worried, too, about what he had said to her mother.

Conscious of his mother watching them both, her own glance fell.

"You did better than okay," Katherine informed her, looking a little concerned herself about whatever was going on. "You handled everything quite well. Especially Helene.

"In fact," she said to Gabe, "Addie handled everything so well, that Helene is now getting back a little of her own."

Gabe's eyebrows merged. "What happened?"

"It apparently got out among the general members that she hadn't wanted Addie on the committee," Katherine explained as she idly picked up a leaf that had fallen from the massive arrangement on the marble-topped table.

"During the meeting," she continued, tucking the leaf into the vase before Ina could get there to take it from her, "one of them commented on Helene having an agenda other than what might be beneficial to the group. Not only has her reputation among the membership now suffered, but she had to deal with reporters asking what her problem was with Addie. The last I heard her, she was madly trying to make it sound as if it had all been a misunderstanding."

"It's hard to say what the press will make of any of it," she murmured philosophically. "But Addie did nothing anyone can criticize."

The last time Addie had seen Gabe, his campaign manager had just arrived to discuss her. Hearing his mother describe the events of the morning, and her own performance in handling them, it seemed she was seeing him now only because he had come home for a report. He wanted to see how much damage she'd done.

The distressing thought had barely occurred when she heard Gabe say, "I didn't think she would."

Confused by the absolute confidence in his tone, Addie's eyes met his.

That confidence was reflected in those steel-gray depths, along with a conflicting sort of uncertainty that had tension radiating from him like sound waves from a sonic boom.

Apparently aware of that tension, too, Ina sucked in an uncomfortable breath.

Mrs. Kendrick arched a curious eyebrow.

"Would you excuse us?" Gabe asked his mother.

"Of course, dear," she replied, bouncing a cautious glance between the two of them. "Ina?" she prodded, and headed through the dining room to see what was going on in the back of the house.

Clearly wanting to do the same thing, but not happy to miss what was going on in the foyer, Ina hurried up the stairs to put Mrs. Kendrick's things away.

Addie didn't doubt for a moment that she would be back down within the minute to see what had happened with Rose. She was far more conscious of Gabe, however, as he slowly crossed toward her.

"I thought you were in Vermont."

"I was. I came back this morning." Sounding far more at ease than she felt, he nodded toward the door. "Do you want to go for a walk?"

Addie looked down at the burgundy leather pumps on her feet. "Can't," she murmured, hating how accusing she'd sounded, grateful that he'd seemed to overlook it. "Wrong shoes."

"You've been shopping."

"Actually, they're your sister's. So is the suit. I couldn't go into town to shop for anything because I was afraid I'd turn into a photo op."

The glint in his eyes as his glance skimmed her body hinted heavily at approval. That glint also died with her last comment.

"Did the cameras bother you today?"

"The reporters bothered me more."

He looked as if he'd been afraid of that. He also looked as if he didn't know whether or not he should touch her.

Keeping his hands in his pockets, he nodded back toward the hall. His carved features held interest and concern, but revealed nothing about why he'd been so silent.

"So how bad was it?"

"It could have been worse. Much worse," she allowed, thinking it should have been more difficult to confide in him as they walked across the foyer. She had no idea what her mother had said to him. She was worried about why he'd gone away. Yet, there wasn't anyone she would rather talk to about the roller coaster of events she'd been riding all day. "I'm still in charge of the project, and Helene will organize a fund-raiser if we can't get the rest of the funding somewhere else. I even got a job offer from the guest speaker.''

The door of the library was open. As they moved through it, Gabe absently gave it a push, almost closing it. ''Who was that?''

''Dr. Richard Albright.'' Addie breathed in the scents of lemon oil and rich leather. It had been weeks since she had been in the decidedly masculine, darkly paneled room. Weeks since she had stood in Gabe's arms by the desk she now passed. She'd had no idea then, how drastically those few moments would alter her future.

''He's head of the National Arboretum in D.C.,'' she explained. ''When he found out I didn't have a job, he asked to see the research I'd done on the garden project. The society secretary had a copy, so he looked at that, asked how much education I had and asked if I'd be interested in a staff position. It doesn't even matter that I don't have my degree. He said they'll help me get it,'' she told him, still scarcely able to believe how impressed the man had been with the scope and thoroughness of her research.

Addie came to a stop by the long, red leather sofa. Gabe stopped an arm's length in front of her.

His incredible smile was the last thing she'd hoped for.

''Addie, that's perfect for you. You've always been happy working with plants. Now you can do what you really want to do.''

He looked genuinely pleased with her news, something that would once have made her smile, too. But she had the awful feeling that there was relief behind his pleasure. Relief that he now didn't have to worry about what she would do with herself. Or worse, relief that she would be leaving.

''When do you move?''

Wishing he would at least have had the decency to pretend he would miss her, she turned away and picked up a brass pineapple from the end table. Drawing her finger over the molded leaves splayed like a small palm tree on top, she bravely pretended the heavy ache in her chest wasn't there.

"Dr. Albright said I can start anytime. I'll start looking for a place right away."

"Where?"

"I'm not exactly sure where the arboretum is, but somewhere around there probably."

For a moment Gabe said nothing. Not sure what she expected him to say, Addie finally looked up from the brass object in her hand.

An uncharacteristic caution marked his features. "Would you consider living in Fredericksburg?"

Puzzled as much by the question as the caution, Addie set the little pineapple down and crossed her arms over the empty ache. "Fredericksburg is an hour's drive from D.C."

"It's also an hour's drive from Richmond. That would put us halfway."

Addie felt her whole body go still.

Us?

Fairly certain her expression now mirrored his, she tipped her head, searched his face. "Just what exactly did you and Leon decide to do about me?"

Gabe had always thought Addie pretty in a soft, nurturing sort of way. Now, without the denim and windblown hair, the softness was still there, only more refined, more gracious. The warmth seemed lost, though. It was hidden from him by the guardedness clouding her beautiful eyes.

"Leon had nothing to do with this," he murmured. Not with the decision he'd made, he thought. The questions the man had asked the other night had definitely helped put matters into perspective for him, though. So had the promises his mom had asked him to make.

Do you want her in your life, or out?

Ask yourself why you're willing to risk your reputation for her.

Think carefully before you do anything you might later regret.

"I know I should have called you," he admitted, knowing where he stood, but not totally sure about her. The way she protectively held herself didn't exactly invite his touch. And the last thing he wanted was for her to pull back from him. "I just didn't know what to say to you that would make any sense. Everything happened so fast," he said, hoping he could make sense of it for her now as he started to pace. "People were wanting answers I didn't have, and I just needed to get away to think. But the place I usually go to do that is here and that's where you've been, so I went to a friend's place up north."

Plowing the fingers of both hands through his hair, he stopped beside the desk with the large painting of a hunting scene hanging above it. Turning, he let his hands fall to his hips and paced back. "I was there two days when I realized it wasn't just being in the woods or walking around a lake that made it easier to focus. It wasn't even the place that mattered. What I needed all those times I came home," he said, his voice dropping as he stopped in front of her, "was the woman I always found here.

"I thought a decision like this would have taken longer," he admitted, needing her wariness of him to go away. "But I was wrong. I've had years to reach the only conclusion I could. I finally realized you were the reason I came home when I needed answers or escape, or just to recharge. You know me, Addie." She was the one person he could truly be himself with. She knew his dreams, his fears, his failings. "And I know you."

With more caution than he knew he possessed, he reached out to touch the ends of her soft, shining hair.

"I've been in love with you for years," he confessed, more relieved than he could believe possible when she stayed where she was. "I just didn't realize it until I faced losing you."

She balanced him. She was his anchor. "You once told me that I needed someone who could help me reach my goals. That's what you've been doing all along." His fingers drifted down the short length of her hair once more. "Like I told your mom, without you, those goals mean nothing."

The wariness in her delicate features had faded. What he saw there now looked more like skepticism, and an oddly encouraging sort of disbelief. "You said that to my mom?"

"I wanted to know what Rose's problem was with me. That's why I came back while you and my mom were gone," he explained, captivated by her softness, relieved to be touching her again. "She told me she thought I would only hurt you, and I made sure she understood that's the last thing I ever intend to do.

"By the way," he murmured, feeling the tension in his body fade as the warmth glowed in her eyes, "she knows the rest of my intentions, too."

Cupping her face in his hands, he smoothed his thumbs over the satin of her cheeks. "I don't need to wait, Addie. But I'll understand if you do. I think we've bought ourselves some time if you'd like to take it slow. But I want to marry you.

"I know you have your own career to consider now," he hurried to say, wanting her to know he had every intention of supporting her the way she always had him. "Especially now that you have a chance to do what you love. But I'd like to share as much of your life with you as you'll let me, and I'd sure like you to be there to share mine."

He'd been in love with her for years. The knowledge had her heart feeling as if it would burst.

"It won't be easy, especially during campaigns," he told her. "Especially if we start a family—"

A family.

The rest of what he said was lost on Addie. Raising on tiptoe, she threw her arms around his neck just as he said something about juggling schedules, and covered his mouth with hers.

She felt his strong arms come around her, slowly at first, as if he didn't quite believe she was actually in them. She could hardly believe she was there herself. She'd been so afraid she'd never be in his arms again. But within a couple of uneven heartbeats he locked them more tightly, drew her harder against him and nearly left her breathless with a kiss that turned soul deep.

Her heart was beating like the wings of a hummingbird when, long moments later, he lifted his head.

She didn't think her heart could possibly beat any faster until she saw his devastating grin.

"What did that mean?" he asked, his deep voice beautifully husky.

"It means I don't need any more time. I want what you want. And by the way," she whispered, touching her hand to his freshly shaved cheek, "I love you, too, Gabe. I've been in love with you all my life."

She felt his body go still against hers. The admission touched him, sobered the smile and turned his eyes the color of molten pewter. But just as his head lowered toward hers, the squeak of the door had them both glancing toward it.

"Ina, get away from there. You, too, Olivia," Mrs. Kendrick scolded, her voice drifting up the hall as a blur of white backed out of sight.

Gabe's mother appeared in the foot-wide crack. "We

just wanted to make sure you had your privacy,'' she said to Addie and Gabe. Addie's mom stood right behind her, her hand at her mouth just as it had been before. It wasn't distress in Rose's expression, though. It was pure happiness. Both mothers were beaming. ''You didn't quite close the door,'' Katherine explained.

Gabe lifted his chin, his arms still around Addie, who'd buried her face against the hard wall of his chest. ''Thanks, Mom.''

''You're welcome,'' she replied, just before the door clicked shut.

''I told you I didn't think he'd wait to ask her,'' Rose said, her voice muffled by the wood.

''I really didn't think he would, either,'' Gabe's mother confessed. ''So now we'd better get busy. You find out what Addie's schedule will be,'' she continued, her voice fading, ''and I'll get Gabe's from his secretary. It looks as if we have ourselves a wedding to plan.''

The voices disappeared as Gabe tucked his finger under Addie's chin. Tipping her face toward his, he chuckled.

''There's no such thing as a private conversation around here.''

''I've noticed that.''

''Are you okay?'' he asked.

Even happier than she'd been in her entire life, she couldn't escape being practical. ''I was just wondering how the press will react to this. We've been telling them there's nothing going on.''

''We'll tell them the truth. That there wasn't anything going on. Not until they started saying there was.'' His arm slipped back around her. ''I think I'll even thank them for that.''

Her smile returned, warm and bright as sunshine. ''Thank them for both of us.''

"With pleasure," he murmured, but as he bent to kiss the only woman he'd ever loved, a press release was absolutely the last thing on Senator Gabriel Kendrick's mind.

* * * * *

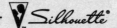

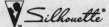

If you enjoyed what you just read,
then we've got an offer you can't resist!

Take 2 bestselling
love stories FREE!
Plus get a FREE surprise gift!

▰▰▰▰▰▰▰▰▰▰▰▰▰▰▰▰▰

Clip this page and mail it to Silhouette Reader Service™

IN U.S.A.
3010 Walden Ave.
P.O. Box 1867
Buffalo, N.Y. 14240-1867

IN CANADA
P.O. Box 609
Fort Erie, Ontario
L2A 5X3

YES! Please send me 2 free Silhouette Special Edition® novels and my free surprise gift. After receiving them, if I don't wish to receive anymore, I can return the shipping statement marked cancel. If I don't cancel, I will receive 6 brand-new novels every month, before they're available in stores! In the U.S.A., bill me at the bargain price of $3.99 plus 25¢ shipping and handling per book and applicable sales tax, if any*. In Canada, bill me at the bargain price of $4.74 plus 25¢ shipping and handling per book and applicable taxes**. That's the complete price and a savings of at least 10% off the cover prices—what a great deal! I understand that accepting the 2 free books and gift places me under no obligation ever to buy any books. I can always return a shipment and cancel at any time. Even if I never buy another book from Silhouette, the 2 free books and gift are mine to keep forever.

235 SDN DNUR
335 SDN DNUS

Name	(PLEASE PRINT)	
Address	Apt.#	
City	State/Prov.	Zip/Postal Code

* Terms and prices subject to change without notice. Sales tax applicable in N.Y.
** Canadian residents will be charged applicable provincial taxes and GST.
  All orders subject to approval. Offer limited to one per household and not valid to
  current Silhouette Special Edition® subscribers.
  ® are registered trademarks of Harlequin Books S.A., used under license.

SPECIAL EDITION™

Don't miss the first title in the exciting new miniseries from award-winning author

Janis Reams Hudson

THE DADDY SURVEY

(Silhouette Special Edition #1619)

When rancher Sloan Chisholm stops at a roadside diner, two adorable little girls think he's the perfect candidate to be their new daddy. After one look at their beautiful waitress mom, Sloan agrees. Can he somehow convince Emily that they're a perfect match?

MEN OF THE CHEROKEE ROSE

Their word is their bond,
and their hearts are forever.

*Available June 2004
at your favorite retail outlet.*

Silhouette®

COMING NEXT MONTH

SPECIAL EDITION

#1615 FIFTY WAYS TO SAY I'M PREGNANT—Christine Rimmer
Bravo Family Ties
Reunited after six long years, Starr Bravo and Beau Tisdale couldn't deny the attraction that had always sizzled between them. But when Starr discovered she was carrying Beau's baby, she panicked and fled the scene. Could Beau find—and forgive—his one true love so they could be a family at last?

#1616 ACCIDENTAL FAMILY—Joan Elliott Pickart
The Baby Bet: MacAllister's Gifts
When Patty Sharpe Clark set out to track down a child's missing father, David Montgomery, she was shocked to learn he'd been in an accident and had amnesia! She vowed to care for Sarah Ann until the girl's father recovered, but would Patty find love where she least expected?

#1617 CAVANAUGH'S WOMAN—Marie Ferrarella
Cavanaugh Justice
Deeply dedicated to his family and work, Shaw Cavanaugh didn't have time for the frivolity of life…until he met Moira McCormick. The charming actress came from a troubled past and longed to be part of a family, but would Shaw accept her into his life…forever?

#1618 HOT AUGUST NIGHTS—Christine Flynn
The Kendricks of Camelot
After CEO Matt Callaway and Ashley Kendrick shared a steamy one-night stand, the fear of scandal had separated them. Ashley had never forgotten the way Matt made her feel, but would he be able to forgive her for keeping their unborn child a secret…?

#1619 THE DADDY SURVEY—Janis Reams Hudson
Men of Cherokee Rose
Rancher Sloan Chisolm had never turned his back on a woman in trouble. So when beautiful Emily Nelson lost her job as a waitress, he was determined that she come work for him at the Cherokee Rose Ranch. He knew she considered being his housekeeper temporary, but their kisses made him hope that this might be a partnership…for life.

#1620 ONE PERFECT MAN—Lynda Sandoval
Years ago Tomas Garza's dreams of a family had fallen apart after his wife abandoned him and their daughter. He'd desperately tried to fill the void in his daughter's life, but the time had come when she needed a woman—someone like the beautiful event planner Erica Goncalves. She'd agreed to help him plan a party for his daughter, but would she be open to something more permanent?